XARES:
Final Countdown

CHRIS TURNER

This is a work of fiction. All the characters and events portrayed in these stories are either fictitious or are used fictitiously.

Published by Innersky Books
www.innersky.ca

Copyright © 2019 Chris Turner

ISBN-13: 978-1-989493-15-1

Chapter 1

Something had startled Star: a sound, some movement, a sinister and deadly rustle in the murk of the god-forsaken tunnels hewn by alien hands. A thick sweat clung to her skin, dripping down her neck and onto the small of her back. She lifted her blaster. Her long blond hair fell limp, in damp clumps down her slim shoulders. The air in her suit was humid and close and would be running out soon. Maybe better that the nightmare was over quickly, that she die here before she was caught and plunged into one of those horrible tanks.

Usk, her locust ally, one of the Mentera race, hung suspended in the luminescent green fluid of one of the eerie tanks in front of her. His locust-shaped head lolled, protected in a kind of scratched and dented grey helmet. A dark red smear ran along the edge of his insectoid brow. The other three tanks were unserviceable, either cracked and drained of their water, or contained alien creatures she could not bear to look at: with horns, pincers and claws the only barely-recognizable features. Usk, human size, bobbed upright in his glass tank like a lab specimen. Though she loathed the very sight of the alien aquarium, she took two steps closer, reached out a trembling hand to the glass. The locust blinked, slowly lifted an answering pincer up in response. Now human finger and locust claw touched on either side of the glass in a classic pose of friendship. The locust's space-suit was shredded, the wounds underneath considerable. The last battle against the Zikri squids had not been kind to the locust, but his hurts were fast healing in the brine. The liquid was like an elixir, some kind of ancient balm of alchemists long dead. It healed flesh and injury like quicksilver flowed over land. Miko and she had seen to it, dunking Usk in the alien liquid

3

before Miko had left to discover a source of replacement oxygen and ways and means off this dismal world.

The pale water rippled in response to Usk's feeble movements. The liquid itself emitted its own eerie greenish glow. A companion locust drifted at his side with unseeing eyes, seemingly dulled from his long captivity in the brine. The stuff, Miko'd told her, had a faint odor like sulfur and peat and something else mixed in. She did not have to remind herself that it was the same brine in which other Mentera could feed off a captive like vampires.

Miko had left her to guard Usk, that the locust should not fall prey to the squid-like Zikri. Damn Miko! She had never felt so alone in her life! Or vulnerable. These creepy tunnels were too much for her to bear. Around every corner lurked death. She was no warrior. No soldier of fortune or freedom fighter like the tales spoken of in the holo books, those crusaders of justice on the fringes of the known universe. Forced, more like it, into this wild, insane venture. Woe the day she had accosted Miko in a desperate plan to get off her home planet, miserable as it was. Followed him into the 'Grand Skull' casino in Skullrox City and practically thrown herself at him. Had she known she was getting herself into this hellhole, she would have gladly kept her old, boring life, rather than face the predacious menace of the Zikri on this dismal world *Kraetoria*.

She stared in horror as several dim forms glided out from the far end of the chamber—Zikri! with their flashing tails and grotesque tentacles, making squishy sounds as they moved, chittering in their abominable voices. On the most furtive of feet, Star ducked in behind a rock pillar, the full weight of terror catching up with her.

How they could survive in this environment without protective suits defied reason...their physiology must be super resilient, or capable of adapting to the thin atmosphere and extreme temperature by metabolic or convectional phenomenon beyond her grasp.

The creatures came in twos and threes, gliding without effort on six tentacles and what could have passed for a set of two hind, lizard-like feet. She crept back deeper behind the cold stone tucked under an overhang of rock. Her heart pounded. Her blaster lay clutched in a quivering hand. Should she use that weapon, even a single burst, the brutes would be alerted and she would have the full wrath of them upon her. Perhaps that was the most frightening thing. Gang-attacked by a monstrous brood of unknown genus, knowing firepower alone would not annihilate them. And yet, she could not let them just maul Usk and do god-knows what to him. She hesitated.

Perhaps a second too long.

A slithering tentacle shot out, leaving a trail of slime across her faceplate. She blasted the first of them full in the face, sending black and grey squid parts airborne in squishy, bloody heaps. Another scrabbled forward, incensed at the death of its peer. It curled a slime-pocked member around her waist and whirled her around. The shriek died in her throat. Seeing that loathsome thing's dusk-grey rubbery face feet away from her sent her into a mad panic. She lifted her E1. Fired point blank. The offending appendage hung limp and half severed, but the rubber-jellied torso came waddling after her. More came in ever fiercer numbers. She scrambled back, a strangled cry catching in her throat.

She clutched her weapon, spraying fire, but a part of her knew it was hopeless. The fiends would surely capture her and kill her. Usk was lost. Though a renegade of his own kind, he had been a valiant ally of her and Miko since the beginning. She caught a brief movement out of the corner of her eye: a Zikri probing with sucker-marked tentacles into Usk's tank, hauling him aloft and glaring at him with a nearly eyeless face. The gobbling gullet of a mouth twitched.

That Usk should fall to these creatures now, after all his courageous efforts, seemed ridiculously unfair. But then, what ever was fair in this nightmarish world ruled by squids and locusts?

Star ran down a tunnel, cutting corners, weaving in and out, trying to evade the creatures fast on her heels. The slightly lower gravity was not helping. It made her overshoot. She banged into walls and pillars of natural rock, wreaking havoc on her scuffed suit, buffeted body and bruised skin.

She recalled the grim prophecy of the Masters, imparted by the proxy left behind to continue the legacy of that cold, clinical diseased race, one that claimed to have created the Zikri and the Mentera. She shuddered.

Where in hell was Miko?

CHRIS TURNER

Chapter 2

Regers frowned down at the nav console on *Xaromar's* bridge. "Amazing this rustbucket is even fly-worthy," he grumbled. "Those gauges ain't looking too good, Creib. Sure, this ship'll make it to *Phallanor*?"

Creib patted the console with a proprietary air. "She'll get us there, Regers, you'll see."

Regers grunted. He smoothed out the lank black hair falling over his receding hairline and turned aside. Confidence. That's what he liked in a crew member. Didn't much like Creib though—too much of a fat boy and a crybaby. Yet he'd keep him in this loose Robin Hood-gone-bad outfit, so long as the chips were favorable. Deakes and Vincent were fine, working away at the weapons grid, perfect Rambo types for this sort of situation. Deakes the older of the two, balding, thickset, saw eye to eye with Regers. Vincent was a close second with his schoolboy face and trim brown curls. Ramra, the stocky Jakru with budding horns protruding from his temples, worked sensors and com console, a good yes man with medium to fair intelligence, loyal to the core. Jennings or 'Jiminy' as he called him, the fair-haired puritan, was the acting science officer or engineer. He'd already used up two, get-out-of-jail-free cards. One more slip and he'd set him loose at the next hub. Maybe troll one of the dives offworld for a replacement. Thugs galore down there. Possibly he could get by with only four recruits. The idea struck a chord. A lot of catchup to do in the next few days.

Regers went over his ideas in his mind, how many explosives he'd need, neurotoxins, sniffers, poison drops, assault rifles, compact flares, the like. A man couldn't be too careful in these troubled times with murderous squids jetting around in their war Orbs and those filthy locusts with their creepo, slimy tanks. He'd slipped up once, got caught by the squids, betrayed by one of his own, that motherfucker Yul, and thrown into a bug tank to die. But that would not happen again. No, not ever. And when dear old Yul and his pals met for a sit down face to face with Uncle Regers, there'd be a fierce reckoning.

Regers relaxed. He flexed his replacement hand. Let the blood simmer down, Charlie. Too much angst was not good for the heart. He laughed. Understatement of the year.

Regers stroked the fake skin on his left hand. The prosthetic looked realistic enough, fingers, nails, the whole deal. Never would he have guessed that hand was once a mutilated mass of jelly after the giant heptadoria had near chewed it off in the Mentera tank he was stuck in down on *Phebis*. He gritted his teeth. The strength of his new mechanical hand was greater than his normal grip, compliments of modern day technology. Hell, why didn't they make all men titanium these days? Regers shrugged off the macabre thought. Heads would roll for that grisliness down there on Phebis in the crashlanded Zikri Orb. Lucky he had escaped and reached *Alastra* station in time to replace the lacerated flesh and have the clinic people install a working prosthetic. Had to dig into the bottom of his savings, what little was left now in his universal bank account.

Next stop, Phallanor City. CEO Mathias had a little explaining to do himself, that same fuck who owed him for the contract out in *The Dim Zone*. If Yul, his faithless crew mate who'd abandoned him on the Orb, had made it back and delivered the alien plant specimens, Uncle Regers was owed his share. If not—well, nothing ventured, nothing gained. Maybe big cheese Mathias of Cyber Corp would compensate him for his injuries incurred. Even contract him for some other work. Though this time he would not sell himself as cheaply.

"We need supplies for this next gig," Regers muttered. "Probably get 'em down on Phallanor, if we're lucky. I sprung for food for a few days. Anybody with a few hundred yols in their back pocket?" He grinned.

Blank stares greeted him.

"It was a joke." Regers mooned his eyes, exhaling a weary breath.

"Not me, boss," said Vincent after a time. "You know me, penniless to the end." He turned to the others. "Anyone up for a couple of robberies to help pay for Regers' replacement hand?—and some food to spare for a few starveling travelers?"

Regers curled his lips. Threadbare funds. This little rogue posse was operating on a shoestring budget. "You're reading my mind, Vincent. There's hock shops everywhere that'll likely go in for a bit of trade."

Jennings opened his mouth but Regers silenced him. "Before you start preaching about the sins of theft, Jiminy, let's get on with the program. Get me full diagnostics on *Xaromar*—also a full report on probable heists on the nearest worlds, Delta sector. Robot parts, household bots, drifting ships, anything salvageable. We move a serial number here or nameplate there, strip out some general signatures, make it clean, saw off some circuits that don't belong and pawn the wares off at the nearest hock shop. Should raise us enough capital to keep us afloat for a time—especially for this next venture."

Jennings tapped keys on the console with little enthusiasm.

Regers coughed. A dry chill ran up his bones. He shivered and gripped the butt of the black, ten-inch E1 at his belt. Ever since he'd come out of the Mentera tank, he felt as if he were in withdrawal from some evil drug. This bridge space was too cramped for his tastes. Grainy holo screens scattered everywhere, low-tech scanners, various other equipment too, and instruments squeezed into a widening L, with dual viewports in fore, Captain's chair set in back. Low ceilings made for a tight space even for midget Daulks. What he wouldn't give for a seat on *Albatross* again, the state-of-the-art Alpha-explorer that Mathias had commissioned them for that doomed mission out in *The Dim Zone*. *Xeses* the uncharted alien world, with its strange, quivering plants and flitting moths, had been a lark. But the ship was dead, back on that forsaken moon Phebis in the belly of a Zikri pirate Orb, like the rest of his crew members. This lightfighter was a cozy fit for six. He preferred the roomier V-Zon cruisers or XL-4 explorers. Beggars couldn't be choosers. This old Daulk model, captured by the Zikri squids who knows how long ago, had sat chained there in the Orb, until his boys had blowtorched it free and started her engines. Still, he'd have to thank his luck they got the lightfighter operational, otherwise they'd have been Zikri fodder. He knocked his metal hand on the steel nav for good luck.

Jennings turned and whipped back his blond-grey hair. His pale eyes glowed. "Deep profile scan indicates Varwol light drive showing a fluctuation of gamma andredine."

"What the fuck does that mean?"

"It means we're losing pressure of atoms—the ones firing on her radial-core. If they don't fire at a specific rate, we get warp fatigue or Varwol misfire then are kicked out of hyperdrive."

Regers groused. "'Varwol misfire' or some shit like that. Hmmn, Jiminy. Sounds bad. Good thing we have you along to explain it."

"Any pursuit by the squids or Class B Orb action?" demanded Deakes.

"Negative," muttered Creib. "No such activity."

"Good, Creib, keep watching," Regers advised. "I don't trust those squidly beasts not to have some new gadget for tracking us." He grimaced. "We gave them hell down there on the Orb but they could come back and squeeze the love out of us."

"How long to Phallanor?" asked Ramra.

"0600. Give or take a half hour, depending on how our andredine fares." Jennings murmured into his scraggly beard. The man was still dressed in his blue spacer uniform from when he was nabbed by the Zikri squids aboard his Aldebaran freighter. "I still say we go to the nearest New Order Alliance base and report all this…the Zikri war Orb and the horrors aboard and everything else we've seen. There were a hundred men and women down there floating in tanks, still alive in suspended animation, though god knows how. Who knows how many more in other bays."

Regers knew how many more there'd been as he'd scouted the lower levels before smashing the glass tanks to release his current crew members…those victims'd numbered around eight hundred.

"I say we don't, Jiminy. We've been through this before. We're not the pirate police or any do-gooder Samaritans. You just sit tight."

Jennings bridled. "Maybe you aren't a 'do-gooder', Regers, but I am and at least have a conscience."

"Sit tight, you dumb fuck. Or I'll sic Vincent on you." He laughed. "He's screaming to unleash a bashing on someone's head. Look at him, wringing his wrists and eyeing you with those black killer eyes of his. We do things my way, Jiminy. You should be bending over kissing my ass, the way I see it. Rescuing your pansy ass from those tanks."

Jennings snorted, but he glowered and shut up.

"We got a hock shop errand to run and it's looming up fast," Regers intoned.

Jennings's ears perked up, jarred once more out of his listlessness. "Why? You still haven't told us what this big 'plan' of yours is, Regers—"

"No need for it. Just pipe down and monitor those damn control gauges. I don't want *Xaromar* crapping out on us any time soon. Clear avenue to Phallanor through the light drive tunnel. You and Ramra are our early bird sensors. Anything looks sour, like it's going to bird shit, I want to know all about it well in advance. We've made it this far. Hell, we've even made it out of those bitching tanks—elevated to free rogues on our own personal starship. That's quite a feat. It should go in some galactic record—"

"Are you about done? What about customs, authorities, jail time, that kind of thing—surely you—"

"There's no worry here, Jiminy. We just ride through everything." Regers pushed Jennings back down toward the console. "Keep your mouth shut and keep monitoring."

CHRIS TURNER

Chapter 3

The next hours passed with the Jakru humming a dull tune. From the sounds of it, it was starting to drive Deakes out of his mind. "Could you please knock it off?" Deakes growled. "This ain't no karaoke carousel."

"Right." Ramra licked his lips and mumbled dark words into his scanners.

Regers popped out of his reverie. "Listen. We get supplies, fuel up on food and beverages, get some meat on our bones. We gather us some weaponry and gear, then head out to pay good old Mathias a visit. I've got spoils coming to me."

"That's it?" said Vincent.

"What else to say, Vincent? Should there be more?"

Vincent frowned. "I guess it'll all work out. Not sure about this Cyborg Core place though."

"Cyber Corp. Simplest means is the direct one."

Vincent blinked. Ramra threw up his hands.

"Trust me, I'm an old dog that follows his nose." Regers grinned, a smile that quickly turned into a sour grimace. *Yeah, and one that got you thrown into a fucking tank with fishy brutes nibbling at your arm. Regers, you're a dumb ass. Don't be too sure.* He looked down yet again at his once-mangled wrist whose stringy flesh had somehow cauterized and healed over in the greenish brine. Damnedest thing. Could never figure out how those tanks worked their magic or where those locusts got the crazy idea to build such macabre briny prisons.

Salma always said he was a magnet for trouble. If she could only see him now… Regers grimaced. She'd never see him again though, as she was six feet under, wasted by those brutes out in *Meslon* he used to be affiliated with. Olg and his motherfucking gang. He stuck the memory of her deep down. And that spidery script of Olg's, written in Salma's own blood on a note pinned to her mangled corpse, the still-warm blood caking her glossy blond hair decked with flowers.

That life was over, a million miles away. A personal promise lingered deep in his gut that Olg would be the next to fall after Yul.

Phallanor came up on the holo nav. *Xaromar* dropped out of hyperdrive. The Varwol eased out of its monotonous hum, allowing the ship to settle into a high orbit around the industrial planet of Phallanor, a greenish-blue disc that glowed beneath the ship.

Creib eased the vessel in close to *Baltar* station on impulse thrust, the checkpoint for all offworld ships…also the center of customs which scanned each vessel's drive codes and processed arrival craft for stolen machinery. Regers had long since overridden the drive codes of *Xaromar's* registration with another. Automatic scan from the station searched for contraband. Not that they were carrying anything illegal, but just to be safe. No warning blared over the com's general frequency. All smooth sailing.

"You and Creib hold the fort, Jiminy," muttered Regers. "Deakes, you, Vincent, me and the Jakru will go down. I may need muscle, if Mathias turns out to be a little girl about things. The man's a tricky son of a bitch. Cold as a snake. Rich fucker though. Probably owns half of the planet down there."

"What, and you're just going to walk in there and make demands of him?" Jennings jeered.

Regers flashed him a dark gaze. "Mathias made a contract and has to honor it. By Jesus, I'm here, alive. I'll hold him to it."

Jennings' eyes rolled. "And if he doesn't want to pay out, he's just going to lawyer up and loose his team of attorneys on you."

Regers spat out a curse. "Yeah, and I'll shit down his throat."

Jennings shook his head with disgust. "That'll surely work."

"What else you got planned, boss?" Deakes asked.

"Just playing it by ear, Deakes. If Mathias doesn't play ball, I'll have to get more creative." Regers gave a little laugh. Judging by the stony look on the Jakru's face, he guessed horn head was not liking much the current turn of events.

"Relax, Ramra, you're too tense." Regers patted the Jakru on the back.

"You're like a buck with a hide full of buckshot. All bottled up like you got a corn cob up your ass. We need to get you out of your box. Get you laid, some nice piece of exotic ass. I'll see to it, once I get some cash." Regers chuckled. Vincent burst out in a peal of laughter.

Ramra only grinned.

Poor fool. Jakru boy didn't know what he'd gotten himself into, signing up for Uncle Regers' brigade. These bastards would all have to wisen up, recognize who was in charge. Ramra got it, in his formal oath of obedience kind of way, though he looked half stoned, still grinning like a languid sheep from his long spell dunked in a bug tank. Creib was shaping up, but slowly. Vincent and Deakes were fine; Jennings, of course, was a complete tight ass. If he didn't get it, he'd get a caving in of his skull like that poor wanker down on Phebis, the one he'd had to put in his place. Spoke out of line once too often and got his head split for riling up the others. Too much sass. That wouldn't do, especially to one in a position of command. A leader had to exercise authority. The juniors either had to join and fight, or die at the hands of fiends like those ugly Zikri squids. A lot of them already had died; his initial wedding party of ten had gotten mauled down to half by those everloving squids on Phebis. Busted up skulls, broken bones, guts popping out of space suits. Not a pretty sight.

Chapter 4

On Regers' order, *Xaromar* touched down on the outskirts of the city in an abandoned service yard of a crating company.

"We rendezvous on the other side of town," he said, "unless I radio in with different instructions. Clear?" He glared at Jennings. "And no cute stuff, Jiminy, like running to mommy, or getting on the horn and waxing on about squid injustice." Jennings uttered a curse and Regers sneered at him. "Try it and you'll see. The wrath of Uncle Regers'll come down on your delicate hide. Watch over him, Creib. Stay glued to that damn com."

Jennings gave no comment, just stared at him in stony silence.

Creib gave a lukewarm nod, a moony smile creeping over his chubby, pale face.

Regers stepped down from the cargo hold, his boots crunching on the gravel. Ramra stood beside him with Deakes, inhaling the dry, warm air. The sky shone a deep azure. To the east, a parade of mile high towers hung in balance in a light haze. *Xaromar* banked off and disappeared from sight into the cloudless sky.

Vincent stood blinking in the bright light beside Deakes. "You really got something rigged, boss?"

Regers elbowed him in the ribs. "What do you think?" He grinned. "Come on." He tugged at Vincent's arm. "We head to the surplus shop, get our stuff, get this business over with. Mr. CEO'll play, I know it."

Deakes grunted and winced. "Sure."

"Why out here?" Ramra asked.

"Best place to get quality stuff, Ramra, and cheap. Out in the boondocks. Downtown, twice as expensive, twice as monitored, and fifty times as busy."

Ramra shrugged.

They trudged down the service road perhaps a mile past warehouses and various other outlets: plumbing fixtures, textiles—a real industrial wasteland, then to a rust-fenced yard, with an open gate. Chain and padlock hung off the mesh and a sign tilted over the warehouse's front door.

"Here you are, see? *Lenny's Surplus.*" Regers pointed.

The four pushed past the heavy swinging door and sauntered into Lenny's. A subdued atmosphere greeted them: the spacious depot smelt of charcoal and old sweat, with traces of rubber, oilskin, and old engine parts, and a mixture of oil and lighter fluid. Large warehouse steel girders ran overhead. Guns ranged on the far wall on a rack behind glass cases, good stock—E1s to E4s, efficient instruments, arrayed with hand pistols, energy charge packs, scopes, infrared, even some compact grenades.

An attendant came bustling from behind a steel desk along the far wall. "Sirs, can I help you?"

Regers inclined his head. "You got any spinners?"

The man's lips parted in surprise. He lowered his voice, eyes glinting like pearls. Then motioned to the back room. He sized up Regers, as if his mind churned over the level of commission he could get on a cash sale. "Come with me." He hustled them behind the counter into a back room. No one else was browsing in the shop. At his heels, Regers saw him rummage in a lower, back cupboard then turned to lay three out on another counter. Silver nines. An activator came with them, a small hand remote with three settings—stun, high heat and kill. "Those are imported, manufactured offworld," he said. "Contraband in Phallanor."

"Like I could give a shit." Regers examined the silver pellet, the size of his thumbnail, with a grunt of acknowledgement. Vincent craned his neck to get a better look. "Anything else I should be buying here?"

The man cleared his throat. Smoothing his small goatee, he gave a salesman's nod. "There are poison pills over there. Heavy duty...if that's what you're looking for." He eyed Regers with an inquisitive glare.

Regers dipped hands in an open crate, rummaged about. "I am. What of these thumb charges here? What's the latency?"

The salesman paused before answering. "A second to two. On sale now. Army surplus. Probably a 1 in 50 chance one of them's a dud so you're better off taking two or more."

Regers shrugged. "If I double my weapons with my boys here that halves the odds."

"You know your business." The man screwed up his eyes in a frown. "Can I ask—"

"No, you may not ask. Just play the dutiful salesman, please. Keep showing us the good stuff." Regers turned his back on him, then continued to sift through the explosive stock at his leisure. He frowned at one oblong deformed piece and rejected others out of hand. "I'll take five of these cadmium flares. Plus three poison pills. No, wait make that four and throw in a couple of sniffers."

The vendor beamed with appreciation. "Good choice. How many spinners? This bag is on sale, four of them for fifty yols.

"We'll take 'em all."

"Shall I bag 'em up?"

"No need. We got hands here. Nobody around your grubby yard's going to get wise to us." He stuffed the bag in his pocket, distributed the excess flares to Deakes and Vincent. After paying the 212 yols, Regers, Vincent, and the others left.

They walked some more in the rising heat, another mile before Ramra huffed out a complaint. "Seems a waste of time, Regers. All this walking about. We're going to hoof our way into town? It's twenty miles. Isn't there a better way?"

"You got something against a little exercise and fresh air, Ramra?"

"I mean—"

"There's a method to this madness. I don't want the ship anywhere near the city core. Too many damn gendarmes and cops, and I don't know Phallanor well enough to know her rhythms. You got to be smart about this. We could hire an air car, but I don't want a paper trail. We do it the simple way, and the slow and right way. Cash transactions. We take our time."

Ramra grunted and gave a silent nod. "What's the big deal, Regers? You're going all cautious on us. Aren't you just going to ask Mr. bigshot Cybercore for the payout and then scram? Why all the sneaking about?"

Deakes gave a coarse laugh. "Where've you been the last hour, Jakru? Head up your ass?"

Regers chuckled. "It's always a big deal, Ramra—when Uncle Regers is on the job."

They caught the first feeder tram heading into the city. Not much of a wait, half an hour, no more, but enough to keep Regers restless. By the time the four got closer to the city center, the traffic had thickened considerably.

The middle carriage was full, brimming with passengers, all at the height of the day's kerfuffle. Folks of all denominations—rich, poor, loud, quiet—business people, chatty types, students, office employees and the odd blue collar worker taking a time out for a kebab or donut, whatever they ate on this tinsel-town world.

Magno trams raced everywhere, crisscrossing each other on levels up to eight stories high. Regers craned his neck to look through the tinted glass. Blue streaks of light whisked people off to their destinations. Always in a rush. Busy world with nobody having the time for anybody or anything. So unaware these people were of the menace lurking in the background, those perilous squids and bugs, waiting to ravage and enslave a privileged planet like this.

At Armington station they debarked and emerged into Monastria's bustling square with four stone statues commemorating the planet's 'terra-forming-fathers' in some distant century. Regers gave a devil-may-care shrug and herded Ramra and the others on. They had taken no firearms with them. Useless. They'd never get past Cyber Corp security anyway. He had other plans in mind. The sniffers and spinners could come in handy. Then again they might not. He'd memorized the city's layout, essentially a dense grid with a wide oval roundabout sweeping the central core around the tallest buildings.

The mile-high sky towers soared above like things of fantasy. Past the inner circle down a few side streets, they strode, pushing past milling folks, then to an old brick and steel building, showing its signs of age. Part of the old quarter. More heritage shops and apartments rose overtop. The magno trams continued to rumble overhead.

Aside from the brief heritage architecture, the streets were cold, sterile, and clean. Lots of activity here but everybody just going through the motions, blinking, speaking, gesturing like a mechanical horde of robots. He guessed this conformity is what cities bred and birthed these days. Good old Regers'd take a starship with a working light drive and the open universe any day.

The impossibly high sky towers glinted in the harsh sunlight: chrome, glass, plexicene. One of those massive towers had a sprawling green and white logo pasted to its side, that of an eagle and robot with a bright yellow halo over them. Cyber Corp.

Regers exhaled a sharp breath. How long had he waited for this moment?

He motioned his men inside the lobby of the giant corporate headquarters. Exotic plants with leafy ferns ranged around the octagon, some twined around poles running a hundred feet up into the sun-dazzled glass cathedral ceilings of the atrium. Marble floors, men in suits, some of the women in business skirts walking around in important poses, dark blue, plain brown or plain white. A tight ship here.

Regers sauntered up to the main desk and flashed the pretty receptionist his most disarming smile.

"Sir, may I help you?"

"Yes, I'd like to speak to Mathias."

She blinked, coughed, as if such were the most outrageous request today. "Sir, Mr. Mathias is indisposed. Are you sure you wish Mr. Mathias? He's the CEO. You'll need an appointment and he's booked months in advance."

Regers flashed another shark-toothed smile. "I know he's the CEO, miss prissy pants. Do I look like an imbecile? We're just wanting a few minutes of Mr. Mathias's time. I think he'll make an exception. You need only mention the name, 'Regers'."

The woman scowled. She consulted a register. Busy fingers. She spoke into a com, a private line with a red receiver, tapping the rim of a holo screen.

"Sir, a Mr. Regers to see Mr. Mathias."

There was a long pause before a voice replied.

"Bring him to the office—immediately."

"Very well." She motioned Regers and his men on. "Down the hall to the elevators. Third floor. You can't miss the signs."

Regers saluted her and winked at Deakes. "See, that easy."

Vincent and Ramra blinked. Deakes only smiled.

They all got off on the third floor and entered a lush office with plush carpet. Regers' heart beat with anticipation. How to play it? Cool? Smarmy? Come on like gangbusters? With fists flying? No, kid stuff like that wouldn't work here. He'd have to play this one more subtly, with a heavy emphasis on 'impromptu'. He leveled a toothy glare at Vincent, then one at Deakes, warning them to keep their mouths shut.

They stepped past an auburn-haired secretary toward a mahogany door labeled 'CEO Mathias'. She leapt up. "Sirs, you can't go in there. Wait here, please." She pushed past Regers and his nose caught the whiff of styerethelene and new plastic. Something odd about this woman. The eyes too glazed. Hair too perfect, like a doll's. A female bot? With stiff ceremony she ushered them into the CEO's private chambers only to saunter briskly out, busy butt wagging, closing the door behind her. Regers shook his head in bafflement.

A man jerked himself up from behind a desk. He had a round, red-cheeked face with wispy, straw-colored hair, the color of old sea oats. Blue suit and tie encased a portly body and thickset neck. The man looked more used to being in a lab surrounded by high-tech equipment than in an office. Though he looked familiar, Regers couldn't quite place him.

"Who the fuck are you?" came Regers' derisive croak.

"Language, please. I'm Desmond Yadley, Mathias's senior science officer. I'm subbing in for him." His lips parted in a prim half sickle. "Regers, I remember you. One of those seedy mercs we hired, who supposedly died out there in *The Dim Zone*. I see I was wrong. Last we heard, you were stuffed in a Mentera tank, effectively dead."

"For all intents and purposes, that was true, and yet here I am."

Yadley shook his head. "I don't get—"

"Where the fuck is Mathias?"

"Sorry, not here. Been gone for weeks now. I've been designated acting CEO. Don't like the job much, but I don't mind the pay. I'd rather be researching the samples Yul brought back for us."

"I'm sure you would."

Yadley stirred. "So Yul was lying to us. He had some distorted story about you choking to death on a crash-landed Zikri Orb on a dead moon. Said he tried to save you, smashed the glass and all, but there weren't enough suits to go around. I see he was wrong."

"Did he now? My old friend Yul. See, Dezzy, that's the problem with the world as it is, too many lying, cheating, backbiting fucks who abandon ship mates to die." He clenched his white-knuckled fist and rapped it hard on the water dispenser. "I'm here to get my money owed for services rendered. Also 10 times more for damages, like my mekkie arm and a dozen years of stress from being dumped in a Mentera tank. Speaking of which, where is my old pal, Yul? He and I have some words to share."

"Even if I knew that information, it's classified," said the acting CEO with cool hauteur.

Regers sighed. He put an arm around Dez as if consoling an old beer buddy at the karaoke bar. His clown-like grimace did nothing to reassure Desmond. "Nothing's impossible, Dez. This is the 26th century, ain't it? I mean look around you. We have robots, radio fried pizza, air bots, remote control, dial a date, robocops, robomaids to clean floors, shake your hand, massage your dick if you want, wipe your smelly, brown-stained ass, console you when you're down, like a true Mother Milly."

Dez licked his lips with a scowl. "No need to get vulgar, Regers. I didn't let you in here just to get browbeaten by a pack of dirty—"

Regers snarled and lifted a menacing fist, "I'll ask you again, where's Mathias?"

"Don't know. Please, leave now. I'm calling security! He reached for an intercom on his desk.

Regers swept eyes about the room looking for cameras. One little spyhole to left north, possibly another to west. He grabbed tape from his pocket and pasted it over the sweephole. Then ran to the other. There could be more. A risk, but he'd have to take it. On a quick nod to Deakes, he and Vincent turned on Dez.

Dez paled, clutching the com but Deakes got hold of his wrist and twisted hard.

"Ow! Okay, okay, Jesus, that hurts." He loosed a painful bray. "Last we heard was a transmission come in from Mathias on the trail of Sigmund Hresh's secret lab on *Remus* in *The Dim Zone*."

"That's more like it, Dez. Well, guess we'd better set a course for this secret lab and get a head start."

The CEO gaped. "What do you mean, we? Are you crazy?"

"I've been to hell and back, Dez. Crazy has no meaning for me." He reached in his spacer's jacket and lifted a device, a small, glinting pellet, the size of a prune pit. A maniacal grin spread over his features. "Now before you get any idea of summoning your pretty synthetic secretary or security people, let's get a few facts in order. This here's a flash flare. Make mincemeat of your face. And this here's a spinner." He held up his other hand, showing something similar, but smaller and silver. "We'll get to that one in a second." He moved toward the desk while the sweating Dez made fish gulping sounds and Ramra, the horn-headed Jakru, stared bug-eyed. "We're going to need to go over the details of Mathias nice and slow. A few questions, that's all." His eyes gleamed. "I remember you now. A puffier face, longer hair to the shoulder in a white lab coat, running around that mechno lab, spewing numbers and chemical formulae like a high school geek. Who are you to take over Mathias's job anyway? Thought you were just a lab rat."

"There was nobody else, what with Hresh, our senior scientist and geneticist, gone. I was next in line."

Regers blinked, thought for some time. "Hresh, that other brainiac who set us on that voyage to *The Dim Zone* to collect samples? This poses an inconvenience to us, Dez. Provided you're not lying to me."

"Why should I lie?"

"Why indeed?"

"Ask around," Dez protested. "There's the door."

Deakes swore. "Wasted trip here, Regers. This is bad."

Regers whipped back his unruly mop of black hair. "Maybe not. Think about it, Deakes. Why not just beetle out of here? We can take Dez along as collateral, in case we have more questions for him, or he's lying to save his neck."

"Wha—what do you mean?" Dez laughed. "You're joking, right?"

"Do I look like it?"

Dez squirmed out of Deakes's grip. Fast as a rabbit, he made a break for the door but Vincent hammer-locked him and twisted the executive's arm behind his back. Dez howled as Deakes grinned and Regers exhaled an explosive breath. "Control this fool!"

He scanned the room, looking for more cameras. None that he could see. "Hold him, Vincent. Me and the Jakru have to get this spinner down his gullet."

"No, wait!"

Deakes and Vincent forced the struggling executive to the rug while Regers and the Jakru got the spinner into his mouth.

"W-what the hell are you doing—?" His bewildered cry was cut short. Regers chopped him on the back of the head.

"What you can't know, Dez, can't hurt you."

Regers worked Dez's larynx in a jigsaw pattern then plugged his nose. "Swallow your medicine. Attaboy."

Dez gulped with horror. Regers fingered the remote. "Let's give it a little test. Oops." Dez nearly keeled over as something smote him from inside.

"So, reckon the stun is working. We got a day before our boy shits it out," he murmured to Deakes. "Should he try anything funny, we blast him. That said, I have a whole bag of these spinner devices to keep feeding him. Consider it an incentive to answer when I tell you, Dez, or we shove more down your throat. For example, when we pass through these cameras at checkpoints out of here, you better make it real casual, or your liver's rat fodder. One touch of this button and it goes into kill mode."

Dez nodded, a strangled noise issuing from his nose. He licked his pink lips and scowled.

They walked out of the office, Deakes to one side, Vincent and Ramra to the other. Regers brought up the rear.

The secretary lifted her coiffured head and frowned, removed her headset. "Sir? Going out so soon? There's a file on Veramax that needs a signature."

Dez waved it off, his face a pale shade of wax. "I'll be away on business, Clara, for a few hours—" Regers gave him a painful nudge in the ribs "—I mean for some time with Mr. Regers and his colleagues. Keep me apprised about the files and the upcoming roster on the universal holo. We're expecting new shipments of robot parts from Rangenkro any day soon."

"As you wish, sir." Clara flashed Regers and his grimy ruffians a dubious glance, but she donned her head gear and went back to her work, furrowing her brow, scanning the intra-holo roster.

The unlikely group walked down the hall, an opulent spread of chrome, modern art, aquaria filled with tropical fish, flanked by holovision corporate ads and slogans. Dez's knees were shaking.

"Slow down, Dez, you're getting ahead of us. Keep smiling and don't look back like a frightened mouse. Tends to alarm the security people. Uncle Regers and his boys'll take care of you. My itchy finger might swipe this here activator by accident if you try something cute. I'm fidgety, nerves not as steady after being dunked in a bug tank. Oops, sorry, slipped again."

Dez doubled over in pain.

A security guard approached from down the hall. Regers didn't fail to notice the compact black E2 hanging at his belt and the stilted stride and nodded at Dez. Dez made an odd motion and grimacing face which aroused the guard's suspicion. The guard halted in midstride.

"Afternoon, sir. Anything wrong here?"

"I—" Dez hunched again in pain upon Regers' finger movement.

"You okay? You don't look well."

Deakes shouldered his way in. "No worries, chief. Mr. Yadley here just got some bad news—a death in the family. We're in from out of town, trying to comfort him."

The security man frowned and flashed Dez a quizzical glance, as if demanding corroboration of such a claim.

Regers scowled. Another bot? Not too bright. Wooden grip to the hands. Slight stiff movements to the legs. Probably another of Mathias's fucking mechnos. Or maybe a defective prototype.

Dez held up a shaky hand. "Nothing, Balsen. Just a little under the weather."

"We're taking CEO Yadley to the cafeteria to get a little hot soup," Regers explained. "It works wonders, just as Granny always said."

The security guard's frown deepened. "Yeah, well the cafeteria's back the other way."

"We know, just giving Mr. Yadley a bit of leg exercise. He seems to have stiffened up all of a sudden. Wanted to work out the kinks." Regers smiled. He hustled Dez along like an errant calf. "No fast ones, you dipshit fucking toad," he hissed. "It's you who'll get clipped, not us. Me and my men can blast our way out of here, if we have to."

"You don't even have rifles," Dez gasped.

"Your men do. And easier than apples to get one of those pistols off them. Think I can't do it? Watch. Been in this business long enough."

Dez sagged. He nodded his head in despair, a defeated man. "Brutes." He mumbled under his breath.

"You got that right." Regers tipped his head in salute. "Pipe down. We're going on a little walk out of here." He cast Dez a menacing look.

They exited the glass foyer without mishap. Across the busy street they shepherded Dez down another side street away from the hubbub. They merged into the crowd and for a brief moment, Regers gusted a relieved breath. Despite his bravado, even his nerves had a limit. Now that the worst was over, the rest would be easy. Provided his accomplices on *Xaromar* didn't do something stupid and fuck up what was essentially a simple operation from here on in.

Even as he pondered this, Regers wondered how many of these munchkins running about the streets like headless chickens, were bots. Wouldn't surprise him if Cyber Corp had unleashed an army of them—testing them out on the streets, ready to take over the planet.

The magno tram, Blue Line C1, approached, hovering a foot off the ground. Its blue, aerodynamic housing, capable of high speeds through the city, was low noise, economical. Regers marveled at the efficiency. The reinforced fiberglass doors slid back, admitting new citizens, disgorging others. Regers and crew piled in, taking seats at the back of the car, two on either side of Dez. He tried to mouth some words but Deakes silenced him with fingers digging into his side.

No words were spoken. A couple of route changes got them out of the city and on to some abandoned lots on the east end of town where Regers had told Creib and Jennings to meet them with *Xaromar*. Regers had deliberately picked an out-of-the-way spot, far from their dropoff. Helped throw off snoopers.

The tram door opened at a penultimate station. Dez tried to make a run for it but Deakes flung himself forth and kidney-punched him good, dragging him back to the seat. "There, there, little birdie has frisky wings." Two middle-aged female passengers in nearby seats blinked in owlish astonishment and Deakes graced them with an open-faced grin. While Dez doubled over, groaning, Deakes patted Dez on the back, shaking his head and clucking like a bird. "Escaped mental patient from the institute," Deakes explained. He flashed the old ID from his transpo job out of the grey coveralls he still wore. "We have our orders to use excessive force." He growled between his teeth.

"Yes, seems our patient's learning though." Regers leaned back in his seat, exhaling a confident breath. Not long now. He nodded in approval as Deakes and Vincent kept a close eye on Dez.

Last stop was Portmouth on the Red C Line. The train slowed up with a metallic hum. They exited the tram, cleared the station and headed toward a row of stark, cinder block warehouses. Regers radioed ahead to Creib. Within minutes *Xaromar* arched out of the sky, a dull grey-black blob with curved prow and blue glow flaring from its lateral impulse jets.

"You know this scheme of yours is never going to work," Dez rasped.

Regers shrugged. "Looks as if it is, Dez. What I want to know is why didn't Mathias fill you in on his plans, you being his senior scientist and all?"

Dez snarled, wiping his puffed, sweating face. "Even to his senior staff, Mathias is protective of his secrets. He tells me only what he wants me to know."

"Is that right?"

"So many schemes in the man's mind. Makes one's head spin. The man's ruthless. Twice I've thought of turning tail like Hresh did, getting out while I could, but I'm scared to death of what he'd do. Now I'm in charge of the company in his absence. A strange irony."

The ship landed on an open space upon the tarmac amidst bins and crates of metal tubing. Regers' and the others' hair tousled in the wind kicked up by the ship's thrusters. They approached the opening cargo door.

Dez's jaw dropped as he saw his fate, then looked at the crazy gleam in Regers' eyes. "What happened to you out there in *The Dim Zone?* You're not the same person I remember some weeks ago in our offices."

Regers, a man beyond caring, conscience or principle, gave a bare-toothed grin. "Let's just say I've gone far beyond fear, Dez. Beyond what you might call 'sane' in this so-called real world you think you live in."

The cargo door closed and they marched Dez to the bridge as the ship lifted off for orbit around Phallanor.

Regers spoke in a cheery voice, "Everybody, meet Dez, acting CEO of Cyber Corp." He swept an arm toward the wide-eyed scientist. "Dez, meet Jennings—aka Jiminy, engineer and navigator, and that there's Creib in charge of piloting. Deakes, Ramra and Vincent you already know."

Dez pursed his lips. He wheezed out a raspy breath.

Jennings snorted. "So this is the CEO? How'd you manage to get him here?"

"Dez's a reliable fellow," said Regers. "Commiserated with my loss and decided to accompany us on our little expedition out to *The Dim Zone*, out of the goodness of his heart. To see that compensations are personally attended to. Didn't you, Dez?"

Dez scowled. "The moment we rendezvous with Mathias on Remus, this is all over. I go back to Phallanor."

"Sure, anything you say, Dez." Regers made a thumbs-up sign. "Seems you've got everything figured out."

"People are going to be wondering where I got to," Dez huffed.

"Asking a lot of questions when I don't return. I am acting director of the firm in Mathias's absence. How far do you think you'll get before they come hunting you down?"

"Well, from where I stand, the universe's a big place."

Dez paled.

"You're insurance, Dezzie, that's all. We get the goods, you go home. We don't—well, it's not looking good for you."

Jennings interrupted with a scowl, "How's badgering this guy going to help out our cause?"

Regers squeezed his eyes shut. He pinched the bridge of his nose. "Jiminy, when the fuck are you going to learn to zip it? Deakes—teach him a lesson."

"My pleasure." An evil grin swept across the bald man's face. He rapped Jennings hard in the kidney, causing Jennings to double over, gasping.

Regers smiled with satisfaction. "Now, you're here as science and engineering counsel, that's all. Not to play security monitor or question my plans. Get it?"

Another sharp rap to the kidneys had Jennings giving a cat-like yowl. The man managed a terse nod, his face burning, as fury rose.

Regers shook his head. When were these fucks going to learn? Should've left Jiminy down on the Orb with the other glassy-eyed floaters.

Chapter 5

Creib turned a wary glance over his shoulder from the nav. "Set course for *Remus*?"

Regers shook his head impatiently. "No, a little recreation time out first. Take us to *Mekeroid* in Cepheus."

"Mekeroid? Why the hell Mekeroid?"

"This calls for a celebration, Creib. Dez, I reckon you'll come with us."

Dez croaked out a protest. "Why? You've got what you came for—a fix on Mathias."

"Got my reasons. Glut our pleasures. Plus it'll put off any snoopers and sleuthers. What kidnapper would ever think of taking his charge and holing up on that scum world?"

Vincent drawled, "I've heard they've got the best pieces of bronze tail this side of Arcturus."

Deakes grinned. "You know how to win over your crew, boss."

"You betcha. But first, I want 10k yols in damages up front. Dez, you're going to pay out and withdraw it on Mekeroid."

Dez let out a plangent wail.

"No squawking. You can use your fancy ID card. Throws off any busybodies on the trail. They track your transactions, see you've been paying for pussy at Mekeroid on company funds, they'll know you've gone rogue and are skylarking. We kill two birds with one stone. We get Ramra some Mekeroid ass, you get us some money to help finance our expedition." Regers chuckled and rubbed his wrists.

Vincent burst out in a boisterous laugh.

Ramra nodded with the green glint of enthusiasm that only a Jakru could have.

* * *

Mekeroid city was a world on the frontier breeding debauchery. Full of black market rings, neon lights, strip joints, every intoxicant and cheap pleasure a man or woman could ask for. Most of the action was down on *Asteroid Boulevard*, with smoky dives, three storied black-shadowed toke-up joints, needle shops, blades, wires, whatever was one's fancy. Some of these came with inviting entrances formed of barely a row of stringed beads. Half-men and offworld hybrids wearing masks and goggles, painted ladies with cat-whiskers and rabbit ears walked the street, cruising for something that couldn't be found, except maybe danger and trouble. Nothing but masquerade night in full parade.

Regers and his crew howled in approval as they sauntered through the streets all keyed up for some carnal festivities. They queued up at a virtual instateller off the main drag at the corner of *Catchy* and *Nozzle*, happy to be out of their confined quarters on *Xaromar*. The sharp sulfur tinge of mezolene tainted the air with a rare muggy mist. Mangy dogs with fur half ripped off scabby backs roamed about the dingy, puddled alleys begging for scraps, snarling when competing for the meager fare. Beggars in the alleys chorused along with them, lolling backs against grimy brick walls, chewing on old dog bones the strays left behind. Regers prodded Dez up to the holo-dispersal unit. The CEO tapped some digits on a pad, entered a passcode, then passed the retina test before he withdrew 10k. Regers prodded him for 5k more, then nodded in happy unison, pocketing the cash and distributing 300 yols to each of his crew as spending money.

"Don't blow it too fast, boys—or you'll have to appeal to Dez for more."

They hoofed it over to a specialty shop between a corner convenience and a fancy-dancy wine shop—or deli. They purchased costumes—big black boots, masks, wrists bands, metal neck collars, the whole shebang, to blend in with the locals. Holo-billboards swung high into the night sky, advertising everything from cotton candy to wide screen holo displays to deluxe dildos. Lewd pictures of female and male parts lay interlaced with ads for mega corporations. Laughter, chatter of droning voices, wails and cries of the intoxicated, jacked on Bandex, Quintox, Verizan, anything they could get their hands on. The whistling rush of magno trams caught Regers' ear as they slewed by, disgorging people of all ages, races and sizes. Sounds, smells, sensations of myriad numbers. Sensory overload compared to the murky confines of *Xaromar* and its cramped hold.

Regers and crew went bar-hopping down *Asteroid* strip, bubbling with laughter, bragging to each other about their escape from the tanks, happy to be alive. All except Jennings. And Dez. Two grumpy embittered souls shaking their heads with contempt at what surrounded them. Appalled at the seedy conditions of Mekeroid. Jennings snarled in Regers' ear, "You could have picked a better world than this bloody, hedonistic cesspool."

Regers shoved him away. "I didn't for a reason, Jiminy." His scowl annoyed Jennings. A source of amusement for Regers. He would have kept the sniveling killjoy on the ship, but he didn't trust him not to fly off to a NOA base, spilling his guts about floaters down on a desolate moon and a crew of mercs breaking laws. Happy hour was on. The brazen crew at last hit the *Hothouse Blues* roundhouse bar.

"Looks more like the respectable establishment we've been hankering for," Regers mused.

Low translucent tables ranged to the sides, with touch-screen menus to order from—synthesized beef jerky, caramel tarts, ranghorn stew. Smoky clouds of dry ice and incense lit up in colors from the dusky lights above—blue, muted orange, red, and grey. A weird stage lurked on a low dais, and weirder band members wearing colored costumes, wielding electro-wind instruments that oozed out a seedy beat while sleek, bronzed, naked women and men paraded around the tables selling their wares. Which weren't bad all in all, considering the low-ball price. Not a shabby little joint, Regers thought.

Everything went as expected. Deakes soaking up the vibes, Vincent wearing a shit-eating grin. Drinks, fun, grab and snatch, time to peel off some layers and hit the back rooms. Until Ramra got too excited and like a hungry wolf, groped for some passing ass and had the unlucky timing of interfering with a musclebound sod's grab. A mean type who objected to Ramra's sweaty paws on the woman he wanted to take to an upstairs room. Deakes moved in fast for his size but Ramra got his horns boxed and staggered back, his eyes glazing over as one who sees stars. "Stay down, you dumb billygoat," roared muscle boy. Deakes stepped in and drew back a fist but Regers held him back, a thick grin on his face.

"Got a problem there, chief?" snarled the angry man.

Regers faced him. "No, do you?" The brute's oiled bald pate gleamed in the sultry light with oily skin smelling like musk.

"Your baby face friend's the problem, chief," spat the man. "Had eyes on my lady."

"Who says it's 'your' lady? You own this joint?"

"I'm a regular paying customer. I come here a lot. First time I've seen you and your yobos' faces."

"Well, whippy doo. I'll just run out and get a merit medal and pin it on your chest."

Joe Atlas took a swing. Regers ducked, leaning in to slam a left jab at the man's chest. The other was big, clumsy and tipsy too, a bad combo, carrying more synthetic whisky than his capacity for his height and weight. The night was still young. Regers was well under the limit.

The brute came in swinging with both fists and a roar in his throat. He overshot and Regers snuck under the hairy arm, flung out his metal hand and knuckle-wiped him under the chin.

The man gasped. Regers snatched up a blue pellet from his pocket and jammed the sniffer in the brute's nostrils.

Blue smoke wafted from his face and sent his world tumbling. The giant went down, gagging and Deakes stomped on his head.

Regers nodded in appreciation. Sensing trouble brewing in the smoky haze, Regers pulled them all back to their table. "Play dumb."

Robot bouncers with reinforced plate metal on their forearms and chests, came to drag the fallen man by his heels and eject him out into the street. Two came to study Regers and his crew. Deakes and Regers put in their pleas how they were minding their business when this brute started hassling them. The two robot bouncers blinked. The offworlders had paid out a lot of yols from Dez's funds, so they let them off with a warning.

Regers nodded. "All's well that ends well, Ramra. You've earned your skin, but don't get too grab-happy next time. Go right on ahead with that sweet gal, and we'll see you in a bit. Vincent and I got our eyes on some choice pieces in the back."

Ramra nodded, Deakes let out a belch. Jennings shook his head, fuming.

Ramra and Vincent came out of back rooms, taking turns, while Creib watched over Dez. Jennings stayed put, scowling into his meal of synthetic fried veal. The man didn't drink or smoke a synth-hash pipe or mix with the ladies. Much to the jeers of Deakes and Vincent.

Dez stared off in stony silence.

The sweat under Regers' mask was starting to make his face itch, so he pulled it off. "Come on, Dezzy, get into the spirit of it," he coaxed. "Join the fun. You're a wet blanket on a dry day. Not likely I'm going to let you out of my sight, even if I had all my buddies aboard like Creib and goody-goody Jennings manning the fort. Might get some fool idea to call the NOA or Santie Claus and report us. Wouldn't want that."

Deakes's whiskey-rich laugh assaulted Regers' nose. "I say we deep six the bastard. Look at him sulking over there like a warmed-over toad in the hot sun. Think of the hassle he could cause us. What do we need him for?"

"We may need him, Deakes." Regers scowled. "For something down the road. Let sleeping dogs lie and let me do the thinking. You do the brawling. Got it?"

"Sure." Deakes shrugged. "Whatever you say." He turned away.

Lots of fresh, oiled and scented meat came by but Dez refused any offer of female company. Or male. Regers smiled at that and shrugged. "Your choice, Dez. You and Jiminy can sit here and twiddle your pricks for all I care. I'm due for another release. Just got to catch my second wind."

Vincent managed a half chuckle but was red-faced enough by the end of the night of carousing that he was slurring his words.

Regers grunted. "Enough for you. I'm cutting you off titty and booze." He slapped Vincent's cheeks. "Celebration's over. All of you!" He pushed Vincent aside who hung off his shoulder, slobbering like a baby. "Back to the ship. The hour's old. Time to get back to work."

CHRIS TURNER

Chapter 6

It was a long haul to *The Dim Zone*. They had plenty of time to dry out, jettison their costumes and recuperate their wits. Nonetheless, Regers was leery about heading to Remus, knowing full well the horrors that haunted this region of space. He had only to remember how *Albatross*, his last ship, had been boarded by Zikri squids that stormed them on the bridge and wiped out most of the crew. Zikri—those octopus-like aliens with motilators that could navigate like walking creatures did and could squeeze the life out of one—grotesque creatures who commanded pirate Orbs, and scavenged ships and stole whatever technology they could, from space stations, floating junk, weapons grids, and abandoned bases. They worked in collusion with the Mentera, the locust race who enslaved man, woman and alien in glass tanks and fed off their life force via some infathomable technology, keeping their victims alive in a state of suspended animation.

Regers had no idea what to expect on Remus, this middle planet of the Dizon system, boasting a dwarf star and dim amber sun.

Xaromar came out of light drive and approached the dim grey planet.

"Full shields. Yellow alert," Regers muttered. "Creib, keep your eyes peeled for hostiles. Jennings, Ramra, the same. Deakes and Vincent, keep weapons at full kill capacity."

"Aye, aye." Grunts of acknowledgement came Regers' way.

"Atmosphere's not breathable," said Creib. "A cold mix of methane, ozone and traces of unstable hydrocarbons."

A dawn's glimmer of burnt orange crept over the alien landscape from the distant sun. Much different topography, yet the terrain gave Regers eerie deja-vu of planet *Xeses* where he and Yul had first harvested the alien plants that so interested Mathias and his research scientists.

A jumble of Mars-like rocks greeted the crew and low black, obsidian outcrops with ghostly plains in between. A desolate world. Why Hresh had picked such a shit-dismal place far from civilized worlds for his research was beyond him—but then, Hresh was an eccentric, according to Dez, who knew only mad schemes and esoteric sciences. Who knew what twisted ideas ran through that brainiac geek's mind? Hresh had worked for Cyber Corp—that was telling enough. From what Regers'd heard, Hresh'd gotten on the wrong side of company policy and incurred Mathias's wrath by going on the lam. Regers stroked his chin. Mathias must have tracked Hresh down, turned up unannounced and gotten a rude surprise.

He curled his thin lip. Served the fucker right. But it didn't help his own situation in terms of getting full payment and restitution from Mathias for his injuries. Unless he milked Dez for all he was worth. Not a bad plan. Another return to Mekeroid or similar scumhole and a double draw of company funds.

A blip showed up on the holo screen. The ship skimmed over the broken landscapes and approached the planet's only settlement—the one that had to be Hresh's hideaway.

Zikri war Orbs lay scattered in ruin—large hulking derelicts with bent spikes on the outside like prickly blowfish. Crumpled mantis-like Mentera craft ranged alongside, twisted and broken from heavy cannon fire. A full-scale war had broken out here—only charred leftovers remained, suited bodies, twisted metal. A huge, rectangular complex, likely Hresh's installation, lay shredded in heaps of blackened metal. The adjoining hangar was also destroyed.

Regers paused, chewing his lip. The ship glided over the rubble on low thrust, each man gazing with awe, drawing his own conclusions. The base was utterly destroyed. What was once Hresh's highly-advanced, hi-tech research lab lay in crumbled ruin.

The lightfighter passed between twin bent control towers then past an upright mechnobot, a hulking inert shape, intact in the middle of the dusky yard. The thing, shaped like an armored tank standing on its end, rose easily two stories high. "What in shit's name is that?" muttered Regers in a dark voice. "Looks untouched."

"Beats me," said Deakes.

"It's Hresh's handiwork," responded Dez in a hoarse whisper. "A new breed of mechnobots… Incredible."

"Those are the marks of heavy duty fire all around, Regers," Ramra muttered. "Zikri war ships. Which indicates Uro bombs."

"I can see that, Ramra. No need for the report."

Regers' eyes scanned the surroundings. Low hills curved out in an S-shape to flank the complex. No vegetation that he could see, only masses of wholesale destruction, toppled barrels and ripped open shipping crates and crumpled heaps of machinery on the hill side, framing them all in a sinister U.

The shadowy derelict of a mechnobot stirred—a pilot light flared to sudden blue life on its hideous turret. Impossible. His eyes must be screwed on wrong. In slow synchrony, the mechno vibrated and rose up to the level of their LV3 lightfighter as if spurred by some eerie force of intelligence.

Regers' jaw dropped. It was as if it were scouting out the incoming vessel in curiosity, not threat.

"What the flaming—? What powers the thing?"

The grotesque vehicle jetted closer to the ship's belvedere as the crew watched in stunned silence.

The ship, or whatever the thing was, suddenly lurched as if concluding *Xaromar* and its crew were hostile, for a robotic appendage spurred out of the armored fuselage, a cannon of sorts, that began spurting fire at *Xaromar*.

The ship's shields flared. A porthole opened. A giant winged insect, more dragonfly than moth, flashed out of the black aperture high on the outerbody with a deft thrust of colored wings.

Regers choked out a yell. What the fuck? Same type of creature he'd been tasked with down on the Zikri Orb. Though this one was slightly different. More iridescent in the wings, longer thorax, redder antenna and blacker, bulgier eyes.

Without warning, the dragonfly flitted right up to the viewport glass to stare at them with glassy abandon. It flew closer to gaze at Regers through the glass, now with a cold depthlessness of expression that could barely be described. Its impossibility of existence, the fabulous dexterity of its alien wings had the other crew members awed, but not Regers—or Dez who knew this type of species all too well. Regers' eyes nearly rolled out of their sockets with the utter horror of it.

"What in fuck's name?" Deakes muttered.

"It's controlling the mechno—" Dez lifted an arm "—like the creatures did down in our labs on Phallanor."

"What, you know about these things?" Jennings croaked.

"It's one of those 'Dim Zone' creatures hatched from the plant bulbs Yul brought back. Hresh must have gotten his hands on one and tried to use it to power his bots, like we did. This time the thing destroyed his lab. Regers, turn this ship around and get the hell out of here."

"Mathias may be down there."

"Forget Mathias. The man's dead if that dragonfly thing is flitting around loose."

Regers grunted. The fact was true enough.

The dragonfly and its avatar came closer. Creib muttered a curse. He tried to gun the engine and strike at the thing. The maneuver only slapped it hard against the glass and sent it buzzing back. The insect, juiced with malicious intent, looped around in a dizzy semicircle and smashed its blunt nose against the glass.

"What in hell are you doing, Creib, you stupid A-hole?"

"I didn't like how it was hovering there mooning at us. The wings could gum up the Varwol antenna or the stabilizer plate."

"You think?"

The insect came buzzing in again to strike at the glass with the mechnobot in tow.

"Shutter the glass! Blast the thing!"

Creib struck a fist on a blue knob. The armored plates slid down over the viewing glass. Deakes let out a lusty howl. He tapped at keypads and set sights on the creature with the fore-cannon.

Dez raced toward him to slap his hand away. "No, you fool. Don't fire at the thing! It'll only retaliate and kill us all!"

"How? A little bug like that?" Deakes snorted.

"Don't underestimate them. The insect already thinks we're a threat to its habitat."

"Why the fuck would it?" Vincent sneered. He turned to look over his shoulder, then zoomed in on the weapons array, touching pads to target the thing. "Does it look like we're going to mess up its crib?"

"They're aliens, you dumbfuck," Regers said, clenching his fist. "What do you think?"

"How do you know all of this?" Jennings demanded of Dez.

"I studied them on Phallanor," panted Dez. "The same type of creature

Yul brought back from *The Dim Zone* as a bulb. It hatched. Two of them. Into one of these dragonfly-moths. They're practically invincible. We tried to control the specimen. It only made a shambles of our lab—like this base. Something must have gone wrong down here. Hresh's experiments gone amok."

A sudden movement had the visual monitor beeping warnings. A bug-shaped prow emerged, lifting over the battered hills to the north of the base.

Deakes gave a low whistle. "A fine parade here. Just what we need. So much for Hresh and Mathias."

The disturbing shape loomed out of the morning stillness and came straight at them. A mantis-shaped craft with high curving bow and sweeping cannons.

"What the fuck?" Vincent swore.

"It's a LY-Mentera fighter." Creib's hands shook as he punched in escape coordinates on the console.

Regers leveled his E1 at Dez's neck. "Some sneaky trick of yours, Dez? If you want your head blown off, then you're off to a good start." He pushed the E1 closer to the man's ear.

"I don't know anything!" Dez babbled. "Christ, Regers! Mathias must have gotten in trouble, like you said, stirred up the Mentera, but it was Zikri he got entangled with before he went missing, not Mentera. I don't get it. Don't blame me."

"I don't believe you, you egg-sucking slime."

Ramra gulped. "The Mentera must have had this place staked out. Either that or this acting CEO friend of yours led us into a trap."

"That'll earn you demerits, Dez," Regers snarled. "A blast to the face." He smashed him in the nose with his rifle. Dez's nose erupted in blood.

"OW! You bloody bastard," choked Dez. "Wasn't me planned this Remus shit."

"Well, those ships are bug ships, not squid ships. Creib," Regers yelled, "get us away from this rock. Max impulse. Now! Wait—take us on a high arc, as far from the planet as possible. We can activate warp as soon as we clear atmosphere. No low looping shit!" Regers reached for the Varwol.

"They're too close," cried Creib. "It'll foul up our grav signature!" The ship rocked to Mentera fire.

"Shit, those bugs are fast," cried Deakes. The ship rocked again, shields holding. The hovering mechnobot turned and swiveled its turret toward the approaching Mentera craft.

Regers thundered, "Blast them!"

Vincent rained heat beams at the offending craft. But the enemy's superior fire lashed back at them, sending them in a tumbling roll. The Mentera mantis-fighter ship, superior in every aspect, was going to crush them. Superior shields, armor, speed, dexterity. Another creepy aphid craft fighter with mantis-like prow sprang up from the same shadow-laced place as its peer. Regers loosed a string of curses. These ships must have been waiting for someone to show up.

At the prospect of being thrown back in a locust tank, Regers clawed at the nav controls. Jennings gave a despaired croak. "Your insanity got us into this mess, Regers—Get us the hell out!"

"They've snagged us in a tractor grip," Ramra breathed. "Ship's impulse diminished to less than 3%."

Regers thought fast. "Creib, reduce the thrust. Let them think we've capitulated. At the point of surrender, Vincent, train our guns on their recon tower. Deakes, aim a second set on her two rear boosters. The moment they try to breach, we blast them full on."

"Damn! We'll never break free," groaned Deakes.

"Throw it off! Blast them for crap sakes!"

"Shields are too strong!"

They're not trying to kill us—they would have blown us out of the air by now," said Jennings.

"Of course, so they can stick us in their tanks and feed off us till the end of time."

"Or they were waiting here for somebody to show up," snarled Regers. "Maybe they want information."

Dez cowered in a ball, all googly-eyed and holding his blood-seeping nose. He clutched his hair, frightened out of his skull.

Deakes growled. "They're not drawing us into the mother ship, Regers. They've put a can opener on us."

"Can opener?" His mind reeled. How the fuck had this happened? He saw the screwnail-shaped bot loosed from the mothership come speeding their way in the rear holo cam. It clamped onto *Xaromar's* port middle, digging into her armored hull. Long, metallic grey spider appendages vibrated with giant magno suckers latched to the hull and its massive titanium stinger rose like an oil-well's pumpjack. It poised to penetrate the hull, maintaining the ship's pressure while locust troopers disgorged into the main hall to capture them.

"Ramra, get the defensive armor down off the wall. Everyone, suit up!" He snatched up a Kevlar vest and others donned armor plates on torsos and vitals. Only six suits to go around so Dez got the short stick. Choking and gibbering, the CEO was already beyond realizing his fate.

"We've got ourselves a fight," Regers rasped. He tossed E1s to the others. "Barricade the bridge. They'll come in and try to blast us. But we'll take down as many as we can."

Chapter 7

Audra stirred from her stupor, spread-eagled in the dimly-lit chamber, smelling of must, alien vermin and ancient death. She started to regain her senses. Each of her six powerful motilators was stretched across a torture board in painful precision, taut and wired to a gridded vise of strange design. The unpleasant memories of being tortured drifted into her consciousness. Yes...she was on *Kraetoria*, legendary home world of her Zikri race. The air and pressure in the room was controlled—a feature on the plus side—easier to breathe than the inhospitable cold air in the tunnels. On the negative side...well, her immobility was only one of the many negatives...

"We want to get to the bottom of this mystery," an accented voice said in her own chittering language. "We will ferret out this human and his meddling friends, never fear, *Griekshj.*" The word, a derogative reference to *ghost* in her native tongue, held a hollow ring—indicating a rebel hovering on the fringes of society. The massive Zikri standing hunched over her splayed body, mouthed the name in a jeering, almost insolent way. Here was some minor captain, eager to make a name for himself, with a manner gloating and carefree. He pulled up some data on a green-pulsing screen, a 3D monitor of some unknown technology. His assistant, a lowly attendant, clearly intimidated by his overseer, shrank back in his ropy pose, cowering under the murky shadow of his superior.

Audra's eyes adjusted to the dimness. She squinted through their narrowed slits at her tormentors. She could handle far worse pain than this, but it was expedient to give the semblance of weakness at this moment. All her training had taught her to employ tricks, however small but significant.

She cowered in as painful a feigned posture as possible, but made careful note of every nook and cranny around her in the hopes of making an escape. This small claustrophobic burrow with walls and ceiling of the same dull grey stone as without, was not to her liking. Several machines sat to either side: monitors and control panels, tower boxes and surgical equipment with crane-like arms, holding hypodermics and incisory tools…adjusted by a technician, a much more wiry and thin Zikri than the leader, with six long, pale tentacles. Two steel doors at either end of the chamber served as exits, with the squidlike logos and motilator motifs characteristic of her race. Black and silver emergency suits, of both squid and locust design, hung on the far wall. Sprinklers and air vents, set in the smooth rock ceiling, oddly complemented a half dozen air tanks sitting under the long, utility counter. Their presence caused more distress than ease. She couldn't quite peg the purpose of this place, as much an experimental hazlab as a torture chamber in her opinion. Maybe both.

Noticing her return to consciousness, the overlord made a gesture of tentacle. "No doubt you are wondering why you are here? You are of the older breed," he said conversationally. "Fascinating, as impossible as that can be."

Audra stiffened. The overlord twitched his polyp of a mouth and prompted his attendant to flick a switch.

Electro-stimulus coursed through her tentacles. She bore the pain, though it sent ripples of agony through her elastic, muscular upper body. Her own polyp of a mouth tightened in a small quivering O.

"Answer the question, *Griekshj*, or you will dance in pain. We've much time to explore your dark little secrets and you will tell us all you know. Why were you there with the human, Miko, attacking Mentera and Zikri soldiers?"

Audra gave a chitter of disgust. This peacock interrogating her was insufferable! No less, torturing her. He and all his kind had already lost the ability to transmit electro-charged energy through their motilators. A critical natural defense and survival mechanism lost in the mists of time. Had all this happened while she and Miko had been cavorting about in spacetime? Evidently they had been propelled into the future after the time drive accident. These Zikri needed machines to help them effect their aggressions! What had become of this modern race of Zikri over the centuries?

An answer came in a moment's introspection. Centuries of inbreeding had weakened the strain of the original Zikri race. The new stock was soft and weak, their bodies no match for her superior strength and her flexible motilators—if only she could break free...

A rumbling chitter came from her throat. "I come from an age long before you—from the time of the Oldevri cycle—on a heisted state-of-the art starship, of human manufacture."

"That can't be. You claim birth origin eight Magellan cycles ago."

Audra remained silent.

"You are certainly a different breed of Zikri. Stronger, faster, more insidious. You took out nine guards of mine before they could even defend themselves. That in itself is impressive, as much as it makes you an item of scientific interest. You'll need to be studied. Tell me how you have developed such strength? Through drugs? Bio-implants?"

Audra's body arched as the vises gripping each tentacle shot electrical surges through her body. Unbearable pain. She jerked to a spasmodic pitch, loosing a spine-chilling howl—a guttural, primeval wail of contorted rage and defiance.

"I passed through a time hole, a warp failure," she chittered. "NAVO craft...they blasted us on warp sequence when we were in the humanoid's experimental ship. I have no idea what century I am in. Though everything is different now. *Zaigua* outpost is gone. This planet is much different from what I remembered."

The overlord spoke in a rapid series of gutturals. "*Zaigua 1* was decommissioned over two hundred years ago. So you claim to be two-hundred years old? Impossible." The overlord swept an upper tentacle out, tickling the upper lip of his grey mottled face, a gesture which implied disbelief. Audra grimaced in contempt. The Zikri overlord's mind was slow. Easy to outwit this pretender. Just a matter of biding her time and playing into his puerile illusion of domination.

"Incredible. Far too incredible for my tastes. You could be lying to us, *Griekshj*. I cannot verify it, because we have no records of names and titles from that long ago. Even your ship, this giant Orb, *Xmrkiw*, you claim to have been science officer aboard, has passed out of record. As too the commanders, officers and crew you worked under."

He continued with a tentacle curled around the smooth egg-dome of his skull. "You followed this humanoid creature, Miko, and became enamored with him and attached yourself to his body in a grotesquely physical way."

Audra gurgled out a protest, but ultimately gave a jiggling gesture in the affirmative. A disturbance came at the door.

She watched while two Zikri guards hauled in a Mentera, a smaller bipedal, locust-like creature. They clamped pincers and legs in the torture board not fifteen feet away from her own miserable hide. The creature, like all of the Mentera race, sported the large greenish-black head of a locust, two arms with lobster-like pincers at the end in place of hands, and a pair of hind, locust-like legs on which it stooped much as an ape would. Its deformed wings had long atrophied. As attendant and guards fussed with the locust's bonds, its black, spiky antennae drooped in defeat. Though in the gleam of that rebellious eye, lurked a ruddy hint of recognition. *Yes, the one who had fought against his own kind in the Hall of Tanks,* thought Audra. *A rebel, a dangerous renegade.* The Zikri's and Mentera's mutual feeling of deviancy was shared in a wayward glance.

"This locust, some spy or rebel, was reported firing on his own in the same battle you were caught in. We recovered him dunked in a Mentera tank. His accomplices must have dragged him in there after suffering battle wounds, no doubt to heal. We will catch up with those perpetrators soon enough. For his crimes, he will die painfully. But not until we pick his brain clean of information, question his motives for rebellion and find out who he was working with." He motioned a tentacle. "Jngken, my young protégé, I am mentoring on the arts of torture and persuasion. So you and the rebel will provide excellent case studies in this regard."

Audra only dimly registered the overseer's words as the next power surge shot up her leathery hide. It coursed into her head and started to dull her mind. Likewise the drug or hypno agent they had injected into the puny creature's bloodstream now seemed to be having a noticeable effect. The attendant hooked up a universal translator device to the locust's antenna, one thin black disc. The overlord began grilling him with questions.

"Why did you blow up the lower level of our installation?"

The locust's red eyes glazed over. "The Master bade us to do so—in return for granting us an escape route."

"What Master?"

"The master race. The Masters were here on this planet before the Zikri and you never knew it. They played god, manipulating the early evolution of both Zikri and Mentera, brewing creatures like you and me in vats, not knowing that one day they would overthrow them."

"Oh, really? Describe this 'Master' species."

The locust paused, his one antenna drooping, as if unsure how to answer.

"Answer the question!" A small surge of current made the locust jerk and utter words that the translator echoed back in Zikri-speak:

"Some humanoid creature! Tall with hollow eyes and hairless hooded skull. A thing neither male nor female, somewhat androgynous, with short forelimbs and long bare feet with four hairy toes like one of the giant, humanoid, primate apes. At one time they called themselves the *Cuyrne*."

The overlord gurgled out an expletive. "Preposterous!"

Audra's mind blanked out for several instants as the attendant ministered to some innovative preparations involving a hypodermic injected into each motilator. Each had its own notable effect: dizziness, a pleasurable tingling from tentacles up, an urge to babble the truth without dissembling. The overseer's voice became a soporific drone like the vague surge of waves on a distant shore. She shook herself alert once again.

"...I refute these masters," said the overlord with a tinge of scorn. "These Cuyrne, you say they engineered the Zikri and Mentera—in vats? that the stronger-engineered Zikri escaped, took over the lab, killing their overseers and claimed the planet but that the so-called Masters were there all the time watching in some underground bunker?"

"It implied as much."

"What do you mean, 'it'?"

"The AI simulacrum that spoke for the long dead Cuyrne Masters."

The overseer gave another chitter of disbelief. "So, you discovered this bunker, fell through the crust while pursued by Mentera troopers. Where is the proof of this claim?"

"The proof, the blue memory module—we destroyed it," said the locust. "The simulacrum compelled us to initiate the destruct sequence. Thus the information would not fall into the hands of either you or the Mentera. We barely escaped with our lives. Only to plunge into the midst of your secret, allied base."

"Why would this AI intelligence do that? And why couldn't it initiate the destruct sequence on its own?"

The locust alien twitched its carapace. Its eyes hardened to a dull coral sheen. Its shoulders, dark plates of green and black, hunched in helpless compliance. "The detonator sequence was designed deliberately so the simulacrum could not initiate it on its own. In case the algorithm went berserk. Or in case it was ever tweaked by outside invaders. Or so it told us. As for keeping this origin of our races secret, that is beyond my knowledge."

"You are an ignorant, foolish creature!" the overlord rasped and smacked a tentacle down on the torture console. He signaled the attendant with a brisk flicking motion. The attendant zapped the locust with a dose of current. The locust howled, a keening, whining cry, folding its long atrophied wings in weak flutters.

"The Zikri are masters of the universe! Much older than any locusts, humanoids or apes, or the smattering of mutant intelligent species littered throughout the galaxy. Our dominance on this planet proves it. Where is this module you describe with its databank of proof of these Masters and our manufactured origin? I would kill you now for your lies, bug, had the Mentera not recently discovered a similar blue box as you described in the aftermath of the blast. They are busy trying to penetrate its secrets. For that reason you still live. Your motives regarding this fabricated story, or whatever else you're hiding, I do not know. Possibly to delay your inevitable fate. War is upon us and we are called to duty, to crush the humans once and for all and enslave the populations of their planets. Even now, I am pushing this interrogation beyond my superior's wishes. But I have other intentions in mind, though they're on hold for now..." His eyes scrunched into glittering beads.

"So now, do you still tell the same story, bug?"

The locust did not respond. The overlord puckered his mouth in an ugly O. The locust howled again as current surged through its vitals, causing the hard-shelled pincers to clack and its ovoid head to bob up and down on its chest in anguish. Audra watched in detached curiosity.

The overlord loosed a belligerent chitter. "We're getting nowhere here, Jngken. Up the voltage!"

"As you wish, overlord." Jngken fiddled with the knobs. Audra braced herself for more punishment in parallel to the locust's. Then a sudden idea hit her.

Chapter 8

Jngken, the lab trainee, licked his polyp of a mouth. He stood under the shadow of Hrang, his superior, yet no less caught up in scientific fascination of cracking the mystery of this time-traveling Zikri. She exhibited inexplicable attributes that could not be tossed off as mere mutant side anomalies. Classic muscular lines, toned muscle, a fearsome vitality, all radiating an impressive hyper-awareness. A femme fatale, if any there was. Jngken had never seen such a physically magnificent specimen in such fine, but deadly form...

Lust overcame his reason. Admittedly he felt himself smitten with freakish sexual attraction. The trainee was awed and intimidated at the same time that this Zikri had come from nowhere, having no past and no present. Could this time travel story of hers be true? Why Hrang was treating her so cruelly seemed to be counterproductive to what could be gleaned and enjoyed from her. Whether he wanted Jngken to play the sympathetic role to soften her up remained to be seen. He wouldn't mind that. If the prisoner'd time-traveled, she'd be confused. It stood to reason. Such a queen amongst their race!

As overseer Hrang administered a torture spike to her left lower motilator, Jngken thought he caught her answering stare of burning intensity in response to his gaze of admiration and lust. He quickly looked away. Could she actually be attracted to him? It seemed pure fantasy.

At the height of his youth and having been isolated so long, Jngken could not help but imagine those glistening, ample limbs entwined around his own, squeezing, caressing, all the pleasures of Zikri sin rolled into one. The oily friction, the heightening constriction and the ultimate sultry chittering of the Zikri queen in his ear. Oh, what a thrill! A meeting of minds and bodies, up to and including the release into ecstasy.

Hrang's sharp chitter snapped him out of his reverie. Ending his sex-sotted delirium.

Such desire would only impair his scientific judgment. It would jeopardize his position. A deadly mistake with one so capably ruthless as overseer Hrang.

* * *

In a sudden surge of motion, Hrang bounded over to Audra. "You, *Griekshj*! What have you to say of this utter nonsense the bug babbles? Speak! You knew the other one of this locust's company, this Miko humanoid filth. Did he talk of these Masters to you?"

Audra paused before answering. She was about to utter some nonsense but veered in another direction. Immediately she feigned a cowed gurgle.

The overseer's bullet head jerked around as he pushed in closer. "What's that? Speak up!"

Audra increased the intensity of her plaintive gurgling. As the overseer's head moved in to decipher the gibberish, she struck with incredible force. She tore her upper motilator free from its cincture, shredding flesh and sinew. The electrode flew from its vise. She snapped goblin teeth and sank yellow fangs into Hrang's rheumy eye. While a blood-sopped tentacle whirled around his head, pulling him in closer to her teeth, her muscles rippled and smashed his skull against the empty socket where the motilator had last been fastened.

The device short-circuited. White sparks flew, singeing the tyrant's black, rubbery face. He let out a horrid wail. The cinctures loosened for an instant. In a chain reaction, Audra's lower motilators broke free. She was mobile! The overseer curled in a defensive C. He pushed motilators outward to counteract the monstrous force, but Audra, pitched to a fountain of rage, flung strangling tentacles around Hrang's body.

The assistant Jngken stood frozen. His mouth gobbled, beady eyes gaped, then he was instinctively on the move to save the overseer.

Too late. Audra constricted with a vengeance and sounds of ripping cartilage soon filled the room. The overseer cried out and lay helplessly gasping on the cold floor. Audra straddled him in her triumph, her motilators still gripping and tearing away flesh from his hide while bits of his tentacles lay twitching in gory heaps at his side.

Jngken surged forward. He held aloft the sedative hypodermic in a trembling grip.

Audra caught the movement. She leaped up from her captor's gored body to bat away the syringe. But the needle made contact with her whipping tentacle before she could send the attendant sailing across the room. He smashed into the torture rack. The still-sparking circuits smoked and burned, allowed the captive locust a brief chance to free himself. Tearing at the failing ring mechanism, he ripped his left pincer off. The right pincer slipped free. Tugging and thrashing, he worked to snip the restraining wire from his right leg. He ducked, snapping with sharp teeth at the rings holding his left insect leg. Bedlam, smoke, anguish…all ensued with blood splattering everywhere.

Audra felt a wooziness in her head. That underling Jngken must have pumped her with some somno-drug. She advanced, seeing slightly double. She bore down on him as the locust scuttled out of her way, gibbering in pain.

The Mentera grabbed a suit from the wall and despite its half torn claw, struggled to plunge himself into it. The creature obviously had a plan of action. Soon he was scuttling out the back door. The insect's exit plan was a good one. Audra dimly registered the need to follow such a lead…

In a fit of rage she sprang at the attendant. He was nimbler. Scrambling to the reinforced front door, he heaved it open with a jerk of tentacle, stumbled through, closing it with a clang.

Audra snatched at the iron wheel, still slowed by the injection, but the door was already tightly locked and her tentacles slapped uselessly against the cold metal. She stared at him through the glass window, their eyes shafting daggers at one another. Each was of the same breed but of different eras spanning centuries.

Enough games. Audra turned at the gurgling moan of the overseer, still not quite dead. Her intent, to follow the locust out the back exit, was momentarily forestalled…

* * *

In a painful crouch, Jngken ducked, breathing heavily. He waited several seconds before he frogged his way across the hall; then he halted, having other thoughts. He waddled back to the glass, gaping at the carnage and impossible ruin of the interrogation lab. Three of Hrang's motilators lay twisted and lifeless on the floor. Hrang himself lay on his back, sucking in wheezing breaths. He was straddled by the rebel, mutant Zikri, his beady eyes bulging from their sockets. The Zikri's two foremost tentacles wrapped around the pliable, wattled neck of his superior's, giving the final twist.

Black blood oozed as Hrang let out his last chittering gasp.

Black blood spilled to smoke and sizzle.

Jngken caught a last glimpse of the female Zikri as she gave a chortle of vindication. She turned and withdrew through the back exit where the locust had fled in jerky motions down the dim stone corridor. Perhaps the mutant had reacted to the threat of being injected. The sedative would not last long. Hrang's orders had been to keep the prisoners alive and mentally alert so they could be interrogated to the maximum.

Whatever the cause of her escape, Jngken could not believe the strength of the Zikri. He shuddered when he thought about how easily those motilators had made a ruin of Hrang's tentacles and ripped off his head. Hrang was no weakling.

He struggled with the concept of her improbable presence but was firm in his resolve to avoid a similar fate, both awed and appalled at the prospect of being roughhoused by those meaty motilators and surviving. A dangerous spider-and-fly game. Such distracting thoughts Jngken set aside. What he needed right now was a clear head to handle the current affair. What with his superior Hrang mauled beyond repair, splayed on the detention room floor, Jngken, lab technician, was now leader of the operation.

He turned and glided in silence down the laboratory hall. The research and torture area facility was wide and complex with many side corridors and alcoves, containing machines, decoders, hypno-boxes, pain-inducer units and other interesting gadgets. Half distracted, Jngken wandered on a circuitous path via a back way to the control center, hoping to avoid the creature should it still be lurking. He was still dazed by his near miss of death. Even now, his lustful mind wandered over the lurid fantasy of being wrapped in muscular union with that queenly creature, deadly as she was. A rekindled sexual excitement fluttered up the rubbery mass of his primitive spine and along the sensitive nerves radiating outward toward his carapace. He shook off the lustful urge once again. He must alert Emperor Nrog of Mission Control, tell him of the new developments, the murder of Overseer Hrang and the escape of the rebel Zikri. He must—

He stopped, his ears perked. Odd that the door to the research facility was ajar. Hadn't he closed it when he had last passed this way? Surely the creature hadn't managed to penetrate the inner chamber? No, impossible... And yet, there was that containment room access on level 6, where a cunning creature might bypass the electro-monitored checkpoint then...perhaps—

A bulky form hit him sideways, sending him to the far wall. He reeled, curled in a ball to cushion his fall. He spun around with tentacles upraised to meet those of his attacker's.

Audra advanced. Jngken let out a soft scream. He felt the whoosh of air at his side and the breath fizzle out of his lungs. Before he knew it, he was enveloped in a flurry of whipping tentacles, crushed in a violent embrace. Sexual embrace. Shock, fear, lust and terror all coalesced in one continuum of utter, sensory chaos.

Cartilage bent. Muscle tissue ripped. Jngken felt himself being ravaged, in a thrill of ecstasy, albeit painfully as every corpuscle was crushed to oblivion, every flexible bit of cartilage torn and ruptured from inside out. His male member thrust against her elastic, soft, rubbery-receptive orifice. But Audra denied him that pleasure at the last instant, crushing every bit of fluid and wind out of him.

* * *

Audra paused after her handiwork, letting the mangled heap fall in a lifeless jumble. No one must know how she escaped if she were to capture Miko unhindered. Black blood dripped from her upper left motilator. Her wounds, though not insignificant, would heal soon enough, toughen up with rubbery scar tissue. Hers was a formidable constitution. Now to follow the renegade Mentera. He would lead her straight to Miko, her real quarry. The human who had wronged her. He had a dire reckoning ahead of him.

She reeled back against the cold stone, her motilators skimming the rough surface of the tunnel floor. A minor lapse. The narcotic the Zikri attendant had pricked her with was only a small dose for her enormous bulk. Not enough to hinder her much—already the drug was wearing off. Still, she was aware that she was not in top condition. No matter. She shook off the woozy feeling, the dullness of her mental activity. There was much to do. The future course of events rode on possibilities explored and risks taken.

How she liked these rock-hewn corridors. Perfect for skulking and ambush.

She paused, used her olfactory glands to sniff out the spoor of the fugitive locust. The Mentera was wounded, dripping ichor from a missing left pincer. The locust blood had a metallic odor to it, quite distinctive, like the bog swamps of her distant home planet. A clear path to follow.

Up the tunnels she glided.

A long time later, the sounds of a struggle met her ears, laced with the hint of human activity—short, blaster bursts. At a bend in the tunnel stood an arched entrance granting access to a small cavern hosting several of the Mentera tanks. She crouched at the threshold of the archway, peering within. Several blood-splattered Zikri corpses were scattered about the rough stone floor, obviously taken out by blaster fire.

Further within, the grey-green cloying shadows thickened and she glimpsed one of the Zikri guards carrying a struggling human wearing a spacesuit.

The woman.

Audra's beady eyes narrowed in interest. The same female that Miko found so enchanting. She was wrapped in the tentacles of a Zikri guard, hauling her toward one of the vacant tanks. That was reassuring. More leverage to use against Miko. The Zikri hunter lifted his struggling charge ready to plunge the pitiful specimen into one of the locust tanks.

The rebel locust hunched in the shadows in much distress at his lack of means and weapons. This same one she had shared the torture rack with had been the woman's loyal companion, trying desperately to protect her. What horrid bodies both of them had, human and Mentera. How Miko could find the female thing desirable with her ugly scents, frame so weak and fragile and with hair so fair and long, was a mystery to her.

Without preamble, she acted with a hunter's instinct.

* * *

With a wild yell, Star struck again and again at the loathsome invader's tentacles wrapped around her body. The Zikri lifted her toward the tank that Usk had once occupied. No! This could not be happening! It was of no use—the thing's limbs were like iron, constricting her like pythons. The more she struggled, the more air got sucked out of her lungs. Her suit would rupture at any moment. It would be all over. Yes, maybe that was better and quicker. Die before forced into a more gruesome hell. *Please, kill me! Don't let them thrust me in that tank!*

Yet survival reflex would not let her die. Like a drowning dog she kicked and thrashed and lashed out at the odious brine as she inched closer to its sulfurous oblivion.

The Zikri's face was close to hers now, a black and dusky-grey rubbery thing, like some ancient mask of horror.

In all that terror and the sudden flurry of splashing water, as she touched its filmy surface, she was wrenched back by an inconceivable force.

The sudden ripping of cartilage came to her ears. The strangling grip loosened in an instant and she sank. Some larger hulk was looming behind her, of more massive girth than her captor, something darker and more sinister, a titan of wadded flesh. It clasped her captor in a constricting hold and pulled its motilators up behind its back and bullet head and dragged it backward.

Star gasped, breaking the surface of the water, holding onto the rim of the tank for balance, while dogpaddling with the other gloved hand. She had to get out of this tank!

Could it be? Her defender looked like that grotesque creature that had tried to clasp Miko in an intimate embrace back in the ancient battle hall during the horrible hybrid fight. Why was it killing its own kind? Could it actually be helping her? The concept was as alien to her as the creature, one which turned her stomach and her mind topsy-turvy.

The Zikri in the unknown avenger's grip gave a last agonized chitter before it lay lifeless in a heap on the cold stone. In a blinking daze, Star pulled herself over the rim and dropped down in front of the tank.

Usk, a quivering shape, scuttled up and pulled her away from that perilous place as her mind began its descent into a haze of delirium.

The black-grey skinned creature known as Audra glided in leisurely fashion after them...

Chapter 9

Miko drifted through the creepy tunnels and the tank-rooms that had seen no humans since the beginning of time. His body had disappeared. He was an invisible entity, yet with senses intact.

Blinked out of existence in near airless vacuum with aliens on his tail. How long would this state of suspended animation last?

His senses were on high alert, allowing him to see, hear, even grasp objects, but not smell. He could think and reason—how, he had no idea, outside of the fact that the laws of physics did not apply to him; furthermore, they were not always immutable. Why this was happening or how he was capable of two distinct realities was beyond him. Only that it had happened in a time drive accident with Audra, and a subsequent amalgamator freak misfire, rendering him invisible, or bodiless from time to time. If he were to rematerialize now, he would surely die, choking on the cold, nearly oxygen-less air. He needed to find pressure suits for him and Usk quickly, otherwise…

But where? Just a honeycombed tunnel-maze of miles of cold grey rock with only the odd dim glimmer of phosphorescent light appearing at random around a corner. In this hostile environment, there was nothing to hope for. Only the odd dim glow of perpetual alien twilight shining from an obscure vent.

The last monster encounter shredding his suit lay still thick in memory…a hybrid of tentacles, armored plates and scales. He had 'blinked out' in his usual fashion, eluding it at a crucial moment as he floated out of his mangled suit, thus saving his life. But he could not count on such luck again. Surely there would be more of those foul creatures lurking about this rocky labyrinth. Not to mention...*Audra*. She had been captured by her own kind, dragged away to some unknown doom. He did not know how he felt about that. Relief? Emptiness? Disbelief? She seemed impossible to kill. Perhaps she was no longer around, but a sixth sense told him otherwise, mixed with a vestige of hollowness and sadness permeating his core. Inexplicable. That was the only word for it. They had been joined for months in *Sitty II*, that experimental craft of the NAVO, the New Avionic Vanguard Order. Those memories coupled in a ship were dark and disgusting, ones he'd rather never revisit. Crash landing on *Rogos* with its primitive brood of creatures formed another dim nightmare in the back of his brain. Those desperate moments in a sinking ship in a fetid bog, cutting himself free from her muscled wads of flesh while she was under attack by some alien swordfish, were some of the most vivid of his life. But she had survived and was still hunting him down like a bloodhound its prey.

He hated to leave Star with Usk but he had no choice. He had to find a ship or oxygen, or both, or they were all dead. How much time remained? Six hours for the lot of them? Before her pressure suit's life support system faded out? It seemed an impossible deadline. Impossible odds.

Usk had to heal. He shuddered to think what would happen if Zikri caught up with Usk or Star. He hoped Star could protect herself against them.

Fat lot of good he was doing them now—bodiless, lost, without means or weapon. At least he held the advantage of stealth with his sheath of invisibility. That could prove lethal to an aggressor unable to detect his presence. For now, he moved unseen in the dark windless tunnels of the Zikri and Mentera, until he blinked back at random or someone threw some liquid on him. Liquid seemed to uncloak the spell and reveal his outer human form.

What was this place? Some antediluvian tunnels, rough-hewn haunts of the Zikri and the Mentera still in nefarious use today? Evidently they were using it now as some base or research site, for activities unknown. Probably something related to the two races' recent alliance.

A buzz of motion alerted him. Busy echoes reminiscent of the locusts' excited chatter. He glided on, willing his spirit by mental effort alone to propel him through the tunnels of emptiness. The buzz-like chatter of Mentera voices grew more distinct. Residuals through voice com. Excited and wary. Two locusts in dun-colored space-suits guarded the upcoming control post.

Miko silently glided past them. He debated snatching one of their weapons, a lumo-baton that zapped like a taser as well as fired a stun ray, but that would only alert them to an intruder's presence and complicate matters. If he were to blink back to bodily form without warning, even with a weapon he would be vulnerable.

Rounding a corner, Miko's essence drew to a dead halt.

A hundred or more Mentera craft. Mantis stealth ships. What were these locusts up to?

A burst of fire flashed from somewhere half way up the secret hangar. Resistance? Allies? Haters of the Mentera like himself?

Miko's heart flared in hope. The disturbance had erupted near the first parked ships. With speed, and without second thought, he willed himself up the tunnel toward the praying mantis-shaped-ships and the source of the chaos.

CHRIS TURNER

Chapter 10

Space mercenary Yul peered past his three companions to the twilight ridge several miles distant. A maroon-grey tint gave back a hint of eeriness unsettling to the eye. The sight of its summit, riddled with projections, made it look like a collection of devils' horns whose shadows fell with cold disfavor. Such a sight tickled the hairs on the back of his neck. What lay beneath that ridge? Several enemy vessels had glided into its bowels but had not pulled out, as if mysteriously gobbled up. Others had banked in offensive pursuit of one another, firing live weapons and countering with shield defenses. He did not like this planet, Kraetoria. Who would? It was some home planet of the Zikri or insectoid Mentera, with its hobgoblin hybrids of alien creatures lurking about the rock pits and moon-like craters and dusty plains. Half squid, half locust creatures engaged in obscene rituals. Fenli, their newest companion, and crashland victim, had been lucky. Pulled out from one of the nearly frozen mud pools, he was standing, but by all rights he should be dead. The alien waters the hybrids had thrust him into had kept him alive despite his punctured suit—in some state of suspended animation, though that was a loose term. No doubt the pools were connected somehow to the alchemic mystery of the Mentera tanks and their green fluids' healing technology. He hoped never to see the inside of one of those tanks. Or land face to face with one of those crab-like aliens that had jumped out of the water after them when they had pulled Fenli free.

Under the lower gravity, all their strides were longer, Yul's the longest, being tallest and bulkiest of them all. But there was a danger of tripping or sprawling headlong, thus ripping a hole in one's suit.

Yul lay a gloved hand on Fenli's shoulder. "On your guard there. Easy to overshoot." He'd have to watch this Fenli. The man was still tracking poorly, still woozy from his supine pose in the freezing water. He hoped the replacement helmet would hold, the one they had plucked off the nearby dead astronaut. It had taken them a while to revive Fenli when he passed out the last time.

Fenli's piercing blue eyes studied Yul with a curious amusement, one that Yul did not like.

The ridge loomed nearer, grown higher and more menacing. They'd better hurry before the air ran out of their pressure suits. Shelter and resources may be within reach. They pushed on.

Yul's massive chest heaved under the stress of the last hours. His short, dirty blond hair lay plastered to his scalp from the fresh sweat budding under his thermal suit. His stocky, muscular arms were assets in this space rogue game, particularly his left arm, completely prosthetic.

His wrist brushed over the blaster at his hip as he signaled Cloye, his female companion, to close in on his left.

Cloye was much too impulsive. Sexy as could be, and certainly no coward. He admired her voluptuous wide-hipped frame, a fiery bundle of amber-haired woman. A skilled martial arts fighter too, mercenary spy turned ally, after being hired by his nemesis, CEO Mathias, to track him down and murder him if he screwed up the mission to *Remus*. He had fucked up, alas, resulting in their being stranded on this forsaken planet, a fact of which he had reminded himself all too many times.

Hresh, Mathias's middle-aged research scientist turned rogue, labored at their side. Here was a man with dark complexion, curly brown hair and radiant gold eyes. A genius of unknown caliber, as eccentric as the weather. The destruction of his secret research facility on Remus had no doubt set cybernetics back a few years, if not a hundred, but better that than having those feral alien butterflies roving around, terrorizing the galaxy. All of them had been lucky to escape Remus as it was. Only to get nearly blasted out of the sky by Mentera lightfighters on a surprise approach to the Mentera-Zikri alliance fleet, namely, several thousands of vessels strong, including L-16 Mentera destroyers. What treachery their captive Mentera pilot had unleashed, flying them straight into a hornets' nest. The miracle was that they were still alive. Without a ship, in this hostile environment, meant doom. But that could be remedied, if they snatched any opportunity that came their way. Plenty of ships here for the picking, any one of those that were flying into that ridge.

His eyes darted uneasily about. If any more of those crab-like aliens should jump out and tear at their suits…He clutched his E1 assault rifle in a gloved palm, teeth gritted. Grim comfort washed over him at the sleek, black, ten-inch instrument of death.

"How much air you got left?" he asked Fenli.

Fenli scanned his pressure gauge. "Unit's dodgy. Keeps fluctuating, maybe malfunctioning after that helmet replacement you did. Anywhere from three to five hours. I'd wager not a lot of time to pull a rabbit out of a hat."

"Kinda eerie knowing you only have three hours left to live." Hresh's offhand remark earned him no popularity among the others.

"Not as eerie as knowing you only have two hours and 59 minutes," remarked Cloye. "Hoof it up, Hresh, you're lagging." She hustled him along with her blaster prodding his shoulder.

Hresh upped his pace, seemingly in awe of the woman.

A low roar came rumbling over the ridge. Two Mentera craft pursuing a smaller Zikri Orb flew into sight.

Yul pulled Cloye down behind some boulders while Fenli and Hresh instinctively ducked. They crouched in the dust before a cluster of boulders, hardly daring to breathe. The three ships came buzzing up and over the horn-speckled ridge then dove, screaming down the valley that ran parallel to the base of the cliff. Blue rays trailed from the locust craft. The Orb's tail end lit up in red.

"Jesus, that was close." Yul wiped dust from his faceplate.

"Those are Zikri and Mentera vessels," Cloye muttered. "Killing each other, snapping at each other's tails like rabid dogs. I thought this was an alliance?"

"Funny how they're not getting shot down," mused Hresh.

"Ever hear of shields?" said Fenli.

"Where they disappear to though? Makes no sense." Cloye's eyes arched skyward. "More coming." A bright flash trailed across the sky between two horned peaks. Two Zikri Orbs in pursuit of the attacking Mentera craft.

"They're aliens!" Fenli croaked. "How do we expect to understand them?" He threw up his hands. "I say we get the hell out of here. We're too exposed."

"Yeah, and where you want to run to?" Yul demanded. "The open desert?" He gritted his teeth.

"They're not likely going to be searching for humans down here while they're up to their eyeballs in enemy ship fire," Hresh pointed out.

"I don't want to be the one to find out otherwise." Yul stumbled to his feet. The others grudgingly followed.

On they trod toward a blemish in the cliff that might have been a crude opening. Hresh huffed and puffed into his faceplate, fogging it up, not used to the sudden brisk exercise despite the lower gravity. The older man would slow them down. He'd better not slow them down too much. Fenli could turn into a problem, too, Yul thought, for other reasons.

Before them, the base of the ridge loomed, a near sheer cliff, and they approached with wary steps. The place was layered with crumbled rock and scree. Fenli confirmed this was the place his wingmen had flown over before they crashlanded. "The rest of my team came hurtling down somewhere over there. Sket burned up before he crashed. I'm sure of it. I don't know where Miko ended up." He pointed a shaky finger to a distant bend off to the right. "The man saved my life—rescued me from a bug tank on some distant Mentera station. Sorry I couldn't do the same for him."

Like ghosts, they moved toward a crude opening in the moon-like, dust-grey cliff. What looked like massive carven ox horns curled around the arched top, creeping them out: disturbing, top-heavy things, but were actually alien tentacles carved in some bygone past.

Awe and unease left Yul groping for words. He shuddered, recognizing the eerie iconography of the squid-like Zikri.

A quick peek within revealed a long tunnel laced with sepulchral shadows, large enough to accommodate a mid-sized starship. Yul clambered forward to investigate, despite his qualms.

"Wait!" Fenli grabbed his shoulder. "You sure you want us to go in there? Doesn't look that inviting to me."

Yul looked at him with strained patience. "What is inviting in this wretched place?"

"Your ship—the one that went down, maybe you can salvage something—"

"Forget it, Fenli," Cloye snapped. "The ship is lost. You'd better have some good reason to steer us this way. Nowhere else to go and we're running out of air."

"Me? What are you on? I've no plan. Been stuck in a frozen pool since crash-landing on this dunghill slagheap."

Cloye cursed in acknowledgement.

Yul motioned them on. "Quit bickering. We move on into this opening in the ridge. We hope it'll lead us to where the smoke and ships came from, as planned. There must be some life-support systems where those Zikri and Mentera have their creep meets. Oxygen, water, food. Beg, borrow or steal, we'll get food and shelter."

Hresh looked on with wide-eyed curiosity. Yul stared back at him, wondering what went on in the scientist's square head. Everything seemed like an intellectual puzzle to him—death, deadly plant species, mechnobots of horror. Did the man not realize the danger they were in? Obviously not, or some side of his persona was as warped as could be. Considering the mechno-bio fusion of horrors he'd engineered on Remus that was not unlikely. No time to dwell on that now.

"We're lucky to get two hours more out of these suits. Better hope your info is reliable," he growled at Fenli through the com.

Fenli waved it off with an air of confidence. "Your call, Yul baby. Nowhere else to go. I'm thinking this is as good a place to die as any."

Cloye swore under her breath. "Is this clown for real?"

Yul inclined his head. Not a few dozen feet into the tunnel, he kicked at the pale grey rubble at his feet. Skulls and vertebrae were mixed in of unlucky animals, shells too, that looked like the last macabre hybrids they'd been forced to slaughter, maybe one of the scuttling, crab-like aliens they'd blasted back at the site where they had pulled Fenli from his black frozen pool.

Zikri squiggles and symbols marked the sides of the tunnel. A wide path showed ahead, jumbles of loose rock and occasional boulders to either side, a honeycomb of passageways left and right. The dim light grew dimmer behind them.

Yul gripped his blaster in his gloved palm. Under no circumstances must they screw this up. One misstep and their chances of survival dipped even lower into birdshit.

All good so far. No alien patrols or checkpoint. Odd though. His sharp eyes narrowed, brows bristling. Obviously the squids and their bug friends were not expecting company from this quarter. Maybe they'd even forgotten about this access point? Maybe too much to expect.

Distant booms sounded in the thin atmosphere, registering through their suit receivers. The sound of gunfire? Yul frowned. Rocks caving? There was definite activity ahead. "Let's move in," he hissed.

Hresh looked on with white eyes—the only one without a weapon.

"What, we're going right to the hot spot?" said Fenli.

"Where else? You want to do the scenic tour here and run out of air?"

"I mean—"

"I know what you mean, Fenli," said Yul. "But let me do the thinking. Playing it cautious and namby-pambying around is not going to win us a blue ribbon. We need air, supplies and ship-power if we're to survive."

"No kidding."

"And where there's guns, there's ships," put in Cloye.

Fenli saluted. "Yeah, got it, Sarge. Thanks for clueing me in."

Yul gave a loose-limbed shrug.

"I know, I'm a pain in the ass." Fenli's rangy figure did an odd scarecrow-like twist.

The others ignored him. At least he was regaining some of his mojo.

Down the rough-hewn corridor they moved like restless wraiths. Eyes wide in the dim light from the back tunnels, Yul took the lead, E1 raised. Cloye padded two steps behind while Fenli and Hresh brought up the rear. Fenli thought to tap Yul on the shoulder, ready to offer some advice but Yul silenced him, drawing a finger across his throat. He needed to think. He couldn't have radio noise polluting his head. There was a possibility these aliens were monitoring channels within the tunnels. Why, he could not imagine, just a funny feeling he had.

These wide, snaky passageways looked like an ancient seabed. Strange snail and fish-like fossils stuck in the walls, with curlicued backs and herring-bone spines, some embedded in the shell-like chunks of rock on the pebbly ground. Their feet stirred up a chalky dust as they moved onwards. Now they passed a cross tunnel, leading to an abandoned open chamber with alien bones inside that offered eerie possibilities. A combo of squid and bug motifs were carved on the walls. At one time this place must have been occupied by both races.

The sounds of activity intensified and Yul brought them to a halt. On quiet feet, he crept round a bend where a pale glow issued out from a wide entrance. His jaw dropped as he thrust his head around. Below in a giant oval cavern sat a hundred ships shining in what was an otherworldly glow. All were arranged in neat rows. Mostly Mentera craft from what he could see. Wide, flaring mantis-bodies supporting sleek necks with smooth-curved globelike turrets. The tumult turned out to be not gunfire, but Mentera in space-suits loading supply trains of barrels, bins and various bulky equipment into the lightfighters. Packing up shop. Of course. That seemed to be in sync with events thus far, a Zikri and Mentera allied invasion of the colonized human worlds.

The bangs and booms continued, a discordant jumble of unchoreographed noise. Judging by the aerials and tower boxes, the equipment seemed to be tracking and simulation hardware. Military Mentera—they bobbed around on their hind legs, in their black and silver helmets and suits, taking orders from a few selected captains. All in all, a wash of alien menace.

This vast underground cavern, full of lethal firepower sported a primitive potpourri of elements. High tech, military locusts, scattered boulders and pegmatite rock formations poking up on either side.

Yul's mind raced as he rubbed the side of his helmet. So…this was their base. The Mentera had secured a toehold here, with their small fleet of a hundred lightfighters and messenger craft. Why in this desolate, dry wasteland and cavework labyrinth of tunnels? Their presence mystified Yul.

Maybe Mentera and Zikri deployed joint training maneuvers within the parameters of this new, secret alliance? That would explain the ships dog-fighting over the ridge and disappearing within for debrief and cooperative discussion.

Cloye nudged up to Yul's elbow, her broad face etched in a grimace. The others clambered at her heels.

They sidled closer to gape at the scene, crouched behind some porous rock formations from a somewhat higher vantage point. Yul's breath came out in a harsh, aspirated echo in the com.

Fenli moved in to get a closer look, his weapon cocked in his hand. "Plenty of ships down there."

Yul rasped, "Those are Mentera lightfighters and our ticket out of here. If we can ambush one of their crew and steal their craft…"

Fenli nodded. "Good idea. How though? Only four of us and little air left."

"Fight our way through, how else?" Cloye grumbled. "You a chicken shit?"

"No, I'm not chicken shit. Just a little more cautious in my old age. After nearly dying out in ice and spending time in a Mentera tank for about twenty years, my days of kamikazeing are over, lady. You may want to throw yourself into enemy jaws, but not I, said chicken little—"

"Shut the hell up," Yul hissed at him. "We don't have much time." He turned to the research scientist crouched white-faced and jittery. "Hresh, you got a read on those bugs over there?"

"They're suiting up nicely, Yul, likely getting ready for a mission. I estimate they have orders to join the L-16s orbiting somewhere up there."

"Not a bad guess. So, time to make our—Here, wait now." Yul craned his neck. Three Mentera worked at carrying a strange crate pulsing with a blue glow into one of the Mentera lightfighters. "What the hell's that all about?"

"Who knows? Some bomb or devious weapon, I expect."

"No doubt, Fenli. Whatever's brewing, we have to sandbag these miserable creatures before they enslave the human colonies."

Cloye crouched panther-like. She was ready to move down the slope to pick off Mentera but Yul held her back. "Until the rest of the ships fly off, stay put. See that last ship with the funny box they're bringing on board? Seems to have extra priority. More protocol in order.

"Hresh, you keep a distance behind us. No sense you getting shot up for no reason."

"I feel kind of useless here," he mumbled. "No weapon or commando training."

Fenli hissed, "Be glad you don't have to waste yourself uselessly, old man, like us in the front line."

A massive eye in the ceiling opened like an iris, exposing a patch of pale sky to the cavern. Mentera engines powered up, a high-pitched whining mixed with a subaural roar painful to the ears. The first row of ships took off and headed toward the open dome to fly out into the twilight gloom of Kraetoria.

Twenty ships had gone and counting. All were revving up, leaving in a hell of a hurry. Yul rocked from foot to foot. If he and his company did nothing ...

"Now!" he rasped. Two ships were still on the ground, one of them accepting aboard the crate. The last three were up in the air, making for the eye-shaped dome.

"Fenli you sneak down there and draw them out with firepower—"

"Why me?"

"Because I said so. Why the fuck not? Keep your ears peeled and your guard up. Earn your keep, spaceman. You're a distraction until we get into place for an ambush. Remember, we fished you out of that frozen frog pond."

Fenli grunted. "Just wanted a reason for my soon-to-come demise." He took off in a shambling run.

"Fucking rabbit." Cloye shook her head and glanced at Yul. Yul shrugged and looked to the three ships disappearing in the open dome. This plan had better work.

CHRIS TURNER

Chapter 11

A score of locusts scuttled about loading the last ships. In a running sweep, Fenli fired point blank, taking out the first Mentera hostiles a bit shy of twenty feet from the nearest mantis ship. Then he sprang back and forth like a spider, spraying fire and whooping into the com, waving his other hand to attract attention his way. He dove for cover behind some boulders just as streams of lurid green fire lashed out at him.

"Idiot," mouthed Cloye.

Mentera heads turned. Yul surged into motion. "Now!" He nudged Cloye forward and they came sprinting in to gun down the startled enemy.

A half-dozen Mentera who had been loading the ships dropped like flies. Yul roared a cry of triumph.

Blue-green fire lasered up at them from the loading platforms, smashing chunks of rock behind them. Yul ducked. The splatter smacked his suit and he paled thinking of the consequences.

Gauges still holding. Lucky. Gritting his teeth, he came in charging like a bull. He smashed edgewise into a locust distracted by Fenli and looking the other way. The bug face stared up at him in bewilderment as he stomped on its faceplate. The glass cracked, depressurizing the suit. The insect's mouth opened in a rictus of horror as its black-green chitin iced up. The thing froze on the spot. Yul kept moving. Cloye covered him from the side. Mentera streamed from the cargo bay of the nearest ship, many more than Yul imagined or thought possible at this time. "Kill them quickly!" he wheezed. "This is not turning out as planned. Cloye, ream those bastards to your left!"

Cloye turned. She blasted Mentera flesh to shreds, then crouched and roundhouse-kicked an unarmed Mentera in the faceplate. The glass cracked. The air hissed out of its suit as it writhed on the ground dying. "Yul, behind you!" she cried.

He ducked as fire flared and rock splintered from above his ear. A jagged shard nearly skewered him. His weapon shot up, pegged a Mentera on the run, firing his way.

But they were not killing them quickly enough. More were streaming out from the second ship.

This free-for-all blast fest was turning sour. Death was just a breath away.

Yul's head turned to some inexplicable movement. No, it couldn't be. A Mentera lumo-blaster lifted of its own accord in midair. It started pegging off its own kind. What the hell? How was that even possible?

Mentera from the second mantis ship pitched over in agony. The Mentera were in an uproar. Pincers pointing, fire lashing out at the strange weapon that moved by some invisible hand and fired in their direction. But the moving lumo-rifle sent still more bursts in rapid succession, shooting point blank at Mentera's faces, shattering faceplates, shredding suits, reducing alien flesh to bloodied green and yellow chunks. Mentera blood sizzled on the dusty rock, forming ice crystals in the cold air.

Yul grimaced. Mentera body parts piled up in a long cold line of blood and shredded meat. No further movement.

"What the fuck! Yul?" Cloye gasped. Both she and Yul saw the alien blaster rise and aim, ready to take out and kill more enemy Mentera that came out of the woodwork.

"I know that signature," croaked Fenli through the com. He came running over to where Yul and Cloye gazed uncertainly at the upraised gun. "Miko! You sly bastard. I'll be damned if you're not still alive. Up to your old tricks."

"Who the hell is he talking to?" Cloye roared, bug-eyed. Yul just shook his head in perplexity.

Hresh spoke up in a wise voice. "Stress, post-traumatic anxiety, not uncommon in trauma victims. He's hallucinating."

"Shut up, old man," said Fenli. "You think this blaster is a hallucination?" He leveled his weapon at the scientist huddled behind the pegmatite and Hresh shrank back. "That's my friend, Miko."

"Easy, you fool, we still need Hresh," Yul grunted, slapping Fenli's weapon aside.

Fenli looked around wild-eyed as if a window of opportunity was closing. "I don't have to waste time on you here, chief." With a surly grunt, he sprinted toward the second ship, now unprotected. Activity loomed in the iris-shaped escape portal far above. Yul swore. "Quick, get into the other ship!"

Almost as soon as he'd said it, *Bzt*, a human figure came shimmering into existence before their eyes with the mysterious lumo-blaster clutched in his hand. Yul's jaw dropped. The mystery man, Miko?

How in hell? Unsuited and quickly asphyxiating, the man opened his mouth, face congested in blue. His hands groped to his throat.

Cloye wasted not a moment. She grabbed the struggling man and hauled him into the nearby cargo bay of the mantis vessel. Hresh got the door closed just as Yul ducked in. The last image he saw was Fenli taking the other ship to the tunnels. *Damn that cheeky bastard. Give him B for balls though.* "Where you going, Fenli?" he mused.

"He'll get shot down," croaked Hresh.

"No, he's heading for the tunnels, playing possum, like we should," said Yul.

"Okay, we'll do the same."

Yul blinked. His eyes adjusted to the bright amber light. The layout of this ship was familiar, having crash-landed in a craft not dissimilar to this one hours ago. He raced to the bridge, and fiddling at the controls, cursed as his nerve-frayed fingers quivered. Soon the thrusters were aimed and the ship lifted off. Down the main tunnel they surged. It was suicide to soar out the dome and show their faces.

Grumbling and cursing, Cloye pulled Miko onto the bridge. Hresh was on his other side. The man's face was still somewhat blue.

Yul turned. He stared at a man willowy as a scarecrow with brown hair and pale grey eyes. "Who the hell are you?"

"I'm Miko Almstran," Miko choked, regaining some breath.

"Yeah, and who's that?"

"First lieutenant—of NAVO core explorations, patrol officer. Who are you?"

"Yul Vrean. That's Cloye over there, and Hresh beside her. NAVO? Did you say NAVO? They've been gone a long time, friend. Like a century or two. You trying to mess with me?"

"No—"

"Fenli said he knew this guy," piped up Hresh.

"Fenli? He's alive?" croaked the newcomer.

"Is this for real?" Cloye spat. "Some nut from a hundred years ago knows another one from some wrecked ship nearly gobbled up by aliens?" She snapped up her E1. "Too many coincidences. Let's waste this fucker, Yul. The invisible man and his friend would have hijacked the only ride we had out of here and left us high and dry. Don't trust either of them."

"Easy, Cloye," Yul cautioned. "You've always been a hothead. Let's—wait, and sort out the facts."

"What facts? Don't patronize me, Yul."

He shook his head and grimaced while Miko held up a hand. "Can I speak in my own defense?"

"Fast, flyboy," snarled Cloye. "Or we blow your skull off. Too many traitors in this bitched up universe."

"I understand you're hair-triggered but—"

"You think?"

"Listen, I've got to find my companions," Miko said. He hobbled over to the rack of bug suits hanging on the wall. "Their names are Star and Usk. Both are dying out there somewhere. Maybe already dead. I promised I'd come back for them." He gusted a sigh of grief.

"You crazy or something? You don't even have a working suit. How are you going to help them? Those bugs out there are going to come back and blast all of our asses." Cloye waved her gun around in a wild arc.

Miko shook his head. "You don't get it, miss. I'll use one of these Mentera suits. They're elasticized. Let me off, Yul, please! If you have any decency, you'll help me find them." He snatched down one of the locust suits hanging on the wall.

Yul growled a softer note. "Miko's extra firepower did save our hides. I should have anticipated the extra guards."

Cloye just laughed. "Your choice, Yul." She turned and showed her teeth. "Our plan is to get the crap out of here."

Yul frowned. "Cloye, calm down. We'll help you, if we can, Miko."

"How you plan to do that?" blustered Cloye.

"Shut up and let me think." Yul slapped hard on the console. He tried to get the auxiliary impulse working. Cross tunnels and pale glimpses of tanks in a row whizzed by. They'd have to fly faster than this to escape pursuit.

He slapped a gloved hand to his faceplate. "Cloye, Hresh, get over there and man the weapons. I see we have company."

He motioned to the holo view. Hresh's and Cloye's eyes darted to two bogies, red and yellow blips that had entered their safe zone. With a harsh laugh, Yul gunned the engines, sending them recklessly down the main tunnel, swaying from side to side as he maneuvered corners and narrowing spaces. He hoped to hell it didn't narrow down to nothing.

Mentera in silver suits came out from cross-corridors blasting weapons at them. The green flares bounced harmlessly off their shields.

But the ships behind them were an entirely other matter.

Chapter 12

Yul gripped the nav stick and worked the controls with precision, his teeth clamped in an unpleasant grin. He ran his tongue over his lower lip. The ship careened through the grey tunnels, churning up dust, leaving a trail behind them. The shields took the brunt of the abuse, the mantis-wings grazing off the coarse rock, taking small chunks with it, their speed tempered by Yul's newness at flying an alien ship.

"Shields holding, but won't forever," he warned. "We've got to lose these bugs or they'll bury us. Bring the whole Mentera fleet down on our heads. Cloye, talk to me. What's wrong? Can't you figure out these bloody weapons?"

"Trying, Yul. Locusts must have locked something down. Everything's different."

"Hresh, get your ass over there!" Yul croaked. "You're the tech wizard here. Do something!" Miko was still looking blue in the face and somewhat dazed as he zipped up his borrowed bug suit.

Hresh stumbled over, clumsy in his suit. His quaking fingers danced over the weapons controls. Fire spat out from an incoming bogy. Yul swore. The enemy ship clung to their stern like a vine, as the two ships careened down the narrowing corridors with barely feet to spare. Hresh tapped a holo pad. Rear fire lashed out. Cloye picked up his lead and pushed him aside with a grudging grunt. She made better aim and tagged the enemy's frontal shields.

"Attagirl, Cloye!" rasped Yul. "Keep nailing those bastards!"

Hresh beamed at the result of his handiwork.

Luck was not on their side, however. The ship swooped up toward the stony ceiling in an attempt to evade enemy fire. At an especially wide turn opening into a larger cavern, enemy torpedoes locked on their hull. A Mentera attack ship came screaming out of a cross corridor. A bright flash exploded from behind. Nailed the rear vents, blowing out the mantis's tail.

Yul cursed into the com. "Shit, that bastard came out of nowhere! Brace yourselves. We're gonna hit!"

The ship yawed like one of those obsolete jets out of the past. More enemy ship fire came from the side. Their lightfighter went spinning out of control, and bounced and skimmed across the rough stone of the tunnel floor.

Emergency lights flickered on, buzzers sounded. Sparks flew from the console, green rays peppered the hull and sent them skidding sideways, missing the connecting tunnel by yards, smashing into the wall twenty feet away. They all went flying forward.

Yul stumbled up from his broken seat as bits of wreckage burned and the ship engine's died. "Cloye!" He grabbed her waist. "You alright?"

She mumbled something incoherent, a sprawl of arms and legs beside him. Hresh looked in no better condition as he massaged his shoulder. Miko stirred somewhere behind him from under the rubble.

"Now we're cooked," croaked Cloye.

The nav panel smoked like a campfire.

Yul swept away the smoke from his faceplate. "I admit, we're a little screwed here," he rumbled. "Looks as if our only chance is a shootout. We hold the fort, hope they mess up." He sucked in a heavy breath. "Bring down as many as we can."

Miko shook his head, "It's a suicide run."

"What isn't in this funny farm?" grumbled Cloye.

"They're not blasting us, which means they want to take us prisoners," Hresh hissed. "Orders from above maybe."

"Stick us into their tanks."

"Think, Hresh, think. You're the brainiac here."

"I'm thinking. Hard to think under pressure, Yul."

"Hard to think when you're dead," sneered Cloye. "Snap it up."

Yul groaned, catching a look out the port glass. "Now we're done."

The enemy ship had doubled back. Another mantis fighter came at its heels, its nose and forward cannons pointed with destructive force.

Tense moments passed. Everyone waited to get barbecued. Yet the enemy ships waited, as if in indecision. Maybe orders from above?

Yul blinked in the murky haze tinted amber by the emergency lights. A sharp hint of ozone came through the filtered air into his now malfunctioning suit. The bridge leaned on a thirty degree angle, exposing the port bow side. He dragged himself across the debris-littered bridge to the port hole, shaking out his stiffening knee. The glass was tilted, offering a view of the dust-speckled junction, rapidly filling as Mentera infantry drifted out of the two ships to surround their ship, lumo-blasters trained their way. One of the approaching captains flicked an upraised claw.

Yul hissed, "Showtime. Hope you guys're ready for one hell of a fight."

Cloye pulled extra blasters down from the crumpled weapons rack, "Nothing ventured, nothing gained." She tossed an E1 to Yul who caught it in midair. Miko caught the next one aimed his way. Yul braced himself for the violent inevitability that could only go one way.

But a new development came. Booms issued from the area immediately outside the ship, then the staccato sounds of exploding metal racking the hull. Their muscles tensed in anticipation of doom. Yul craned his neck for a better look.

A ship came careening out of the dust cloud, slamming the junction area with killing force.

Yul stared, stunned. Another Mentera vessel. Could it be—?

He cried out in mad glee as the dozen or so Mentera ground troops fell, struck by blasts.

Fenli! The bastard had come to save the day.

The rogue ship limited its rain of destruction to the suited figures outside, leaving the other ships intact.

Fenli's sardonic voice broke over the com. "Don't say I never did anything for you, Yul. You okay over there? Cloye? Talk to me."

"We're here," she rasped. "You got any more tricks to share?"

"Sure, a bag of them," Fenli cried. "Shit!"

They winced as a bright green arc flashed past their ship to zone in on Fenli's craft. The Mentera beam blazed off his shields.

"Love to chat but another bogie is sniffing me out. Gotta run—" Fenli cut the channel. He sent his own smoking ship buzzing off low through the connecting cross corridor. The new vessel chased after, leaving behind the parked ships and mangled Mentera bodies silent in the murky dimness.

Yul exhaled a wheezing breath. They all blinked at one other, stunned.

"That flyboy's full of shit-for-brain surprises," mumbled Cloye.

"Good that he is."

Miko just gave a grey-faced nod.

"How the hell can Fenli fly and shoot bullets at the same time?" marveled Cloye.

"Mentera mantises are designed for dual operation," Miko explained. "Better design than our lightfighters. Fenli and I were both trained on Mentera tech before we attacked their fleet."

"You attacked them?"

"In the end, we got them to attack one another."

"Whatever…the crafty bastard didn't nail the other ships parked out there," Yul rumbled. "Now's our chance to ambush one. Quick. Out in the tunnel."

He and Cloye gathered their guns and gear and threaded their way through the wreckage to the exit port. Hresh blundered after them, befuddlement writ in his eyes.

Miko trailed, with a frown on his face. He seemed plagued with doubt about the course of action, as if a heavy weight hung on his shoulders. Was the spaceman getting cold feet, losing his nerve? Yul grunted. Or was another of those invisibility bouts about to overtake the pilot?

Yul exited the hatch. He crouched, blaster on the ready. A cough frogged his throat as the air thinned in his damaged suit. The two ships sat parked somewhere vaguely ahead, their mantis prows etched dimly in the settling dust clouds. Off to the sides, insect-shaped loaders sat inert, aside triangular bins, odd-oblong crates, and various other tech supplies at the mouth of the cross tunnel. A meeting place or loading-unloading point, no doubt. At the moment, the grounds were empty of moving forms.

Yul stepped past the ruin of locust bodies and shredded suits, sidling over to the open port on the first vessel. The grotesque mantis-headed prow rose over him like an eerie living thing. The others trailed back behind him. Only a pilot light of greenish hue glowed from the bridge. Fortune prevailed: the dust kicked up from Fenli's bullets had concealed their movements from anyone aboard.

Yul trooped over to the air lock and worked the buttons. "Get to the bridge," he ordered. "We take over this vessel. Kill any hostiles on sight. Face the wall and hide your hands, in case they have cameras here." Seeing Miko hesitate, he rasped into his com. "We make our move now, spaceman.

Let's go!"

Hresh and Cloye stepped inside before Yul hit the button to get the door sliding closed. Each prepared himself grimly to commandeer the ship, but Miko held his ground, eyes beetling over the other ship not fifty yards away.

The tug of other duties seemed to be eating at his heart. Reluctantly, he stepped into the air lock. The air pressurized. While the others rushed forward to sweep the ship's interior, he turned abruptly back toward the hatch door.

In a moment's decision he hit the airlock release and ducked under the door. All this before Yul could raise an alarm. He broke out in a dead run through the settling dust cloud toward the other Mentera vessel before his window of opportunity expired. He ignored the chatter of expletives crackling through his com while deliberately dimming the volume.

This ship, like Yul's was ripe for the picking. Fenli's taking the last enemy on a merry chase had presented opportunities to all of them. He'd snatch the enemy lightfighter.

With grim precision, Miko worked the controls on the air lock and stepped through. He turned his head away toward the wall and tucked in his arms to minimize any camera exposure. With any luck, if there were any pilots aboard they'd think the air lock light was being activated by one of their own surviving soldiers returning. Like Yul he was banking on the fact that anyone aboard hadn't seen any hostiles creep out of the disabled ship through the dust cloud. A thin hope, but he had nothing else to go on.

He crept down the hall up to the bridge. Simple layout, like the Mentera ship they'd come in on. A straight corridor, with grey shielded plates to either side. A ceiling of soundproofed baffler cubes. No guards. They must have all gone out to get slaughtered by Fenli.

Miko paused, crouched at the bridge's threshold, a narrow V-shaped arch. Risking a glance, he saw two locusts manning the helm. Their eyes were glued on the smoking ship they'd gunned down, squinting through the diminishing dust cloud, headsets over their olive-colored plated skulls. One abruptly rose, antennae twitching in suspicion.

Luck don't fail me now. In a kamikaze run, Miko stormed in, opening fire on the suited figures, shredding Mentera suits and flesh.

The two pilots fell in mangled heaps.

Miko took over the controls, flicked dials and tapped buttons, got the engines revving up. The craft rumbled to life, its nose pointed to the cross tunnel from where Fenli's pursuer had emerged.

Miko plunked himself in the chair vacated by one of the pilots. The green-black alien was bleeding out, gazing up at him with bulging eyes. He ignored the grotesque posture and amped up the volume on his com. He hissed into the receiver. "I'm going after Star."

A voice answered: "What do you mean, you can't just—"

Cloye's voice rasped. "He already has, Yul. Let him go. We've got our own fish to fry and a getaway ship. Let's quit this hellhole."

Miko heard no answer, only ominous silence, but he saw in his rear sights Yul and Cloye's commandeered craft lifting in mimicry of his own. Yul had made the right decision. Without a second thought, Miko focused on the task ahead. His mission was clear...a plan of action was already brewing in his fertile brain.

Chapter 13

Miko stared past the weapons console to the glass tank containing the floating Mentera. A shiver tickled up his spine. He knew the crew would use such a live specimen, possibly a condemned criminal, as food during their long space voyages. The details of the Mentera's vampirish feeding rushed back to him in a flash of grisly recollection: attaching the cable to the circuit box on top of the tank to their own navels then allowing the sustenance that passed down that apparatus to glut their own energetic need. The trapped creature's life force waned, only to be rejuvenated daily by the pale green witch water.

Beside the tank stood the box still radiating its blue glow. He'd noticed the Mentera soldiers carrying the odd blue package into this vessel when he'd been invisible. Obviously something about it was important. It had that distinctive look, like something he had experienced earlier...yes, he remembered, those mysterious tower components in the underground bunker of the Masters who had impelled Usk, him and Star to blow up the secret command base.

Miko grimaced at the memory and pulled his attention back to the controls. That Fenli had even made it to this forsaken place after crashlanding defied understanding. Now to witness him blasting Mentera lightfighters in a ship of his own? No secret that Fenli was a phenomenon in his own right. A man who just wouldn't die. But then what of himself?

Miko's lip curled in a crooked grimace. He steered the mantis-shaped craft through the gloomy tunnels, as best as his memory allowed in the general direction of the tanks where he'd last left Star. With any luck she'd still be there. Then they could make their getaway. These lightfighters were ultra narrow and sleek in design in order to negotiate the rough-hewn tunnels. Yet a sinking feeling gnawed at his gut; it told him she wouldn't be there. He tried not to think of that. All these tunnels looked the same. If he had to backtrack, so be it.

At last Miko recognized a familiar landmark: a set of boulders piled on top of one another set at a wider junction of the rough tunnel. He dreaded what he might find. He parked the ship and took his blaster with him, slowly emerging from the cargo hold and depressurization chamber.

A silence gripped this strange cavern that even his ill-fitted locust suit with its multiple sensors did not fail to report. No movement, sound or radio transmissions. Just empty space, cold desolation, sterility.

A sprawl of bodies littered the grey stone. Mangled corpses of Zikri and masses and hunks of tentacles sprawled in inglorious death.

He swallowed the lump in his throat. A battle had been fought here. With no mercy given. Blaster fire had won out, wreaking havoc on squid flesh. Star's handiwork? There was no sign of her.

At the far end of the chamber loomed four squat glass vats huddled in the icy gloom. The only serviceable one stood empty, its pale waters gleaming in luminous mockery. He threaded past the dead bodies, grimacing in distaste. Approaching the tanks, he felt his heart go cold. He gripped his lumo-blaster, not knowing what horror would jump out at him. He reached out a gloved hand and drew it across the lip of the tank. Some of the pale green liquid had splashed out, leaving puddles at the foot of the glass. Where was Usk? Star? Dragged away by fiendish, blood-hunting Zikri?

Miko's mind whirled. He remembered the last time he had been here and it seemed like an age ago. Everything was the same, minus the fresh gore. Two tanks drained of liquid with only withered husks lying at the bottom; another stained pink and its horned occupants crouched, long dead—creatures of some unknown race. This hall was an old place, long grown in disuse and Miko could not help but suspect that these ancient prisoners had been used to provide fuel for the locust fighters in the Battle Hall not far away. During times of their ancient rituals.

Miko stared in hollow misery. Where could his friends be? This place looked like a war zone. His hopes at finding them plummeted as he brooded. His gut felt heavy as a sack of lead.

Fingers tightened on his blaster. He chided himself for his lack of faith and urged himself on, willing himself not to think about the probability. Where were they? He shuddered to think what lay ahead.

Hurrying along the line of the dead, he stumbled on to the opposite end of the chamber. There he examined a fresh splatter trail. Blood spots continued up the cross corridor on a slight ascent. It looked like a mixture of Mentera and Zikri ichor.

Miko's mind warred with many possibilities. Enemies? Friends? Could it possibly be Usk's blood spilt as he struggled, carried off by some horrific enemy? With only dismal clarity Miko recalled how the Mentera's suit had been manhandled by squids in the gladiatorial chamber. Little chance of survival for Usk if they pulled him out of the water.

He mustn't give up. The two could possibly still be alive.

He hopped back in the ship, turned the nose up the nearby cross tunnel and followed the trail magnified ten-fold on the Mentera camera-eye viewport.

At maddeningly slow speeds, Miko patrolled the passages. He scanned the eerie crossways that appeared and up farther ahead for Star and Usk. Nothing. Just the same endless tracts of cold, grey passages untouched for ages, marked by the occasional green phosphorescence from patches of rocks on the wall or the unsettling glow of a Mentera tank's waters.

Miko began to despair. This was a fool's errand! The squids must have captured her.

Where were Fenli and the others? He hadn't even bothered to check in on his suit com. Maybe they were keeping radio silence?

Around a bend in the tunnel he passed a narrow cross corridor. He swore he caught a flutter of movement. Miko halted. Should he use the ship's com to alert the others? Better not try. The bug fleet might zone in on the frequencies. On a hunch, he set the ship down by the nearest wall. Too narrow to squeeze through there. He scrambled out of the stern bay, his heart pounding. He checked his blaster. Everything good. He sucked in a sharp breath. Yes, his eyes caught a whisk of shadowy movement up the tunnel where it narrowed. What looked like a light-colored suit...Star's? He checked his pace. Careful there, Miko. Patrols could be lurking here. Any number of grisly horrors in wait, as he only too painfully knew from his encounters back in the ancient battle hall with the squids, tanks and their monstrous contents.

There! Usk and Star stumbling up the rock hewn passage. He could have cried out loud in relief. They looked beat up. Both must be starving for oxygen.

Star came bounding toward him, her lips moving in a glad cry. Usk's antenna perked at the sight of a familiar friend. Miko broke out in an answering, shambling run.

Star was thirty feet away, her guard down, when all of a sudden a blurred shape struck out of nowhere. It came hurtling from behind a mass of eroded pillars and caught her broadside, sending her rolling over and over toward the far wall.

Miko froze in dismay. "*Star!*"

He gaped in horror. The thing was starfished with six black-grey motilators and rough, ropy hide, a familiar creature, crouching like a waiting spider. The powerful tentacles rippled like some unholy marauder. It enveloped Star, lifting her off her feet in a jumble of writhing flesh. Star's face stretched in a rictus of horror, then a silent scream lost in her helm.

Audra.

He might have known! His blaster rose in a shaky hand.

Yet he dared not shoot. Star would die, either tagged by his beams or crushed by Audra's powerful tentacles. How they raised grisly memories of old dread in him! Slimy things, clutching, groping at his clammy skin during those shameful moments of bodily joining aboard *Sitty II*.

His legs almost buckled beneath him. He felt his resolve withering to dust.

Usk stood a dozen feet away, frozen in helpless dismay.

Audra glided over and hulked before Miko, her tentacles rippling in vindictive majesty at her prize. In a vise-like grip she hoisted Star high up like a trophy for him to see. Star's legs dangled, her heels striking against the Zikri's rubbery body, kicking like a terrified minnow dragged out of water. Two motilators curled in unison, crossed her helmet, settling on her shoulders.

Miko caught a wild, panicked glimpse of Star's eyes, pale pinpoints, her lips and feverish brow doused in sweat, visible through the faceplate. Her expression was that of a half mad person.

Miko caught his breath, trying to imagine the pure terror she felt, all too aware of his impotence.

He raised his blaster and aimed for Audra's head, but she thrust Star before her like a brazen shield.

"Star, don't struggle! It's me she wants! I'll give myself up—" Even if Audra could hear his babbling, what use were such words against her strength?

Two more motilators arched around Star's legs, stopping those futile kicking motions. The ropy folds of the Zikri's fleshy motilators tightened, squeezing without remorse. The slimed appendages glistening in the eerie light looked more like python coils than squid assists.

An unsaid communication passed between Miko and Audra. As her hypnotic eyes fixed on him in triumph, Miko's blaster fell from his limp grip. Perhaps only he could understand her hold on him in that moment after being under her power for so long during those unending months on *Sitty II*. Like a drugged man in a trance, he walked toward her, offering himself up in exchange. Usk stared in incomprehension. The locust's chitinous mouth worked; he jerked forward, lifting his sole pincer to strike.

But Miko was no more than a few feet away when Audra tossed Star aside like a sack of potatoes. Her front motilators whipped out, to tear a strip in her suit a few inches above the left breast. The air began hissing out of her chest piece and she gave a shriek of anguish.

Miko's hoarse wail went unheard. For the briefest of seconds, he realized he'd been betrayed.

Slimy tentacles whipped out and caught him sideways in a writhing grip. He could not scramble away. His blaster lay useless several paces distant. She pulled him aloft, clutching him with terrible force, as she had Star.

Miko's mind raced a million miles back as familiar Zikri strength smothered him. In a lucid moment, hollow anguish washed over his being, his world suddenly gone to hell. Tentacle tips explored the exterior of his suit in an all too familiar groping, gentle at first then more insistent as the terrible moments passed...much as a master would handle a reluctant pet.

Star crumpled on the stone, her suit punctured. Usk had fled to her side, dragging her with one claw up the tunnel closer to Miko's ship and life-saving oxygen.

Audra drew Miko in, her eyes betraying a savage intensity, mimicking a starving animal hungry for food.

Miko struggled; he writhed, but he knew such was of no use. The breath whooshed out of his lungs, the force crippled him, and his face contorted in horror, his bones at the verge of cracking. She drew his face closer to hers, the glass pressed to her noseless visage. Black beady eyes stared at him with wrath, almost a mad triumph, something that Miko knew had progressed beyond the scope of normality to strike at the demented core that had haunted this creature for all too long.

The almost telepathic communication lasted long instants and somewhere the savage echo in his brain knew this was the last reckoning.

Alas, Miko, you have been very naughty. Remiss in your affections. Your friends cannot help you now, loyal as they are. We've a lot to catch up on, you and me...

The wide, all-seeing eyes kindled a darker shade of ebon and turned baleful in her grizzled face. The ultimate scorn of a jilted lover raged in the heat of frenzy, one spurned and neglected. Now Audra was out to exact her lustful revenge on a careless lover for events long unresolved.

The seconds turned into minutes. Part of Miko's soul crumbled like an old building. Against all odds, she had prevailed, her brute tenacity had triumphed and she had found him on this desolate world. What a loathsome place to face one's end.

Audra's motilators were at last unable to control their twitching and the tips broke through the lining of his suit in a flurry of violent anticipation.

Miko gasped in horror as he braced himself for the inevitable...

Not a score of paces away, two heads popped up from behind a shield of crumbled rock.

"Jesus, what the fuck is that?" Yul gazed in disgust.

"Some mutant squid. It's got our runaway flyboy," Cloye hissed. "Doesn't look too promising. Now would be the time to pull that disappearing act, flyboy."

"Poor bastard."

Cloye lifted her E1. "Fuck that, I'll—"

"No, wait!" Yul grabbed her wrist but it was too late.

A burst of red flared from Cloye's E1's muzzle. "He's already dead."

Down the tunnel the arc flew and peppered Audra's glistening hide. She let out a horrid chitter of anguish. The curled tips of her upper motilator hung limp then flaps of flesh thudded to the floor.

Miko immediately jerked back and squirmed out of her grasp as she relaxed her grip. He fell in a quavering heap.

The fire had further ripped holes in his suit. He choked, his lungs struggling for precious air that didn't exist as the last hissed out from his suit.

In a chitter of rage, Audra flung herself at the unexpected intruders.

She smacked her head into Cloye who could not get off a second shot. She had misjudged the creature's burst of superior speed. Audra slammed her backward as if she were a sack of fluff.

Yul fired but the Zikri was faster, bowling him over in a savage rolling motion. He felt slime-pocked tentacles crawling over his suit, grasping with unforgivable force. He gasped in anguish. Cloye shook the haze out of her head. Reaching to snatch up her blaster, she fired point blank.

Audra sprang back, chittering as red arcs seared her thick hide. Whistling what thin air was available through her gullet, she recovered fast, rolling out of the way. Seconds from death, Miko jerked to his knees, croaking and wheezing. Just as he sucked his last breath, *bzt*, he blipped out of existence.

His bodiless form floated out of his suit like a mutant spirit. Still stunned, though his senses sharpening, Miko traveled with it. In a rush of ghost-like vapors, he drifted past the chittering Audra, immune to her dismay. He snatched up his blaster. The weapon floated eerily in midair. With invisible eyes, he watched wraith-like as Usk got the rear doors of the ship closing. Calmly he swept in behind them, blaster clutched in invisible hand, before they sealed the doors tight.

He had no control over these weird forces that granted him invisibility. It engaged when it would, more often than not, in times of dire peril or extreme stress. When he came back to bodily form was a mystery. If only he could master the power, instead of it mastering him…

Audra, appalled at the chaotic events, staggered for shelter behind the ship's bow. As the hull vibrated to life, she scuttled to safety, crouching behind some scattered boulders just as Cloye sprayed wild fire again her way. Damn that human! The blasts zipped off at all angles, ripping shards from wall and boulder alike. She propelled herself toward the safety of the tunnel, her ropy, rubbery hide smoking with blaster fire. Used to such hurts, she forced herself on. Such damage would kill lesser Zikri, but not her. Her human quarry lay left behind, hunched twitching on the cold, rough floor. She had been so close. Victory had been hers…but snatched away.

"Into the ship," Yul wheezed at Cloye hoarsely. He grabbed at her and hauled her back. Cloye squirmed out of his grasp while spewing a spate of obscenities. "Die, you fucking bitch octopus!"

"Save it for later…" He pulled her back toward the ship.

She drew back grudgingly, spraying a final round for good measure.

Hresh had stayed aboard to watch the ship. Now through the glass, he gaped as the two ducked into the cargo hold and the outer hatch drew down behind them. The chamber depressurized. Cloye and Yul stumbled blindly out of the air lock and down the narrow corridor toward the bridge. Hresh tagged at their heels, wringing his wrists. Miko's ship had long departed.

* * *

Back in the shadows, Audra glared. She nursed her heavy, rubbery chest wounds. They would heal, as they always did. Even with missing tentacle parts, she knew her vitality would take care of the rest. They would regenerate, as would the chunks of flesh off her hide and haunch. She was beyond gangrene and infection. Such was her iron constitution.

A long time after, she stared at the retreating ships, besieged with rage, frustration, and pride. The latter was spurred by her lover's ingenuity in escaping an impossible scenario. She had to compliment him. It had been an all too chaotic escape. Miko was fast improving his game. Last time he had almost gotten himself shredded at her violent ministrations. Perhaps he had learned to control these freakish lapses into non-existence.

She glided over to his vacated Mentera suit and kicked at the empty, shredded husk. He still could be lurking about these tunnels as a bodiless entity. But likely not. The human would connive to get on the ship that the locust had piloted away. She should have crushed that meddling bug when she had a chance.

She twitched. Her head swam with bitterness. Never helpful in these moments of hindsight.

Expelling a gust of cold air, she glided jerkily up the tunnel. She'd been here before at a similar place of deadlock. Immune to the harsh environment and the airless loneliness of this planet, a familiar spite swept through her tingling limbs and dissipated to the familiar tune of 'I told you so'. There would be other places, other times. How much longer could Miko escape her clutches?

Her limbs quavered. Down the empty tunnel she glided, toward the smoking carcass of Miko's earlier ship where his friends had been gunned down by the Mentera. After much wandering she found it. It was some tunnels away. Slaughtered Mentera lay piled in ghastly heaps. She'd bide her time. Waiting in ambush hiding would suffice. When the Mentera showed up to claim their dead, they'd be in for a grisly surprise...

CHRIS TURNER

Chapter 14

Miko glided wraith-like onto the bridge where Usk sat at the helm, guiding the ship down the tunnel with a labored breath. His one claw was badly torn. Star sat hunched beside him, head slumped, her back to the wall by the weapons console. The holo view showed darkened corridors with rough-hewn walls, with the ship passing the occasional cross corridor. Despite his handicap, Usk navigated the lightfighter safely down the gloomy ways. After a time he halted the stolen craft. With insect mouth agape, he rustled through the ship's med kit and wrapped up his claw in a coarse weave of gauze. Then he shuffled on insect hind legs to the nearby Mentera feeding tank. He paused as if toying with the idea of hooking up the intravenous cable to his abdomen. He abandoned the idea and instead snatched up a cup to the side, eyeing the blaster that floated in the air, blinking in a cunning way. The locust lifted the tank's lid, pulled out a brimming cupful of green water and hurled it where Miko clutched the weapon.

The air around Miko sparked and hissed as he buzzed back to visibility. He reeled, clutching at his temple. "Ow! Don't do that, Usk! It's hellish enough coming back into this wretched body." His head felt like a throbbing lead weight. Cold sweats and chills fled up his limbs.

Usk snarled out in bug-speak. Neither Miko nor Star understood a word. The locust dipped another vesselful into the open top and brought it over to the flashing console with him, intending to immerse his stump such that he could regenerate the pincer. That might take some time. Shaking the webs out of his head, Miko stumbled over to Star, who was recovering from her shock with painful slowness. The woman looked totally defeated.

"You okay, Star?"

She stared glaze-eyed past him to the locust-feeding tank. Her eyes registered dim comprehension. She shivered. She still wore her chest-shredded suit. While Usk struggled one-pincered at the controls, as he guided the craft along the narrow tunnels away from the battle grounds, Star stirred, registering Miko for the first time. Her hair, flaxen and damp with sweat, was plastered to her brow. Beads of it funneled down her face. Signs of trauma lurked in those clouded eyes. She looked ten years older, her cheeks hollow, the color of funereal ash. To say the woman was in shock was an understatement. Miko scowled, ashamed that he had put her through this hell. He came over to crouch beside her quivering frame and as gently as possible put his arms around her shoulders, hoping to restore her to some semblance of her former self.

She looked at him, trembling. "Miko...I can hardly believe it's you. Maybe we're all dead here and this is some kind of sick joke."

"No joke, Star. I'm afraid we're all alive here."

She rose to a feeble crouch, groaning. "That squid thing...the one that wanted you," she quavered, "it attacked us in cold blood...it could have...would have killed me."

Miko looked away, his lips pursed. He jerked up and over to the ship's nav, where Usk was busy piloting the ship down a tunnel. Miko flipped on the universal translator, a black-red button above the anti-grav generator. He knew where it was from experience. The unit glowed an operating yellow.

He stared at the Mentera, as if seeing him for the first time. "Good to see you, Usk. That claw looks bad. Hope the witch water works. What happened after I left you at the tanks?"

Usk turned to peer up at him with his sad, timeless expression, insectoid and alien. His mouth opened to disgorge guttural syllables. "The Zikri took me from the tank. Tortured me in some chamber. They chased Star, prepared to torture her too. Your hunter female squid was there. We fought our Zikri jailers. She broke free, killed the overseer. I escaped."

Miko shuddered. "That doesn't surprise me. Nothing can stop Audra."

Star came over to gape at Miko. "Audra? Is that what you call that abomination? What does the squid have on you? How is it you are always blinking in and out like some strobe? Are you a mutant?"

Miko dipped his head in wincing shame. "You could call it that." He swung his gaze away. After tapping some dials, he donned a headset and adjusted the receiver. The incoming signal on the com was flashing. Usk, for obvious reasons, had muted it.

The light had been flashing for some minutes now, likely queries from locust mission control. Nothing good.

Miko set the frequency to the same on his suit's com, a three-way channel, not trusting the open ship frequencies and hoped they were not out of range. "Fenli? You there?"

After a time, a hoarse voice came over the com. "Good to hear your voice, friend. I'm about eight tunnels over. Sorry I couldn't help you out. Had my hands busy."

"Cut the chatter," a familiar voice intruded. Miko recognized the gruff, no-nonsense tone of Yul. "We have to think of some strategy out of here. Nice work, Miko, disappearing back there. That Zikri freak would have killed you in my estimation. I won't even ask how you made it into that ship."

"Plenty more chances to die, Yul."

Yul grunted. "Where the hell are you, Fenli? Our holo tracker isn't reading you. Only Miko's lightfighter."

"This onboard cloaker is a wonder. Saved my ass a few times. Guess your ships don't have one. This must be an experimental model, some special task force ship."

"Lucky you," said Yul. "Your status? Clean?"

"Some smoke and trailing metal, but I'll survive. No bogies that I can see. Ready to bird-dog out of here."

"That's our biggest problem: getting out of here."

"Why's that? Ever hear of impulse power?"

"Impulse isn't getting us far. We can't warp out while we're within *Kraetoria*'s grav field. The bugs've got a fleet up there. Thousands of ships I'll wager that'll figure us out in a fly the moment we show our noses. Unless we can convince them we're not an enemy..."

"We can't stay down here and get pegged off," objected Cloye. "We're lucky to have survived this long. We've got to get the hell out of here!"

Hresh grunted his endorsement.

"All nice on paper, but many things can go wrong the moment we show ourselves outside this mountain ridge."

"Times ticking," Fenli grumbled.

"Impulsive moves will kill us all, so cool your jets, Fenli," said Yul. "Miko, report your status. Your friends okay?"

"Yeah. Two crew members here, Star and Usk. We're shaken but otherwise intact."

Yul clipped out a rumbling query. "Who exactly are your crew—this Star and Usk? They have any combat skills?"

Miko paused. "Star's a street hustler, not savvy with ship tech. Usk, he's…a Mentera, so has some piloting and military training."

A pregnant pause lingered over the com. "Come again? Mentera?"

"A rebel. Prisoner of theirs from long back. I rescued him from a tank—since then he's been an ally."

"Are you mad? You're playing with fire, spaceboy. All the Mentera are feral bloodsuckers. They'll clip your jugular, stick you in a tank and suck you dry."

"Yeah, how many more of these weird friends you have?" mumbled Cloye.

"If you're counting me among those 'weird friends', Cloye," hissed Fenli, "you and I are going to have a conversation."

Hresh interjected. "Let's get serious. We have a major risk here. He's a Mentera."

"Usk's more loyal than any crew member I know," affirmed Miko.

"Okay, Miko, your call." Yul sighed. "Looking as if we need every available helping hand…and to use brute force to get out of this mess. If we try to impulse to planet farside, we'll have a hundred lightfighters on our tail."

"Wait," interrupted Miko. "We can't just blast out of here and let those aliens take over innocent worlds. We've got to try and stop them."

"Right, spaceboy," jeered Yul. "Three rogue ships against a fleet of thousands? Think again."

"We can think of something."

"Like what? Fly in, shout loud enough and order them to call off their invasion?"

Miko went beet red in the face. "That's not exactly what I meant, Yul."

Hresh coughed, his hoarse, raspy breath catching at the edge of the static. "Unless—"

"What?"

"We can use your Mentera. You say he's a dependable ally? Can you communicate?"

"We have a limited communication, using the shipboard translator."

"Good. Get the bug to radio in to fleet command. Tell them our scouts lost the human captives to a ship crash. Tell them we're going to join the fleet as planned and await further orders."

Cloye squawked, "You crazy? We're not going to go up there into the spider's nest."

"No way around it, Cloye. Unless we sit here and die."

"What happens when they try to contact the dead officers that Fenli nuked down there?"

"We'll deal with that when the time comes," Yul muttered. "Hresh's right. We've got a small window of opportunity here to fool them and blast out of Dodge. The old 'hide in the open' trick."

"Yes, it could work," mused Miko. He consulted Usk, who looked at him with intent eyes. Star gazed on, her mind still in a daze.

While Cloye continued to curse and grumble, Yul hissed at her to settle down.

Hresh's voice hissed over the com. "Have your bug make it sound plausible, Miko, or we'll have a swarm of hornets on our asses."

Miko licked his lips. He'd have to switch to open channel and take his chances. From the ship com came a garbled spatter of bug speak. Likely mission control. Miko grabbed the receiver, passed it to Usk while Star stood by, tugging at the shredded folds in her suit. "Radio in, Usk," rasped Miko. "Tell them the intruders were gunned down. Dead. There are no survivors."

The universal translator spat the words into Usk's earpiece while the com continued to stream new orders from mission control. Obviously they were expecting a reply. Usk's antenna twitched. He uttered some words in response.

A tense silence passed. Another blast of alien talk rattled the airwaves and Usk's antenna dipped in a gesture of anxiety.

Miko whispered into the translator clipped to Usk's antenna. "Tell them the others went down, Usk. We're the only survivors."

Usk chittered more words into the com.

Another long and nail-biting pause. "Affirmative Mentera KU6j. Update will be reported to Commander Kruk. Respond."

Miko covered the mouthpiece and spoke to the others. "Progress!"

"Let's hope they buy it," Yul growled.

Usk's antenna perked up once again. The universal translator relayed the message in a broken, robotic tone. *"Report to main fleet, squadron Meijk-JytO—"* the rest was gibberish, even the translator couldn't copy *"—Full investigation of hostiles will proceed as soon as resources are made available...The assault on 'Quenrix' takes priority."*

"Quenrix? That's a frontier world on the fringe of *The Dim Zone*," Hresh mused.

"They're telling us to join the fleet," Miko whispered.

"Good." Yul exhaled relief.

"What do you mean, 'good'?" bawled Fenli.

"Means we can go up there, spy on their operations and hopefully do something to sabotage their efforts."

Fenli threw up his hands. "Are you people insane? You can't win against these locusts. They're insidious. Ruthless killers. They'll throw you in a tank and let you sit there for a hundred years."

Yul spat, "If we don't fight them, Fenli, we're all going to die. Besides we need to find a clear avenue to get our ships out of here. Otherwise we're screwed. Only so many planets we can hide on before both bugs and squids take over this whole galaxy."

Fenli fumed over the com.

"He's right, Fenli," said Miko.

"Don't tell me what's right, Miko," raged Fenli. His staccato curse was harsh on the ear. "Wasn't you lying in a frozen pool on an alien world left to die—freezer food for those crab-locust-squid whatever-the-fuck primitives."

Miko grunted. "I've had my share of them too and dunked in tanks. Don't think that I'm that oblivious to what it's like."

"Sorry, Miko. I forget that. Just a little frayed around the edges."

"I get it."

"Still, the instant this plan goes south, I'm impulsing the hell out of here. Blasting my way to freedom or death."

"Fine, do what you want, Fenli," said Yul. "But in the meantime we have to act as one, be a team and follow through. You go skylarking out of here after we've given them a sob story about the rebels dying, it'll raise suspicion."

"Yeah, sure. Then let's go join the fleet, flyboy, and kick some ass."

"Move out," said Yul with a hint of annoyance.

So it was decided. Fenli worked his way toward them, tracking them on holo radar. Miko's and Yul's ships threaded their way along the tunnels at quarter speed, with Fenli tagging behind. No Mentera patrols were to be seen. The tomblike spaces were deserted enough. Likely all available locust power'd gone up to join the fleet.

The tunnel widened. A grainy yellow light shone with a trace of maroon up ahead. Dusk was drawing near and now an exit into the dry desert wastes beyond.

Yul exhaled a breathy sigh. In a show of confidence, he gunned the engines, blasting out of the cavern. Miko and Fenli dogged at his tail. Miko caught a last backward glimpse of the cave-like orifice shaped like a giant grouper's mouth as they banked out. The ships moved across the desolate landscape as one. The horn-studded ridge stayed to their left, showing bone-pit valleys and skull-haunted bluffs.

Miko spied traces of ruins down there, likely former crude stone dwellings of the hybrid locust and squid mutants that once populated this arid world in plentiful numbers. He was not sad to leave behind such a hellhole: the dreaded cliffs, the plains, and the endless dust craters that kept their dark secrets.

Flashes of the nail-edge space chase that had led to their being stranded in the underground labyrinth shot in and out of Miko's mind. The harrowing escape into the secret bunker of the Masters then the ill-fated refuge in the ancient battle hall. Miko could not help but shudder at memory of Laren, their crew-member, seized by some monstrous squid that lashed out a tentacle from its oversized holding tank. A grisly demise, if ever there was one.

He gripped the controls while Usk labored at his side. Both sat ready to resort to fight or flight tactics should hostile activity swarm upon them. Star stared, as if only half taking in their perilous situation.

All parties of the three-ship convoy held their positions with a grimness reflected by their clipped whispers through the com. Their main advantage was the simplicity of their plan. Just a routine patrol returning from a failed mission to trap the human intruders, now ready to report to fleet command for the upcoming invasion of Quenrix at the cusp of *The Dim Zone.*

Into the dusky tracts of space the trio followed the brightening beacons that led to the ever growing mass of the space fleet orbiting at 300 miles above Kraetoria. A cluster of ships more massive than any had suspected.

Miko gaped. He felt his heart tumble. This armada numbered in the thousands. Three thousand? Four? Still more were amassing by the minute, as they came out of hyperdrive from various bases throughout *The Dim Zone*. Their jagged, eerie, green and orange-spangled light streams trailed behind.

Such a variety of ships! Aphid fighters, mantis craft, Zikri war Orbs, large and small, flagships, drone scout ships, assault craft, all spiked like undersea mines and equipped with deadly uro bombs. Mentera LU-destroyers sat at a distance with their weaves of com towers, cargo ports and launch pads, complex structures at the very least. Then there drifted the Mentera slaver ships with holds a half mile long, shaped like zeppelins, huge to the overwhelmed eye, capable of holding thousands of tanks and prisoners.

At the sight of the incoming ships, Miko's eyes bulged like a drunken man's.

"Team-leader Mekrich lightfighter VH3... Proceed to vanguard manta leg 3 post alpha, beta. Follow the guide beacon on your display. Take up your position! Likewise, VH4 and VH7. We are to launch to Quenrix in T- 2."

Yul joined the tail of a squadron of eight mantises and several aphid-shaped fighters on the wings. Miko and Fenli had no choice but to fall in behind, all now dwarfed by the sheer size of the alien armada.

Miko rasped to the others, "We can't let them unleash that kind of hellish menace on a single human world! They'll devastate it. Enslave millions!"

"Not much we can do, Miko," said Yul.

"Where is NOA?" muttered Hresh.

"They don't even know this alien alliance exists," cursed Miko. "We're a hell of ways out in *The Dim Zone*. We have to alert them."

"How?" wailed Hresh. "Our signals will take forever to reach a civilized, colonized planet and pass through the light-drive tunnels. *Saturnia's* the nearest planet in my estimation. What, a light week away?"

Yul grunted. "Fenli, you hyperdrive into *Winterule*, the nearest NOA base."

"Right, and have them check my credentials? Find out I'm a space wayfarer, dodgier than shit? Two price tags on my head, Yul, a man who should've been dead 40 years ago sitting in a Mentera tank. Why don't you go? Or maybe let Miko and his pals do the dirty work? Wait, I forgot. Miko predates me by a couple hundred years—and he's traveling with a true green Mentera."

"Quit your wise-assing," snapped Yul. "Warp in, send NOA a message, then warp back out. Go wherever the hell you want after that. What does it matter? Sounds as if you don't owe anybody anything and nobody owes you."

"Easy as all that?" said Fenli.

"Yeah, a cake walk."

Hresh cleared his throat. "The moment Fenli warps out, we're all buggered. The Mentera'll be on us like flies. Remember, we came in from the tunnels as a trio."

Yul gave an exasperated sigh. "I'll send the mayday now and hope there's some explorer or surveyor ship that hears us."

"Those're mighty slim odds."

"Better than none. We'll hyperdrive out together, as a group, right after I send the message. Miko, Fenli, pull up your warp grids. Set a course for neutral ground—in Veglos, say *Hasfa's* planet or *Varga*—"

Cloye swore.

"Shit, they locked our warp! We're all targeted for *Quenrix.*"

Every bug ship within radius of the Mentera L-16 destroyers was auto-locked for the target planet.

"Even if we wanted to fly the fuck out of here, we're committed to *Quenrix.*"

"No shit," croaked Fenli. "Happy with your decision now, Yul? We should have just blasted our way from the beginning."

"Maybe, but how could we have known?" said Hresh. "They could have gotten wise to us and torched us all the easier."

"Shut it, Hresh. We're sick of your theorizing," said Cloye.

"Quit arguing!" Yul spoke over the secure-encrypted network, "NOA, this is an urgent call! Repeat, urgent! Large Zikri and Mentera task force plans an assault on *Quenrix.* They're an estimated 3-6 hours away from deployment, max. The next target is a neighboring world, I'm guessing. Maybe *Aljo* or *Baltair*. Repeat *Aljo* or *Baltair*. Put every ship you have into sector 3.115 DZ. Only way to avert a planetwide disaster. Repeat, urgent—"

His ship, along with a thousand others, blazed in a blinding flash of light. All communication went dead.

"Damn!" Yul cried. He banged his fists on the console. He looked hard at Cloye who cringed as the mantis fighter shot down a cone of light toward their destination light years away. He hoped the hell NOA got the message.

* * *

For Audra to outwit the last locust patrol left in the dim tunnels on Kraetoria was an exercise in ease. The mantis lightfighter landed back at the underground base after fruitless hours of searching the tunnels for its mixed bag of fugitives: a rebel Mentera, two humans and one Zikri. The exhausted locust crew awaited further orders. Audra crept round the back of their mantis's silver hull. She made note of the sleek, special scout-model design, ideal for her purposes. Her piloting skills, even in the arena of alien Mentera craft, were not to be faulted. A single guard was posted at the starboard hatch, as was normal procedure. The insectoid was starting to nod off, its locust head dipping in the space helmet.

Audra struck like a viper. The guard fell in a flurry of tentacles, crushed beyond recognition. Audra dragged the mangled corpse into the rocks scattered about the periphery. Waiting for some moments, she kept her eyes trained. No immediate reactions. The hatch opened; another locust emerged and peered about with suspicion, tapping its grey helmet's audio link, lumo blaster raised. Audra struck with no less lightning efficiency. She let motilators guide her through the open hatch and on through the decompression chamber where she made her way to the bridge. In seconds, she disposed of the remaining pilot. With three Mentera neutralized, she had herself a starship.

Chapter 15

Regers' eyes roved in appreciation to the defensive metal sheets hanging across the wall by *Xaromar's* weapons racks. "Get them down!" He swept a brisk hand to Vincent and Deakes. "The horned Daulks had it right by keeping this here fireproof shielding for just such occasions. Slide 'em over to the controls, boys. We'll create ourselves a nice barricade. Ramra—seal that bridge door. Bugs aren't going to be kind to that door. Jiminy...Creib—you two stay close to those controls. Guard them with your life, in case anything comes back online."

The sounds of furious drilling and cutting tools scraped somewhere on the upper hull down the hall. Regers glared up with baleful eyes. His metallic fingers gripped his blaster while Deakes and Vincent dragged the sheeting over past the weapons grid. He tucked himself in behind the makeshift firewall, grumbling his dissatisfaction, racking his brain for ways to win this unwinnable war.

Deakes settled in a wobbly crouch beside him, flush-faced, muttering over the grating noise on the exterior hull. "Regers, you sure you want to do it this way? There may be another option."

"Like what?"

"Blow the oxygen tanks? Fry the fuckers? Get the ship online and moving away and have us gouge the top of that drone against something hard, like the hard rocks down on Remus—"

"You're not thinking, Deakes. The locusts've corkscrewed us. Cut a hole in our hull. Hear that metal-grating and tinkering? That's them piling Mentera soldiers into our ship right now. We blow that drone off us, nuke the air seal and we're suddenly flooded in vacuum. Kills our ship. We can't hyperdrive out with a hull like a honeycomb."

"Yeah, okay, so maybe I was wrong. Scratch that."

Regers clenched teeth. "Yeah, scratch that. What do we have that's working? What resources? Think, you fuckers—Creib? Jiminy?"

Creib pulled at his muff of stringy hair. "Nothing. Just bridge auxiliary power, electrical, oxygen, life support, but that'll do us no good against the locusts. Wait, artificial grav is still up."

"What good is that, ass-fuck?" Vincent snorted. "We're already in grav, being a dove's dive from Remus."

Jennings asked, "Does the AG have a sliding scale?"

"Yeah, why? Quit wasting our time."

Jennings ignored Regers' insult. "Max the AG out. Coupled with Remus's grav, it'll make them heavier than lead."

"Yeah, and us too."

"Well, we'll know it, but they won't."

Regers rubbed his jaw. "We could take them by surprise. Okay, here's what we do. We hole up in the bridge, spike the artificial grav at a key moment. Creib, you stand by and max it when I tell you to. Teach those bugs a lesson. We give them a mouthful of pure hellfire when they come through that door. Vincent, you and Deakes get yourself ready to be 300 pounds heavier. Lay flat on your bellies, fire around each end of the shield. Make sure you blast the shit out of those crickets before they hone in on us or we're dead! Ramra, you'll be backup. Cover 'em like a fly on shit. I'll make sure they can't sneak back to piss on Deakes."

"It might work," Jennings admitted.

"It had better work, Jiminy. We've nothing else. When those bugs come busting through the door, we want to be ready. Creib, you ready? Wait for my signal."

"What about me?" whined Dez, crouching like a spider. "Am I supposed to be the third stooge and die over here?" Regers looked at him with a rueful expression, bordering on bland indifference. "You'd better make yourself scarce, Dez—like hop like a bunny into the forward utility bulkhead—you've no weapon, no armor. Safest place for you is there."

Dez dipped his head, cowering like a whipped puppy. He crept into the crawl space, closing the door behind him.

Regers scowled, tugged at his lower lip. He recalled how he'd been caught in a similar situation aboard *Albatross* with his faithless friend, Yul.

That had ended in disaster. By no means must he fall into a similar situation. Not like his former crew member, Hurd, dragged off kicking and screaming to his death by squids.

He and his roughboys didn't have to wait long. After a quickening series of high-pitched whines and staccato thuds against the hull, there came a space of silence. An ominous interlude that had each man contemplating his own grisly death. They gripped their weapons, staring at the whites of each other's eyes, eyes darting from one grim face to another, sweat beading from gleaming brows. Deakes's muscles bulged enough that his joints creaked; even the air crackled with an intensity that could be cut with a knife.

Regers glanced over at Creib whose pudgy hand clutched the artificial grav controller. He flashed him a reassuring nod. Good to inspire confidence when doom lay so thick in the air. A massive boom assaulted the bridge. The steel door flew outward, over the lip of their shield to ream Creib.

He cried out in pain, his left leg pinched between twisted door metal and console.

Smoke enveloped the bridge, reducing visibility to near zero. Regers croaked out a curse. Hordes of Mentera skittered through that haze-filled gap, a blur of motion flitting amidst the clouds of grey-black smoke. To Regers' eye, those movements were like large rats scuttling out in grey suits.

No rats these. Cannibalistic slaver enemy insectoids born on a faraway planet, with plated heads, antenna like locusts, and pincers for arms, but dressed in man-like suits. "Fire their asses!" Regers roared.

Vincent gave a kamikaze yell. He unleashed a burst of fire that reduced the invading locusts to shredded lumps. Mentera return fire bit back at their metal-shielded barricade. More nimble shapes fanned out to flank them.

Vincent and Deakes loosed deadly volleys, keeping the right flank at bay. Regers and Ramra shot at the other stream flanking them. But a dozen more locusts seemed to replace the ones falling to fire. Regers swore and gnashed his teeth. In seconds they'd be overwhelmed. "Now Creib, now!" he boomed over the chaotic free-for-all.

Creib grasped the grav control despite his blood-streaked shin and quavering hand.

For a brief second, the artificial grav kicked in. Bodies felt the tug of crippling forces. Then they cut out as Creib's fingers slipped and toggled the switch and the man slid to his knees, groaning in pain, clutching his useless leg.

Regers spewed every curse known, firing bolt after bolt into the fray in his frog-hopping crouch while green Mentera fire streamed close to his head. "Peg those fuckers, you dipshits!"

Sounds of blaster fire deafened his ears in the cramped space.

Mentera stun fire at last targeted Creib, sending him sprawling on his side. Three Mentera slavers snatched him up, carting him off through the smoke like a fresh calf to market.

Regers fought like a wild man. Whirling, he lashed out with arms, elbows, fists and boots. A savage lust for survival possessed his resolve, spittle spraying from his mouth, his trigger finger blasting anything that moved through the dim haze, be it bug, chitter or swirling smoke. The bridge had turned into a bloodbath of alien flesh. Two clicking locusts were moving in on him, firing stun rays. He rolled, catching stun fire that numbed his left side. Deakes turned to cover him. Regers rolled away, blasting moving shapes, willing the feeling to return to his left hip. More shapes edged in from the door. *How many of these fucking crickets were there?* He felt claw hooks dig into his back. He cried out in anguish. He whirled with an agonized shriek as another jumped on his back. "Agh, you motherfuckers!"

He twisted aside, lashed out with the serrated edge of his combat knife, gutting the thing before it could claw up higher on his back. He threw the quivering thing off him into the parade of creatures bounding at him. A sneak-pack of cricket menace. He ducked as more Mentera fire sprayed against the ravaged firewall as *Xaromar* did a sudden dip and all bodies went sliding toward the weapons rack.

Regers caught movement in the dimming holo screen: an eerie hulk containing the dragonfly heading toward the Mentera mini-destroyer.

The dragonfly had dipped back into its protective armor. It had perceived the Mentera flagship as a threat, not liking the confusion and invasion of its realm.

The armature, closer now, looked like an ugly, slab-sided molar of blue-grey hue with roots dangling from both bottom ends. The crowning turret had horned ridges, much like the ears of a predatory owl. Between those ears the cannon swiveled and aimed at the Mentera mini-destroyer. In return, red beams sprayed out of the destroyer's forward cannon to lash harmlessly against the avatar's armor-shielded exterior.

That was a mistake.

The dragonfly's protective armor absorbed the hits and flashed crimson. Gunfire spat out from its turret's spray-guns and rained against the Mentera flanks. Some of the blaster energy deflected and smacked into *Xaromar's* own hull.

Regers uttered a grim cry. Deakes scrambled to his side. Thankfully the auxiliary shields held.

The dragonfly gave no quarter. It flew out of the hole in its armor to flit behind its avatar, hovering like some otherworldly ghoul. It dive-bombed the Mentera craft, smashing dents like moon craters in the armored hull. The sight was as improbable as it was impossible. Regers gaped. The insect must consider the locust ship an extreme threat to its habitat to launch such an all-out attack. Why else would it bludgeon the mini-destroyer like that?

He scrambled back through the line of bodies to the command console. Grabbing the grav switch, he jammed it to full capacity.

A terrible weight seized everyone's limbs. Auxiliary power dimmed. The lights flickered, components did a sparking dance. Running figures suddenly toppled like bowling pins. Either they pitched headlong or ground to a quivering halt, thrown to their knees. Regers, forced to a pancake crouch, went ape with his blaster, pegging off sluggish enemies. Somewhere in the smoke, he saw Ramra roll, clutching for his weapon that had been knocked out of his grasp by a blood-hungry locust. Deakes pivoted, raining fire into suited alien bodies.

At last the bridge was still. Only reeking smoke and barbecued cricket coiled up from riddled heaps. The defenders' breaths clung in their throats. Their lungs heaved.

Regers' head turned to the holoview. Crimson beams lashed out from the beleaguered Mentera ship toward the dragonfly to destroy it in one fell swoop. But the creature, as if driven by some freakish sixth sense, dodged in between the death rays and smashed the hull with its bullet-like head, denting plates like blacksmith hammers on sheets of corroded tin. A few more strikes and it would breach that hull.

The Mentera vessel lurched at the punishment of such alien force. The creature's outer carapace, composed of indestructible material, was unlike anything humans had ever seen. Maybe it didn't even have DNA in its cells?

The alien's makeup could be something different than DNA. How could it inflict those blows on metal and evade the bug's ship fire at the same time?

The tractor beam faltered, restoring to *Xaromar* her electro-force. Unpiloted, *Xaromar* dipped, plummeting fast toward Remus.

"Get to the nav!" came Regers' hoarse cry.

In the brightening holo view, he caught a glimpse of gory, serrated teeth in the dragonfly's mouth, chomping on mangled Mentera, suits and all, as the dragonfly plunged through the enemy hull to dispose of the crew. Like an insect mutant gone amok.

Regers crawled to the console with legs like logs. He released the AG. Others of his crew rose from their half crouches.

The bridge was a shambles of blood and guts.

Jennings clawed to take over the nav. With a strangled cry of his own, he stabilized the ship's plummet and lifted the nose, saving them from certain death. With inches to spare *Xaromar* breasted the mangled towers of Hresh's research installation below and leveled out to an even path, cruising parallel to the desolate landscape across the eerie predawn ruins. Regers was thrust back on his heels by the sudden Gs. He crab-crawled his way to the nav. A hook of a hand gripped the console. Most of the Mentera were dead, or quivering or groaning in anguish in distended heaps.

"Good save, Jennings. What's our status?"

Jennings said hoarsely, "Impulse is up, but at min capacity."

"Light drive?"

"Dunno until we try it."

"I'll be optimistic and assume it'll be working."

"That's a dangerous assumption."

"Move!" croaked Regers in a harsh voice. "Configure it for a jump out of here. Vincent, Deakes? You with me? Get to that bug hole in the upper hull and patch it up as best you can. Nuke any aliens you see." He waved his gun then trailed after them with a limp. Vincent hobbled on, his face still etched in an idiot's grin. Man must be in some sort of self-survival autopilot mode.

The hall was bathed in half light on emerg power and permeated by an odor like a grass field of fermented piss, locust spit and pheromones. Regers caught a brisk movement of twitching antenna rounding a bend. "There! Blast that skulking thing."

Vincent fired repeated rounds. Deakes and Ramra scrambled after it.

The four of them rounded the bend. They saw, just as the insect was booting it up a ladder, a circular portal cut in the ceiling through which it was escaping.

Ramra opened fire. The insectoid shape fell from the ladder, some weave of spidery ropes. Its pincer claws snapped at empty air. It fell back on its shell and breathed its last breath. Deakes stomped on its neck, crunching it flat. Vincent clambered up the ropy strands while Deakes covered him, his E1 trained. Vincent lifted blaster to point inside the dark opening where the drone assault craft sat above the hull. Firing blindly, he stirred a peal of agonized chirrups just as the portal started to shutter closed like some great eyelid. Ramra blasted the outer mechanism, the circuit box that sparked and sizzled.

Regers grinned a feral grin. "That'll do, Vincent. Good job, Ramra. Doubt if those bastards'll be able to open that hatch too soon. Back to the bridge."

"What about Creib?"

Regers shook his head. "Creib'll have to fend for himself. That portal's buggered."

They staggered back to the bridge where Jennings worked the controls, sweat beading from his brow. Regers hurried behind him, another plan in mind. But a figure came edging out of the ruin of bodies behind him—

A portly man with a half-crazed look scuttling like a crab to snatch up Creib's fallen rifle. Dez—the fuck. He pointed it with a shaky hand at Regers.

"Turn this ship around, Regers," he croaked.

Regers faced him, cheeks crinkled in amusement. "You'd better put that firecracker down, Dez, if you know what's good for you."

"Shut the hell up. What do you think I am, some kind of moron?"

"Smarter than a moron maybe, but stupider than a dead asshole."

"I said turn this ship around!—wait, I've a better idea." He motioned the gun. "Jennings, set a course toward the dragonfly avatar. Use the claw arm to pick it up. We're going to bring that mechno back to my lab. There's a goldmine in experimental tech in that hardware. Worth its weight in gold."

"You're giving orders now, Dez? Who's going to pilot it? You? With your fancy ass gun in hand? I don't think so. Good luck."

Dez sprayed a line of fire at Regers' and Deakes's feet. "Stay back, fools!"

Regers did a little dance. "Horny toads, Dez! Getting frisky?" He gave a dog-eared, crooked smile.

"Tell Vincent and your other dumb thug with the horns to lower their guns and move slowly over to the controls with Jennings where I can see them."

Regers shook his head, then cast Deakes a sly grin. "Okay, boys...Jiminy, you heard the man."

Jennings licked his lips. Regers leered in distaste as Jennings set the course to rendezvous with the dragonfly's avatar. He clacked away on the console to familiarize himself with the ship's exterior robot arm.

Regers blew air out of his cheeks. "Funny how a gun in hand changes a man, Dez. Makes him think he's bigger than he is, allows him to take more risks, as if he's got a bigger cock or something. When deep down inside that man knows he's either a spineless cur or a fighter. And you ain't no fighter, Dez. Written all over your face. Simple advice, drop the gun, give up this charade and all will be forgotten. Just warning you."

"I'm going to teach you a lesson, Regers. Now get over there with Vincent and the others!" The CEO's veins bulged on his neck, rifle clutched in shaky hands.

A sudden pincer arm poked up from the rubble of shredded Mentera corpses. Dez turned, startled by the movement. He sprang back, a shrill cry in his throat. A gibbering, hissing moan came from the not-yet-dead Mentera. Dez's gun loosed a spray of fire, killing the Mentera and ricocheting off the weapons rack.

Deakes wasted no time. Slamming forward, he crunched both fists into Dez's shoulder. Dez sagged, his mouth wide in a shriek of agony. His weapon arm hung limp. Regers moved in, wrenched the E1 from him.

Regers smiled down at Dez. "Sure glad we settled that little episode. Enough bloodshed today already, Dez. Look around you. You think we need to add your worthless hide to the killing ground? A perfectly decent ship all shot to shit with multiple bug corpses putrefying my space and shedding green blood everywhere. Think I'll elect you number one mop up man to clean up this mess."

Dez sank lower to the floor, moaning, clutching his side.

"Attaboy, Deakes. You always come through. Now it's your turn to be learning a lesson, Dez. I told you, Uncle Regers's gonna take care of us, one big happy family. Why you try to spoil it, Dez, like some A-hole with shit for brains?

"Now, take Jennings for example. He's the only one I'd put a gun in hand, 'cause I know he doesn't have it in him to turn on me. Man's wise enough to know if he did, between Vincent, me and Deakes, he'd end up potato mash."

Jennings firmed his lip, muttering dark monosyllables.

Dez whimpered on his knees. Regers shook his head without sympathy. He motioned his E1 to the holoview where the Mentera were getting their asses kicked, bombarded by the dragonfly. "Would you look at that. Buggie-boo's coming through in the end. Ain't that a pretty sight?"

Jennings shuddered. "Creib would have something different to say."

"I reckon Creib is on a highway to hell right now, Jiminy, so let's have some respect for the dead."

"We could—"

"Bug off, Jiminy. Don't even mention it, or I'll blast your teeth out." He waved his rifle in the man's face, a baleful gleam in his eye.

"Sure, whatever you say, Regers."

Regers' grin turned to ice. "Now get this fucking ship moving." He slammed his metal fist down on the console. "Dez's idea's not a bad one—so we'll forgive him this time and take his suggestion."

"What the hell's that supposed to mean?"

"It means we're gonna take that bug armor with us, use it as collateral and hightail it the fuck out of here."

Deakes stared, starry-eyed. "You crazy?" Ramra and Vincent leaned in with open mouths.

"Move! You heard what I said."

Jennings caught Regers' arm. "The alien bug's dangerous. Look at it. Can't you see—"

"Screw the bug. If it's going to fuck with us, we're going to fuck with it. Make us some money in the meantime. Save us a bunch of piss-assing around in Veglos, working small time cons."

Deakes shook his head, blood trailing from his cheek. "Too risky, Regers. Can't condone it."

"Yeah, well, life's a risk." Regers grimaced. "Besides, don't want that thing getting back in its armor and chasing after us. I've seen what their species can do. I remember it well, back on Phebis. Ain't for the weak of heart."

"It's insane, Regers."

"I've heard that too many times." Regers waved his gun at Dez. "Blame Dezzie here."

They glared at the scientist who cowered in a tighter ball.

The others stood around, still gaping. Ramra scratched his horned head; suddenly Regers lost his cool. He slammed a boot at the console and stuck the rifle end in Jennings's ear.

"Hurry it up, lady Jane. We're not on a sightseeing tour here." He gave Ramra a shove. "You too, hornhead. Go work nav, stick your finger up your ass, plot us a light drive course or something to Tilas or thereabouts. Once we get our cargo I don't want to be dicking around plugging in numbers. Quick, while that bug's distracted."

Mumbling misgivings, Jennings impulsed toward the place where the armored hulk hovered. He guided the ship over its owl-eared turret so the bottom cargo bay and space arm were positioned directly overtop. Tongue to lip, the engineer latched the claw clamp expertly onto a heavy ring on its upper armature and began to lift the armored hulk. The eerie, maroon-shadowed ruins of Hresh's research station loomed below like a jumble of broken sticks. The hydraulics worked and the space arm bore the mechnobot into the lower cargo bay. Dez watched with eager eyes while the others darted anxious looks at the holo view rich with details of the final assault on the doomed Mentera flagship. The dragonfly continued to weave in and out of the battered hull as the ship spewed its last feeble rays. Another mantis-fighter had roared out of the dawn's murk from the distant ridge to aid the mother ship. The dragonfly rose to greet it with no less hostile handling. The invaders too soon fell to the dragonfly's hammerhead assaults and crashed uselessly into the ruins of the research station.

Regers grinned.

But that grin did not remain for long. Even as Jennings turned Xaromar's nose toward deep space to clear planetary gravity, the dragonfly was on the move. When it caught sight of its armored shell being carted away, it came streaking up from planetside like a mad hornet.

"Is this for real?" Vincent murmured.

"Up the power, Jiminy, unless you want to be staring into the eyes of a space bug in one of his cranky moods."

"You see, you can't kill them!" cried Dez, his eyes lit in a maniacal gleam.

"We're almost at warp distance," Ramra hissed. "How fast can the thing fly?"

"*Xaromar's* beat up." Jennings clawed at his brow. "Impulse is shot to hell. Let's just hope the warp isn't screwed too."

"If it is, guess who's going out in a space suit to fix it?" Regers jeered, his lips fixed in an unpleasant grin.

The bug loomed up in the holoview, overtaking them at their slow impulse. With a sudden burst of speed, it smashed its hammerhead nose right through the plated hull of the Mentera assault probe along *Xaromar's* starboard side. Bits and pieces of wreckage and mangled bodies floated out of the newly created hole.

The dragonfly surged in with otherworldly eyes glowing ravenous hues. Its acrid spit cauterized the hole, now small enough so that no human could escape. As more debris flew out, Regers gaped, shuddering to think about Creib's fate out there. Even if they'd attempted to save him, he'd be long gone now.

"How far?" he croaked at Jennings, fingering his blaster.

"One and a half minutes to safe zone."

"Too long! Hurry the fuck up. If that bug smacks through our hull, we're all floating corpses."

Jennings grimaced. Another oil-drum boom came thudding from the port hull.

"Christ, that thing's going to shred us," rasped Deakes. His eyes rolled port-ward to the engine bay. "How much more damage can this ship take?"

The ship lurched to new assaults.

All eyes turned to the holoview. The dragonfly ripped out of the hulk and flew ahead of *Xaromar* and turned back to stare at the crew with iridescent eyes, even though the port glass was shuttered. For a second time, Regers got an unpleasant glimpse of that creature through the holo view, as if it glared through misty veils of evil and on through his soul. The streamlined carapace glimmered rainbow colors under the faint light of Remus's faraway sun. Its near transparent wings buzzed at impossible speeds. Then its bulbous body twitched like a bumblebee on a blossoming flower. The six legs retracted and extended and an extra set of antenna wavered. How could any creature survive in a vacuum? A shudder of apprehension shivered up Regers' spine. He could not help but remember the dragonfly creature he'd named *Shredder* that had torn through as many Zikri squids as he could count on Phebis.

Jennings gave a sudden gust of triumph as he slammed the Varwol drive to engage. The ship lurched in response and hurtled through the light highways to impossible places. The crew gaped as the holoviews showed a wall of white light to either side.

Safety.

Silence.

Regers loosed a strangled breath. "That's not a creature I want to mess with. Good work, boys. Let's crack out the Daulk ale." He glared at Dez. "See, Dez, your shitass prank of delaying us, nearly got us killed."

Dez's lips peeled back in an angry scowl. He held his tongue, forgoing to mention that Regers had already implemented his original plan to capture the armor.

Regers stepped through the pile of Mentera bodies, whistling a happy tune, kicking at corpses as he passed. "Let's get this mess cleaned up. We'll shove this filth in the trash compactor. Hate the smell of their yellow, green-goblin blooded hides."

Regers took little heed of Dez's droopy misery as he hunched amidst the bloody masses of locust husks that lay strewn across the bridge. Ramra lifted his weapon to blast one of the last twitching insects, but Jennings held up a hand. "Don't nuke that one yet." His face was flushed, cheeks blood-smeared. "Hear that? Radio chatter. We can patch in his communications to the ship's universal translators and figure out what these bugs were up to. Seems a dismal place to crouch and hide. If the locust is still alive, maybe it's receiving some kind of messages or last transmission from its superiors."

"Good plan, Jiminy." Regers turned to Ramra. "Help Deakes." They dragged the weak creature over to the com console, ripped off its cracked helmet and patched the battered headset into the main computer. Raspy, clicking, insect sounds played through the ship's audio. The computer began to analyze and decode the garbled scratches and hisses.

"Mantis one, can you read? Intercept humans. (Pause). Bring all aboard with the others. (Staticky pause). Once you have acquired targets, rendezvous to Kraetoria with the mother ship at sector A34.7765#953154. Other humans have been intercepted on old world. Invasion of human worlds is proceeding to plan..."

The message cut off and repeated.

Only a recording. Regers mulled it over. More static, then the message faded out to background. White noise. The Mentera's life extinguished with it.

"What's that all about 'Kraetoria'?" muttered Deakes.

Regers curled his lip. "Guessing that my good friend Yul went to that *Dim Zone* shithole. Narrows down my search then. Once we pawn off this tech, we'll head to Kraetoria."

"No way, Regers," said Deakes. "Why insist on one-upping this fucker Yul? You're alive, can't you just leave it at that?"

Regers fingers twitched on his E1. "This is my ship, my way, Deakes."

"You're asking for trouble. Those bugs will cut us up and eat us for breakfast."

Regers grinned a toothy grin. "Not while me and my blaster are on duty. I'll be kicking some bug ass before long, you wait. Jiminy, cut that annoying bug signal."

Jennings flipped the switch. The circuit went dead.

Dez vaulted over to grasp at Regers' arm, mouthing words in a strained voice. Regers winced at the man's breath and his unwholesome pallor.

"You have to turn this thing around, Regers! You heard about the alien invasion of human worlds. This tech is all the more important. Mathias is dead. You'll not find Yul here or on Kraetoria. A waste to keep me hostage here."

"Pay me my money, you fucking bastard, then we'll talk."

"You'll get your damn money, Regers. Seems that's all you care about."

"Damn right. I'll tell you what, I'll sell the mechno to you, even deliver it. Price is a million yols."

"A million yols?" Dez gaped, a strangled croak gurgling from his mouth. "No bloody way, Regers, that's highway robbery."

"What happened to 'worth its weight in gold'?" Regers smirked. He mimed quotation marks and knew by the feigned outcry that the CEO would pay more for it if he had to. Sell his own mother on the streets, considering the scope of the mechno's application. The dragonfly-driven tech would be worth a hundred-fold more than his asking price once Cyber Corp got its marketing machine going.

"Take the offer now, Dez, before it goes up another million."

Dez bit his lip. He looked here and there, flush-faced, like a snared rabbit.

"Price just went up," Regers said after the man's hesitation. "A new ship too, an Alpha Roamer X4 or better. One mil yols plus ship payable on delivery."

Dez squirmed like a worm on a hook. "Okay, deal." He wiped at the sweat gathering at the bags under his eyes. "Why am I going along with this?"

"Because Mathias'll give you a cherry, maybe even suck your dick as a bonus, if he ever surfaces from his hiding."

Vincent choked out a laugh. Dez grimaced and hissed between his teeth.

"So we're good, one million plus a new ship? I'll throw in *Xaromar* as a freebie once you hand over my Roamer."

Dez nodded, clawing at his pale ruff of sea-oat hair.

Regers slapped his thigh. "Now there's business I can feel good about. I'm getting all tingly and warm thinking about it. Practically getting a hard on. Dez, you drive a hard bargain. So, let's say we haul ass back to Phallanor with your bug armor. Perfect timing now, that old butterfly boy is left light years behind." He grinned.

Regers stepped closer to the quivering man and spoke in an amiable voice. "Let's firm it up, our deal, before you go changing your mind, like a little chicken shit bastard turned tail. You're a slippery fellow, Dez, and I gotta keep my eye on you. Some time later you'll send a gaggle of lawyers on me and weasel your way out. A man can never be too careful."

Regers rummaged through the forward bin. He pulled out a lumo pen and phosphor pad and scrawled some hasty words on the back of what looked like an old parts requisition form. "Sign," he said.

"As if I had any choice," Dez panted, puckering up his mouth. He scribbled his signature.

Regers scribbled his own mark while the others looked on in wonder. Regers signaled both Deakes and Vincent over to sign as witnesses.

"If it makes you feel better, Dez, if you hadn't agreed to those terms I'd have sicced Vincent on you, had him shove this rifle end down your throat till you were chirping birdshit like a big fat robin hunting worms in the morning dew."

"You're a pig, Regers. If I ever—"

Regers held up a hand. "Save it. Just a lot of windy air, we both know it."

Dez fumed, his eyes blazing like a man who knew he was powerless in Regers' clutches.

* * *

Far away somewhere in the ruins of the forgotten research station, CEO Mathias hung suspended like a dead fish in his brine-filled tank, huddled in the murk of a broken Zikri Orb. He had missed his chance of rescue by a thin hair. In universal terms, this was significant, considering the billions of unknown worlds in the galaxy and the zero likelihood of any human venturing to these remote planets on the edge of *The Dim Zone*. As Regers and crew, oblivious to the CEO's presence trapped in the tank, scooted off down the light highways at inconceivable speeds, never to return to Remus, Mathis continued his dreamless vigil. Luckily, for him, the brine would keep him alive indefinitely. Unluckily, there was no reason for human, alien, or anything else to ever return to that primitive, mysterious world.

CHRIS TURNER

Chapter 16

A few days later, *Xaromar* made a pit stop at Vendrome planet. They acquired food and battle gear, then headed straight for Phallanor. The planet's blue-green disc yawned below them, a human hub of hubs expanding from horizon to horizon, getting larger by the minute. The ship impulsed down on its still weak power, transporting its precious cargo, Hresh's mechnobot. Regers, making due note on the ship's computer his private bank account a million yols the richer, smoothed his stubbled jowl, feeling a wash of satisfaction.

Dez seemed unusually energetic, parading about like a spring chicken. He stared hard at Regers. "Radioed into Caz, our security officer. The loading dock on bay E5 is all cleared for landing. Acquisitions building, R & D West tower, East wing. We can land at the heliport, and deposit the armature, then see to *Xaromar's* repair. I said I owed you a ship, and I'll keep my word."

Regers peered at him through slitted eyes. "Not repair, a new ship. Hate to burst your bubble, Dez, but home may not be as rosy for you as you may think. See—" he wrapped an arm around the CEO's shoulder "— I know, you're thinking that here's dumb fuck Regers, strutting around like some lame, sloe-eyed ox, sticking his nose into armed forces, security, E1s, tasers, pepper spray, electro-nets, lawyers, judges, you name it. Just giving himself up so easy here on Phallanor like a prodigal son. But been doing some thinking. Had Jennings do a little research on you while we were at the last station, getting supplies and all. Seems you have a pretty wife and daughter back home. Ain't that nice. Alizia and Beatrix. Mighty fine-looking gals too. Be a shame if anything happened to them." He let the thought dangle then held up a hand in reproach. "Don't get all bug-eyed on me, Dez. I put the word out to a couple of associates of mine out in Veglos, no-nonsense types, to pay them gals of yours a visit, should I not happen to report in at a certain hour of each day. How long you think you can hide your loved ones, Dez, you being big, acting CEO? Vespasie and Furad aka 'Dogfir' are thorough fellows."

Dez paled. He gulped, nodding slowly.

Regers patted him on the back. "That's good, Dez. I like it when a man sees eye to eye with his superior and there's no fucking about like a couple of cat-clawing bitches putting out each other's eyes."

Dez slumped. Events proceeded smoothly, more to Regers' liking than Dez would have expected after the last disclosure. Regers and his crew were given royal treatment by Cyber Corp staff, ushered in as high-end VIPs, given luxury suites and unlimited booze, service and amenities.

Ramra blinked at the shag carpet, the crystal glassware, the cathedral ceilings, chrome fixtures and unlimited holo media channels. "Wow, never seen anything like this!"

Vincent flopped on a queen-sized bed with his boots on, loosing a contented breath. "At last, some payback."

"Told you, I'd take care of you," said Regers.

Jennings muttered, scratching his cheek with the heel of his hand. "I can't seem to get Creib out of my mind. Poor bastard, frying out there in *The Dim Zone* with those locusts and that dragonfly. All some horrible nightmare."

"Best you forget about Creib, Jennings," said Regers. "An unfortunate incident, one that Dez'll have on his conscience, fucking around as he was back there. This is in part, his way of making it up."

Jennings grunted. "Keep on believing that, Regers."

"I like to believe my lullabies more than any other knob's bullshit. Tomorrow we're hauling ass out of here, once we get our new ship. To Kraetoria, unless new leads crop up."

Jennings shook his head. "This scheme of yours stinks."

"Shut it, Jiminy. No one cares about your bleeding heart opinions."

"Everything's business first, pleasure after with Regers," Deakes laughed.

"Hear, hear," Ramra cheered, tipping his wine glass, spilling some on the carpet while he toasted Regers' skullduggery in landing them riches and a new ship.

Jennings became irritated with the praise and clenched his fists, furrowing his brow, only another source of private amusement for Regers.

Vincent called up for room service—local surf and turf—giant turtle-like crustaceans of some ilk and yak meat straight from the choicest factory farms. "Too bad we couldn't get some dames up here too," Vincent mused.

"We probably could, Vincent, but I don't want to push Dez too hard. The man might crack. Do something stupid like call the law on us, despite the warnings I've given him. Yes, it's important to keep Dez focused and balanced."

Regers frowned. The man was smart. Wise enough to know that once the bugs and squids crawled down upon Phallanor, there would be no Cyber Corp to speak of. An extra incentive for him to put special 'efforts' into putting the armor to good use, or financing an exit plan, or at least a strategy to defend this world. As for himself, he could give a rat's ass who ruled the universe. Plenty of despots and shysters among the human race to go around ten times. Men who'd sell their own mothers, little rat bastards—and others, men and women included, who'd kill and torture for gain.

"Don't like not having weapons," mumbled Vincent. "Feel naked without one."

"You and me both, Vince," croaked Regers. "I've got enough leverage on Dez that he won't get too cute too fast. As long as we don't tempt him."

Deakes harrumphed. "Is it true that you jammed up his wife and kid? Don't recall Jennings doing any research on Vendrome."

"What do you think, Deakes?" grunted Regers.

Deakes faced the engineer who had turned and was staring out the window. "Well, Jennings, what about it?"

Jennings continued to blink and stare at the hustle and bustle of magno-trams, hordes of pedestrians and air-speeders vaulting across the cityscape below. He just shook his head and lifted a hand toward Regers who flashed him a smug look.

* * *

Dez was, if anything, eager to see Regers off Phallanor asap, yet Regers would not be dismissed so easily. Two ships of Dez's choice did not appeal to Regers who rejected them out of hand. "These are poor picks and inferior quality, Dez. I told you—an Alpha Roamer X4 or better. Don't cheat me on firepower. This Manga 6 here is an early bird model with impulse jets that even *Xaromar* in her wounded capacity could outpower."

"Those are rare ships, Regers!" objected Dez, gritting his teeth. "I'm trying to get an equivalent starship for you."

"Try harder."

Dez shook his head and marched off in a huff.

Deakes and the others were content to live in the lap of luxury, enjoying the downtime from risking their hides out in *The Dim Zone*. Breaking heads, running cons, fooling with underground thug rings, blowing up installations, stealing goods...all tough and dangerous work. "Why not stay here and milk Dez for all he's worth?" Deakes rumbled.

"Because it's boring," said Regers. "Dez's going to figure out a way to get out from under my thumb. Then we'll face waking up with ice picks in our heads."

Ramra grimaced. "Always thinking two steps ahead, eh, boss?"

"That's what I'm here for, Ramra, and why I'm still alive."

Jennings rolled his eyes.

By the end of the week, Dez had procured a lightfighter which met Regers' approval—a buffed and polished Alpha Roamer berthed in the research hangar, ready to go. Deakes was in awe of the vessel as he and Vincent scrutinized the sleek grey fuselage, its twin jets and roomy forward belvedere with expanded bridge, stocked with custom features like enhanced hyperdrive targeting, AI tactical and weapons deployment. Ramra and the others held Regers in even higher stead while Dez stood strangely aloof. "Vintage, Reg. How'd you manage to pull this off?" praised Ramra. "Equipped with turbo impulse ion drive and four cannons, versus the usual two—a lean, mean fighting machine."

Regers showed a set of flashing teeth. "Only the best for the best."

Even Jennings had to grumble his approval, though the man was doubtful their luck would hold up. "Haven't seen one of these classics for ten years. Not convinced there won't be some repercussions."

Regers waved it off.

Dez addressed Regers with cold formality. "Your new ship is called *Grendel*. I named it myself, felt it was appropriate, considering the nature of your 'brigade'."

Regers gave a grunting laugh. He slapped his thigh. "Good call, Dez."

"The armor is topnotch. Ample range and heavy fire, the shields force 4. Guns able to stand up to L16 destroyers. It comes with an amphibious assault vehicle, a two-man craft for light excursions on-world...air, water, sky. A recent model in Cyber Corp's long line of portable amphibious vehicles, APVs we call them."

"Mighty fine, Dez. Appreciate the gesture."

"When's it ready?" asked Deakes.

Dez scrunched up his mouth. "Tomorrow around noon."

"Good, we'll hold you to it," said Regers.

Chapter 17

The flagship destroyer Orb, *Viscurg*, hurtled down the light highways toward Quenrix. Admiral Nrog of the Zikri armada faced his sparring partner with a rippling snap of his strongest left motilator. The combat took place in a special war room enlivened with creeping bottle-green foliage growing hydroponically from the walls. Nrog's pocked, rubbery face was alive in a feral grin. A low, warbling chitter rumbled in his wattled throat and depths of his chest. The robust young pup bobbing before him was a splendid specimen. Also an accomplished wrestler whose elongated motilators, thick with rigid muscle, rippled and constricted in the menacing patterns of time-honored intimidation. Normally, intimidating one's supreme commanding officer wasn't recommended, yet the Zikri were notorious for parading their physical prowess in front of one another, like those of old in the gladiator pens, regardless of consequences.

A chittering voice from the spectators intruded on Nrog's concentration. "Consul Jnedz wishes to speak with you, Admiral Nrog. He is here, aboard this vessel, transported across by amalgamator to see you, as proxy for *Princeps* Jring.

Nrog scowled. "I know for whom he is proxy." He resisted the urge to lash out and punish his officious aide for distracting him at an inopportune time. "Tell the skulking Mentera to wait." With a flick of stinging tentacle, Nrog sent him on his way.

Nrog let his own seven-foot long, sucker-marked motilators rise high over his head as he glided forth to assess better his first opponent. Let the youngblood do his dance. The only reason he allowed such cocky displays in his private battle chamber—and aspirants as arrogant as this pup—was because they were worthy adversaries. They tested his mettle, kept him sharp, fit, and his fighting skills honed. Too many of his fellow Zikri had gone the way of softness over the generations, even the well-intentioned ones, weakened by technology and overindulgence. He would not fall prey to such enticements. That was why he was 'admiral' and other competitors of his race remained shredded pulps in the unfolding drama of his constant intrigue, assassinations and machinations.

The memories of the warm blood spilled in the dark, agonized chitters, squads of many hapless contenders as they fell under his crushing motilators revitalized his soul. Even more so while he had worked his way up the ranks, from lowly marine to squad commander, to stormtrooper, death squad overseer, weapons deployment monitor, intelligence officer, and finally commander of his own fleet.

Nrog had marked and mapped the steps in his mind—the small, deliberate sacrifices, the shady betrayals, the well-timed trysts and the bloodshed, all necessary manipulations on his road to supremacy.

Nrog's wide, inverted-V-shaped upper body gleamed with muscular strength. A robust vessel built up from obsessive conditioning. He locked motilators with the youngblood, Baglaiksh. A freakish pinkish tinge clung to Nrog's flesh and set him apart from his peers. That and his more massive rubbery build marked him a special breed.

Four spectators hovered to either side of the sand pit and now scuttled closer to check that no transgressions were committed amid the chittering gasps and slimy heaves of tentacle and torso…Rules must be obeyed…and more importantly, should Nrog lose or start to suffer appreciable injury, the attendants would leap in to kill the overzealous combatant.

Nrog cleaned himself up with aromatic suds in tubs of water set to the side. Soon these had grown murky with darkened blood. The wrestling match had been a violent one and quick. Baglaiksh overestimated himself; he had foolishly wasted himself on a half lock to Nrog's upper motilators, the strongest. Easily Nrog had twisted out of that strangling hold and unleashed his own paralyzing grip. The error had cost the pup dearly. Baglaiksh lay sprawled in his own filth with two mangled motilators and much blood. The upstart crawled with difficulty, rasping wheezes along the way, amid sand and sawdust spread upon the floor.

The aide, fluttering tentacle tips, had crept back to wait expectantly.

Let the Consul wait. These Mentera were far too officious as it was. They demanded this and that like petty dictators, as if they owned the whole of space.

Nrog glided through the weapons bay of his Orb battle cruiser. He ran eager eyes over the deployment of his armaments. One by one the warships came out of light drive before Quenrix.

One thousand attack Orbs! With half as many stealth Orbs for dogfighting and recon. The Mentera were left with the dirty task of rounding up human slaves planet-wide to appease their vampirish hungers. The Zikri kept the Quenrix space clear and secure of any defending space fleet. The Mentera got their choice of the slaves, the Zikri got the planet's resources—the mines, the factories and the remaining humans as slaves. A mutual win-win for both sides.

Nrog was under no illusion as to how the Mentera were using the Zikri's muscle to subjugate the galaxy. He had confidence that his armada of Orbs could defeat the Mentera lightfighters if it ever came to an all-out skirmish. Zikri-Mentera past relations had not been free of incidents of mutual aggression, each had never trusted the other. Too often Mentera raiders would initiate an attack and enslave Zikri in their despicable tanks. He would not allow such practices to continue, nor would he put his faith in any sworn treaties or promises, or any overt displays of cooperation. All just lip service. Zikri and Mentera had been enemies since the beginning. It was a miracle that this alliance had even taken shape—only by his own diplomacy in promising the Mentera a hefty booty of slaves and territory. Personally, he did not like the idea of Mentera infantry amassing so much power in the acquisition of new slaves. It could fuel their race for centuries, if not a millennium.

"Sir, our forces are ready to strike—"

Nrog stared at his aide, as if nothing could be more obvious.

"—yet we have reported irregularities among the Mentera ranks."

"What irregularities?"

"Three lightfighters on the right flank. Fighters Meijk, Breulk and Kiuk wing breaking rank, drifting in uncharacteristic patterns. Transmissions have been routed on unauthorized encrypted channel."

"Who are they?"

"Our database reports them as scouts from Kraetoria."

Betrayal? Nrog's eyes narrowed. "Scouts? Investigate it. We don't want any security leaks or anomalies," he said with a dangerous edge.

The aide snuffled and turned away.

"Incompetent locusts. Monitor them, Fuxifix. Inform Consul Jnedz and have him talk to First Officer Jring. It could be just technical glitches. But maybe not."

"As you wish, sir." The aide departed, gliding out on sleek motilators.

Nrog chittered under his raspy breath. Sloppy, stupid locusts. The invasion's assured success relied on clockwork precision. The assault must go as planned. There must not be anything to impede it. Odd that Jring and his captains had not dealt with the anomaly. They probably did not consider it a threat. No matter. All would be settled before long.

* * *

The arrogance of Nrog's communication did not cease to amaze *Princeps* Jring, commander of the Mentera army. He looked out to the stars from his stateroom on the LU destroyer with the same pride he always had. Though with more doubt and perhaps critical apprehension than usual. This allied venture could go all wrong, if proper protocols were not observed. Everything executed according to protocol and logic. No stone left unturned. He mustn't underestimate these humans. They'd eluded subjugation before and thwarted Mentera manifest destiny. But with those staggering numbers of lightfighters and Orbs out there, how could the invasion fail? Eight thousand attack craft gathered already. And more by the minute as the Zikri forces hyperdrived in from distant destinations.

The Zikri troubled him. Merciless, ruthless savages, half squid, half amphipod, beings who kill first, ask questions later. Creatures known for their superior strength and brutality, but they were nowhere near as intelligent as was he, or his race in general. He would see that they remain subjugated, kept in their place, mere tools to serve the Mentera's purpose. This ambitious leader of theirs, Nrog, was by no means stupid…the squid was a threat and not to be treated lightly. A dangerous ally who could turn on them when the moment was ripe. He must ensure this did not happen.

Jring both dreaded and was titillated by the thought of their first meeting. That would be soon enough.

He exited his private lodging, leaving behind the commanding view of the stars, and clacked down the U-shaped halls, pausing to scrutinize and examine the attack plans posted on the walls of various crew and engineers. He jingled along, bands of resinous gold metal clipped to his hind legs to show his exalted rank. As far as male locusts went, Jring was short and slender; for this reason, he walked on his hind legs with less of a stoop and crouching gait to compensate. He kept his chitinous carapace oiled and gleaming a slick, fulsome green. More a deep, disturbing jade than his blackish-green or copper-plated Mentera compatriots. An impressive presence nonetheless.

At last he came to the great arch of the central drive of the destroyer's hub. An unfathomable construction…a massive dome stretching as high as the eye could see only to plunge into dim blackness below. There at the rail's edge of the chasm's threshold, Jring peered 800 feet below to a massive weave of countless human and alien victims caught in a sticky web of interconnectivity—like flies. Linked as one, to create a pool of mental energy, a vast psychic voltage which powered the time-drive and the internal engines of the Mentera destroyer, a technology superior to the Varwol technology of the anthropomorphic races.

Jring's reverie, like Nrog's, was interrupted by the entrance of the First Acolyte.

"What is the destination of the first round of human slaves from Quenrix, *Princeps?*" The Acolyte's long, locust-shaped head towered a full six inches above Jring's own insectoid skull. A fact Jring didn't mind, not at all embarrassed by his own inferior height, as might others of his rank. He used his diminutive size as a spur to advance his other skills and rise above his competitors. Now he was the most powerful of the locusts. No one could deny him his rule or question his authority.

"They will go to *Barboryle*, the secret world, as planned, put in their tanks. The Mother locust will feed off the first ten thousand humans and thrive. Regard, Acolyte, a master plan, a millennium supply of non-stop feeding. The Queen Mother needs enough food to complete her incubation of the future hordes, that her children might fly to all corners of the galaxy and lay their own eggs."

"What is the Zikri's role in all this?" the Acolyte asked.

The Mentera uttered a staccato hiss and twitched his antennae in an attitude of indifference. "As slaves. They will serve us, or they will perish."

The aide said with some discomfort, "But they will create war with us. Our allies will then become our enemies."

"Your grasp of these affairs is deficient. Go now and keep me apprised of the invasion's progress."

The Acolyte pinched his locust lips into a penitent scowl. He bowed and took his leave of the *Princeps'* presence.

Princeps Jring occupied himself with other matters of protocol, namely the sending of assurances to the Queen Mother that their mission would be soon underway. It was too late to investigate the offending ships Nrog had mentioned. Upon the successful completion of the invasion, the three careless captains would be punished for being out of sync with the others and making him look foolish in front of the Zikri.

Chapter 18

The untold thousands of alien ships came out of hyperdrive on auto-deploy. Mentera lightfighters speckled space as far as the eye could see. Lethal flagships and destroyers formed larger pods of light within the smaller swarms, and then the ugly Zikri Orbs materialized out of nowhere, spiked black like morningstars.

Yul blinked, hardly daring to believe he was still in the midst of this nightmare. At his side, Cloye glared, pointing a finger at the innumerable red dots on the holo screen. There were enough enemy ships to decimate an entire world. Her strident curse snapped him out of his daydream. It seemed so long ago that he had met her—in the cramped hold on the terraformer bound for Remus. The odds of her turning from enemy to ally had been so slim as to be nonexistent. She'd been ready to zap him and take his head back to Mathias. Mathias! Where was the bastard, the financial mogul of Cyber Corp? The same shyster who, to ensure his steadfast cooperation in *The Dim Zone* espionage, had inserted the painful nanoparticles in his blood stream that stabbed him with agony on a single press of a remote control.

The blue-grey disc of Quenrix hung below like some detached eyeball. Some 30k miles above the planet the alien armada poised in a slow orbit. Thousands of assault fighters ready to launch their terror on the innocent multitudes below.

No visible resistance came in view or on the holo radar within ten thousand miles. Why did this not surprise him? The world below was easy prey for these alien predators.

Miko's voice rasped over the com, "They're lambs to the slaughter, Yul!

I'm calling NOA."

"No, spaceboy—I'll do it. They'll never believe you."

Fenli snorted a curse. "Pray that they don't catch wind of our spying and meddling and kill us all."

"We're walking an impossible tightrope as it is," Yul muttered.

Orders from Mentera command crackled through the ship's com. Yul scowled. That could be nothing good. "Miko, translate." Even engineer whiz Hresh hadn't been able to get their universal translator working.

Miko parroted what Usk translated: "They tell us to move out. That all mantis craft are to act as advance guard. The Zikri Orbs are to remain behind to safeguard the sky. The next world on their list is a nearby planet on the fringe of the outer zone, a mere hop skip away."

Yul bit his knuckles. "Not good." Not even a moment to collect his wits and flesh out a plan. "We're going to have to play along until we figure something out."

Fenli griped, "How long are we going to play this stupid charade before we blast out of here?"

"Maybe until the bugs give us back control of our ships, dumbfuck?" snapped Cloye. "Look, they've hardwired our impulse to Quenrix. They're taking no chances with screw-ups."

Fenli swore. Yul stiffened in horror at the reality of Cloye's assertion. The nose of their craft tilted slowly planetward along with the bee-swarm of brightly-colored dots in near space.

Miko gave a startled cry. "Our nav is up and running!"

"Wait, so's mine," said Fenli. "And my hyperdrive is suddenly active. Well I'll be… What do you know?" He laughed. "See you suckers!"

A bright flash lit across the horizon as his ship entered the light highways and was gone.

"Lucky bastard," grumbled Yul.

"The more we talk like this over open wire is a risk," hissed Hresh.

"The invasion is unprecedented and insane," Miko persisted. "We can't just go down and stand idly by while they kill and enslave our fellow human beings! I can't let this happen."

"Easy, spaceboy," said Yul. "There's nothing you can do."

"Screw that. I'm breaking away—"

Yul swore. But Miko was already gone.

"Fool!" Yul groaned. "He's going to give us away."

"Let him go, Yul." Cloye gave a bitter laugh. "He's on a death mission as it is. So is that flyboy Fenli of his. But the cocky bastard managed to get away as we should've."

Yul shook his head, gritting his teeth. "Those two may end up being the only ones keeping us alive, Cloye. We'd better hope they survive. United we stand, divided we fall."

"Fancy words." But Cloye was not so hotheaded as to deny that he spoke truth.

Yul stared helplessly at the alien controls. Dire frustration smoked in his brain, directed at the squiggles, knobs, strange symbols. "Evidently our last mayday didn't get through."

He hissed into the com. "NOA, this is top priority, do you read?"

A prolonged silence passed as the carrier signal ping-ponged through the light tunnels.

"Over. Private Bjen Stone, NOA command control here. Who am I talking to?"

Yul rasped, "Zikri and Mentera forces are ready to move in on Quenrix. We're three of us in spy ships, Mentera lightfighters in the middle of the attack fleet! Repeat. We're in a three-ship convoy amid enemy vessels. The next target is likely a nearby world. Put every ship you have into sector 3.156DZ. Thwart this disaster before—"

"Who is this? We've confirmed you as an enemy Mentera lightfighter."

"Yeah, I know that, Stone. Name's Vrean, Yul Vrean."

"What are your channels, your credentials? Who do you work for?"

Yul hesitated. Was this guy for real? He spoke in a low, angry voice, "I work for Cyber Corp. Contracted by Mathias."

"Mathias? Man's been missing for a month."

"We know. And he's likely dead. Forget Mathias. We came from *The Dim Zone,* planet *Remus.* Place is a shambles. Bugs and squids have taken over. And something else, some feral alien hellbringer. Mathias's ex-researcher, Sigmund Hresh—his base, is toast, demolished. We made it to *Kraetoria*—"

"Kraetoria? What are you on? That's a dead world, Vrean. Wait, Quenrix, you say? Reports are coming in from Quenrix's defense grid now. Picking up large numbers of enemy craft. Okay...We're on our way."

* * *

Miko's fingers played over the locust nav console. How he despised this prison of a ship, his throbbing brain scanning for options. Impulse drive was still operational, unlike the hyperdrive and his companions' light drives. He watched as Yul floated down planetside cosseted with the locust swarm.

Miko looked over at Usk whose black-plated insectoid head bobbed in frustration. The locust's red eyes gleamed. Hard enough to navigate this Mentera ship. Without Usk they'd be rat bait by now. Star gazed on in apathy at the holo view and its endless blips of enemies. A blank look hung on her face, not even the briefest strangled cry issued from her throat. What would it take to snap the woman out of her lethargy?

Miko's heart thumped in his chest as a wild plan surfaced. Reaching past Usk's pincer, he set the ship skimming over the line of aphids and mantises streaming like lemmings down to planetside. His lips curled in vindictive defiance.

"Usk! We'll linger here as long as we can fake it...might be able to sabotage those ships, put a monkey wrench in their launch plans. There! Look, that Mentera slaver over there." Usk's eyes roved to where Miko pointed: a dark blue, balloon-like hull filled a portion of the viewscreen. "The ship lags behind. If we can sabotage it or drop bombs on its com towers..."

"How?" chittered Usk's voice through the translator. "Those ships have defenses. Once we fire, they'll think we turned traitor and neutralize us in short order." Though Miko noticed he jerked his head up in a faint hope.

Miko gnawed at his knuckles. "I'm open to ideas, Usk. Think of something!"

"Don't do it," Yul hissed over the com, overhearing their conversation. "It's suicide. Stay at the fringes of the Mentera fleet and watch your back and ours."

Miko shook his head, a defiant gleam in his eyes. His hand fled to the impulse slider. They could dip and dodge at top speed, nuke as many as they could then make their break from the fleet...but his fingers held back.

The hesitation cost him. Miko's ship was out of line with the others. The principal Mentera squad leader's craft veered in while a barrage of locust talk crackled over their receiver, translated in real time:

"Mentera lightfighter Meijk! You are out of order. Report to mission control on the double. Interrogation crew and boarding party are on its way. Dock immediately."

Miko hissed, his heart a lead weight. "Bastards. Now we're in a pickle,

Usk. Get this ship out of here! Draw the squad leader toward that nearby Zikri Orb. If we can raise some havoc over there, it'll buy us some time. Damn it! I wish they hadn't jammed up our light drive."

"Don't worry, Yul," Miko hissed in response to Yul's groan over the com. "We'll distract them away from you, and Fenli. Oh, I forgot, he's already gone."

Star shook her head in defeat, at last roused from her daze. "Is this what I think this is?"

"Yes, and worse. Work the auxiliary weapons controls. Now!" he barked. "Target the Mentera slaver. We have no time for hysterics."

She hurried to obey, her survival instinct returning.

The com chattered on with fresh new bug speak. Miko punched it off. Usk blinked at him. Miko worked the forward cannon and sprayed blasts upon the locust slaver, then he maxed the impulse toward one of the giant Orb flagships at the edge of the Zikri fleet, a craft with thick, bristling spikes and heavy cannons. A defiant snarl curled over his lips. Usk's beak of a mouth parted, mouthing an almost vindictive chirrup.

"If we're going to go out, might as well go out with a bang, Usk!" Teeth biting lip, Miko worked the controls as they came coursing up over the looming attack Orb. A host of locust aphid defense fighters dogged their tail, firing beams wantonly.

Deafening booms wracked the hull. Their shields got pounded, pitching to 40% integrity. Star wailed, the whites of her eyes a testament of her fear. All awaited sudden death only seconds away.

Orbs came streaming in from all quarters to surround them, like an eerie array of dark magnets. Miko and Usk lay into them with fore and aft cannon. Return fire knocked their hull, blasting shields to dangerous levels, but not before Usk sent a series of well-timed blasts into the hulls of a locust team leader and two flanking Orbs. The ships burned red then burst into doomed flames.

Usk gave a chirrup of triumph.

Shortlived triumph.

The dire tug of something oppressive gripped their starboard vanes. A tractor beam. The invisible magnetrons gnawed at their glowing hot fuselage and dragged them toward the massive spiked Orb flagship. A jagged landing portal opened. Saw-edged flanks swallowed them up, like the jaws of a giant steel trap.

They were going to take them alive.

Chapter 19

Yul had lost track of Miko as he swept planetside. Nausea pooled in the pit of his gut. A bad feeling grew. All paths and possibilities on this coaster ride seemed to lead to a predetermined outcome.

"I hate just sitting here," grumbled Cloye.

"Yeah, you and me both. But what else is there? Break formation and waste ourselves like Miko? We contacted NOA. If they get themselves together, our job's done. We can contrive to escape."

"Where are those fuckers anyways?"

"We just contacted them," sighed Yul.

"Don't they have reserves somewhere nearby?"

"Why would they? Look at our location, Cloye, a stone's throw away from *The Dim Zone*."

The swarm of alien ships entered the atmosphere over the polar ice cap then spread out across the doomed planet. Yul's wing headed for the foremost continent due south which showed as a brown mass in an illimitable ocean of green. Two other wings split to converge on the remaining continents and their plump cities.

The five thousand enemy ships surged in as one: the fiercest locust swarm in the history of the galaxy. The intent, to take the cities one by one.

The capital, *Gibras*, loomed up Yul's sight: sky towers, ore refineries, parks and monuments. He gripped the controls, refusing to believe this holocaust was in progress. Skyscrapers and executive buildings, air rail and tram skyways, outlined on the pale saffron horizon. It was a lazy afternoon, and the unsuspecting targets went about their daily business.

The Mentera ships skimmed above the clouds then glided down in S-shaped units, a dark menace hovering above the air cars in the streets, unleashing stun rays on the bewildered and panicking citizens. Convoys landed to discharge Mentera troops to hunt down and capture live human specimens. The giant Mentera slaver ships hung in the cloudy air above like great bloated zeppelins, waiting for their moments to descend and collect their mass prizes.

The hollow pit in Yul's stomach grew. He gaped in dismay as the ships unleashed their respective horrors. Miko was lost, Fenli had bailed. Now his ship skimmed the main boulevard with the rest of the horde. His fingers worked the holo pad, firing forward cannon aimlessly, hoping to keep up the illusion of an invader. Apparently their mission was to eliminate ground resistance while scouts and raider craft dropped to secure hapless human victims and transport them to their wide-bodied slaver ships.

Central control gave orders in a spate of bug-speak. Navigation had been given back to the lightfighters; now they could maneuver through the streets and conduct their grisly guerrilla warfare and ship-to-ship combat that was the logical next step. Yul's ship swept across the panic-stricken masses in the streets. His metal fingers tightened in dismay as white fire lashed out at the hull. The mantis ship rocked and shield levels dipped as Quenrix air guard defense fired back at the invading aliens. But this local resistance, too few in numbers, though valiant to the core, was shot down in smoldering heaps upon the teeming streets below.

"Change fire to light payloads," Yul hissed. "Miss as many of the locals as you can, Cloye. We need to keep up the pretense we're part of the fleet—otherwise that'll be us smoking on the ground."

She fired round after round from the rear cannons as close to the fleeing citizens as she dared.

Wholesale slavery. Yul cringed at the subjugation of a nation. While the spiked Orbs hovered far above the clouds like undersea mines, the Mentera lightfighters and slavers did their dirty work on the ground. Local resistance ships were tractored in or destroyed. Crews and pilots forced into slave holds. The great Mentera slave vessels at last made their way landward and Quenrixian citizens by the hundreds were herded into waiting raider craft. A gargantuan hulk, the shape of a massive blue zeppelin, descended in a central park adjoining a public square. It crushed old manicured trees and service buildings under its landing struts and infathomable weight. Mentera raiders in grey space suits spread out to capture the panicked civilians and cull any armed resistance. Several collectors, or aphid-shaped vessels, landed amidst the ruins, unleashing green stun fire. *Scout-raiders.* More grey-suited figures piled out and scuttled to snatch fleeing humans and bring them to the smaller vessels or directly to a slaver craft, whichever was closer.

Yul watched in helpless frustration. Unable to take direct action except to keep up with the pack, he lagged further and further behind the horde that swept through the streets. Cloye, working weapons grid, misfired and shot down locusts collecting victims.

Angry bug chatter rang out from the com. Cloye only laughed.

Guerrilla fighting erupted on in the streets, organized by trained Quenrix militia. But this was sporadic and ineffectual, compared to the better organized offense of the locusts. The defenders were unprepared for the scale of the invasion and fell to the locusts' stun rays. The Quenrix fleet converging on the Zikri Orbs covering the skies had at last been shot down. The Orbs cut off support and waited for any NOA resistance that might come. But it never did. Not in time. A neat package, this alien alliance, mused Yul grimly. The ground militia had likewise been neutralized.

* * *

As Fenli's mantis fighter hurtled down the light highways toward *Veglos* he slapped the controls in glee and let out a big yeehaw. Freedom! Master of a starship. What more could a freebooter want? Except maybe some cash? Easy to rustle up yols. A few wheels and deals back in the old haunts and he'd be back in business.

Hypderdrive into *Zostor*, work some angles. Spin the bottle and see what happened. Things may have changed in his old digs but at the core it was the same universe, the same old characters, stage and drama, and ways to play the game and capitalize.

Several ideas raced through Fenli's mind: the baths at *Pompledoris*, the dog fights on *Agrina*, the kinky dives at *Mekeroid*. The baths, their endless variation of harems, with hot oil, sun, massage…Lot of pigeons there. The dog fights…a prime betting ground and quick ticket to some easy, greasy yols. Mekeroid, well, Mekeroid was Mekeroid…

Friends of his out in *Elsian* would be long dead, a tragedy, alas, what with his being stuck in a bug tank for 40 to 50 years or so. But it would be a good world to start to explore some cash ventures and trade, like starships. Maybe resell, snatch up some used starships at good prices before the universe collapsed, all the wonderful worlds gobbled up by squids and locusts.

A pang hit him at the thought. But he could not dwell on the concept now. He'd have to ditch this starship. Too conspicuous a mark with a bug shape and a bug war now in full swing. Smart thing would be to trade it in for a friendlier craft and not look back.

The idea brought a hollow feeling to his stomach.

Too bad about Miko. Bleeding heart was trying to save the universe. When would people like him ever realize that it was impossible to win against these bugs? He'd seen it first hand, stuck in a tank for decades and almost checking out back on *Kraetoria* in that frozen pool.

But a sour feeling still ground at his innards.

What the hell are you thinking, Fenli? A pang of conscience sprang up at him like a hardwood burl grinding at an old wound in the back.

Fenli, developing a conscience? Certainly a record. Images flashed in his head, Miko saving his ass on the Mentera station so long ago, Yul fishing him out of that frozen bug pool back on Kraetoria...

He heaved a sigh. Against his better judgment, he dropped out of light drive, violating every practical instinct of self-preservation, and set a course for *Quenrix.*

* * *

Swarms of enemy lightfighters swept through the city. Down a wide street blocked by concrete rubble and buried in the ruins of a fallen building, Yul guided the ship. His eyes scanned for a place of concealment. But they registered something else instead. An aphid command vessel parked at the end by a ruined apartment block where several locust marines in grey suits clambered out to haul the screaming captives toward the waiting slaver vessel. Women and children kicked and fought in the aliens' pincered grips. No doubt their minds laid bare to the terror of the green-watered tanks.

Yul grimaced. He glided in, unable to stand the oppression any longer. Hresh, his face a pale mirror of what he expected to come, stared blank-eyed.

Cloye swore as she cinched her lip and cracked off shots at the nearby parked mantis raider. The ship erupted in ruin, its shields nonexistent from the firefight on approach.

"Cloye!" rumbled Yul.

"Oops."

He laughed, lips twisted in mockery. The startled Mentera ground troops dropped their wriggling charges and scuttled back, blinking at the inferno of their ship. The human captives staggered off to safety.

"They won't miss one ship," muttered Yul. With a vindictive grin, he banked the ship in closer while Cloye worked the weapons grid and more bright white flashes spat from the starboard cannons to peg off the slavers on the ground.

"Nuked us some bugs," Cloye sang out.

Hresh's jaw clenched. "How long you think that's going to work before the locusts peg us off?"

"Who cares?" Cloye grumbled. "We're living on borrowed time. Put your mind to work on figuring out a way for us to take out more bugs."

Hresh clutched at his hair, his face dripping with sweat. He searched through the ship's computer for some weakness or loophole that could gain them an advantage.

An aphid-prowed ship came rocketing from above, lacing heavy fire down at them. Apparently they'd been spotted in the middle of their mutinous act. Its pilot and crew came blitzing in to neutralize the potential sympathizers and spies masquerading in a rogue ship. Yul gunned the impulse thrust down the alley and up, but he knew their chance at escape was slim.

At that moment, a ship with a menacing blue-and-green mantis prow burst in on the scene: a special task force model, double the size of the invader. It came looping up and over the tops of buildings at breakneck speed. With full force it reamed the enemy vessel broadside, sending it corkscrewing out of control into the street to explode in a blinding flash of molten metal. Yul and Cloye both cried oaths of gratitude. Below, the aftershock rained debris and red hot metal on the littered streets. Bedraggled citizens with grimed faces and torn clothes ran tottering to shelter.

Yul's ship banked to safety. He breathed a sigh of relief. "What the hell was that?"

Cloye whistled. "Our flyboy, if it was anybody. I'll be damned!"

Yul grunted into the com, "Thanks, Fenli."

"Don't mention it. You saved my ass earlier, Yul, but you owe me one."

"Thought you'd abandoned us for greener pastures."

"Started to get lonesome."

"Yeah, I bet."

Yul grinned. These were desperate times with small victories. Hardly enough to win the day. But their bombing that slaver and giving the people a chance at escape had at least made a difference. A few ships against many. Fenli had saved them by nuking that ship. It appeared the enemy aphid hadn't radioed out in time to alert central command. Without NOA support, the invaders would quickly steamroll the planet. At least Hresh had managed to get the universal translator operational. According to reports streaming over the translator, the aliens had neutralized all major capital cities of the continent. Yul didn't doubt the other wing forces sent to Quenrix's distant continents had achieved any less appalling devastation and slavery.

Yul's heart sank at the sight of the number of blue and grey slavers rising with their bloated bellies full of humans up into the clouds from the ashes of the city. There must have been a hundred or more of them en route to some secret bug colony.

Orders crackled over the com, *"A job well done, lightfighters! Prepare to move out."*

Lightfighters and mantis craft lifted their noses to join the Zikri fleet in orbit around Quenrix. The grim, toneless robotic voice echoed in everyone's brain:

"Assemble your squads. Prepare for the next jump, to Xares."

Yul opened a channel to NOA before the ships hyperdrived out.

"NOA, Quenrix is lost," he rasped. "The next target is *Xares*. *Xares*, I repeat! Out." He cut the channel as a flood of light swept by the viewports and myriads upon myriads of ships disappeared down the light highways.

Chapter 20

Dez had more troubles on his mind than Regers' manipulations. NOA had contacted him personally and requested a private audience. A certain colonel, Grescon, a tawny-haired officious man, had papers requesting disclosure of all top-secret R & D files and company technology. After taking an invasive tour of primary R & D lab #1 and grilling his senior scientists with questions, Grescon, short on manners and invested with a pair of piercing hawk eyes, faced Dez. Dez indulged the man, but remained no pushover. "Under what authority can you request classified information?"

"Under NOA's new intel directive. Unless you want to have a time bomb up your ass, you'd better comply, Hadley, and don't hold anything back."

Dez scrutinized the hard, angry face in front of him. He gazed afar for some moments. "Very well, follow me."

In a secret command booth off a simulation room, the two watched a holoscreen offering a bird's eye view of a giant test arena. There, a great grey and black-speckled moth flitted about before a rectangular mechnobot. The latter was man-sized, floating impassively in its path. On cue from the technicians, the test mechno glided through the air, smashed the alien moth hard against the titanium wall.

Grescon frowned and recoiled. "Well, that looks like the end of your specimen," he said in a critical voice. "Anything else to show me, Hadley? Why're you wasting my time? Bio-weaponry? These are not military grade items."

Dez pointed. "Watch. And the name's Yadley."

Grescon turned his head. The moth, or rather the alien menace hatched from a plant pod on a faraway planet, miraculously revived. Rather than being sandwiched between hard metal and wall, it sent the mechno surging backward with a sudden burst of strength and hovered in the air before its adversary. Its eerie hummingbird wings worked a mile a minute. How it did so was infathomable to the eye, at least Grescon's as it sped out once again at incomprehensible speed and knocked the mechno tumbling to the floor. To say Grescon was impressed was an understatement. "What—How in hell did it do that?"

"That, colonel, is alien tech."

While Grescon pulled at his chin, Dez went on, "You ready to talk now? What's all this bullshit of demanding to see top-secret material? Imagine one of those lethal insects inside a protected armor and owned by your little old self."

The colonel's jaw dropped. A wet tongue passed over his upper lip. "Why didn't the moth finish the mechno while it had a chance?"

"It protected its habitat." Dez shrugged. "That's all it needed. Maybe it sees the hulk as a mechanism to use to its advantage, a type of protective shell."

"You were out there on Remus, Yadley. How much damage can these things do, or sustain? Better yet, how many bio-weapons like the one you're describing can you provide?"

"Four—five at the most…"

Grescon scowled, tugged at his nose. "That's not nearly enough."

"We're preparing more as we speak. You talked to my chief engineers, saw the work they are putting in at the machine shop. Dimensions, specifications, the like, so you know they produce quality merchandise…and that I'm not exaggerating."

The colonel nodded with animation. "That was before I saw a demonstration with a live specimen. We're putting everything we have into this operation, Yadley. Ships, manpower, drones, lightfighters, intelligence, the whole kit and caboodle, any other ideas are welcome. All plans are welcome. You, a senior scientist at a top-grade military research firm, can help us. If the human-colonized planets are to survive this alien invasion, we have to put in an all-out effort." He grunted. "There'll be huge kickbacks for you."

"I know, Colonel. It's just that the last models are purely experimental.

Results can't be guaranteed. There are still small glitches that might hamper—"

"Bullshit! Our intel indicates this is the biggest invasion in human history." The colonel's face turned red. His breath exploded in a violent gust. "An unprecedented 10k ships are en route to *Xares* as we speak, while we stand here wasting time. Our intelligence confirms reports leaked to us days ago dropped by one of your contractors, Yul Vrean. The squids and locusts plan to attack nearby planets one by one until they've conquered and enslaved the whole fucking galaxy. Nobody knows what they will do with those innocent souls once they get them in their tanks or where they will take them."

Dez shivered and wrung his hands. "Sir, I have a plan. If we can jettison enough of these prototypes into the invaders' war zone and install them in strategic places, they'll act as protector magnets—droid magnets if you will. To be unleashed at our discretion."

The colonel's brows rose. "My people are giving a green light to this. We're sparing no expense in hardware, technology and manpower, whatever it takes. Write up your reports and invoices and submit them to my personnel."

Dez nodded. "I can give you all the Star Class A/F mechnobots we have. They're all trained and programmed to kill. They'll sacrifice themselves too in the line of duty."

"Gather them, and don't stint. We'll hyperdrive them in to the war front."

Dez licked his lips, his mind buzzing with vivid memories of the armored avatar and his trip to Remus. "We can throw in our complete experimental line—from bio sources, alien pods to be exact, acquired from *The Dim Zone*."

The colonel smoothed his jaw. "Any bio-hazard I should know about?"

"Not that we can determine. As I hinted, I can't guarantee the new mechnobots' outcomes, as the moths are completely unpredictable, but that's their strength. They'll protect their habitat at all costs. The good news is our tests have shown them 100% more lethal and effective than our F models—if certain conditions apply."

Grescon nodded, his body more at ease. "Transport them to mission control asap. We can transport them into Fygard base on the high probability they'll prove useful. I haven't time to go over the minutiae. Only that anything that foils these aliens' sick plans is a go with us at NOA."

Dez felt a shiver pass up his back. His mind roved back to the dragonfly from hell. He wondered what havoc this test model with the moth could wreak.

Chapter 21

The next morning, Dez summoned Regers and crew to the main research lab. They came down a complicated series of stairs a few levels below main floor level, escorted by security men taking up the rear. Regers stood with the others in a wide, high-ceilinged lab buzzing with engineers in white coats. Wall-to-wall tech sprawled along the sides: holo monitors, sensors and recording equipment. Regers and CEO faced each other at a healthy distance.

Dez was all cleaned up: a new blue suit, black shoes, white tie, face and cheeks and sideburns scrubbed and trimmed, his pale ruff of hair as cheesy as ever, hollow eyes pits to nowhere, as if the stress of the last days had dug deep rivulets into his soul. Regers wondered if he'd ever fully recover from the ordeal.

A dozen demonstration research rooms stood to one side, all with a thick window reinforced with bulletproof glass and close-set iron bars.

Regers moved toward one and stared at the battered metal hulks within—failed mechnobots. The many white-coated engineers and lab assistants running around and their haggard, stressed looks told a story of its own. "How goes the bug research?" he asked sardonically.

Dez addressed Regers in a thin icy voice. "The armor is responding well to the alien insertion of the Xesian species." He studied Regers with a curious expression, bland and noncommittal, as if wondering how scientifically inclined such an uneducated rogue could be. "Once we part ways, Regers, I don't want to ever see your face again or you laying a hand on my family."

Regers shrugged. "Business is business, and our business is done, Dez.

Both of us have upheld our sides of the bargain. So, you needn't worry."

Dez nodded, as if convinced of the truth. "Then come to my primary lab, I want to show you something. Your friends can tag along if they wish."

Regers shrugged. "Sure, if you have a burning need for it, but don't try to sandbag me, Dez. Remember our little talk."

Dez snorted. "I'm sure you'll be fine, Regers, a big bad boy like you." But the CEO's smile did not reassure Regers.

Vincent and Ramra opted to stay back at the suite and indulge in R-rated holo channels over mugs of dark ale while Jennings and Deakes decided to take the tour.

Security men fell in behind Regers and his two crew members, fingering their E1s. Regers cast them a smirking look. Though that was mostly bluff. Something was off with Dez and that troubled him. The man was too smug.

Cyber Corp was an impressive installation as far as research places went: from its botanical gardens and glass cathedral ceilinged foyers to its wall-to-wall lab tech. Regers mused, overkill with its nests of labs lit with bright fluorescent lights, and geeks running around in white lab coats with pencils tucked behind the ear, carrying punch code gizmos, chipboards and robot parts.

The tense group piled into an elevator and descended several more floors into a secure area, a huge underground complex.

"Here, put these on." Dez motioned to a rack of hanging white lab coats and hard hats for everyone.

"You turning us into a construction crew?" grunted Regers.

"No, the helmets are for your safety. The white coats are for alerting my security men not to blow you away."

"Sounds logical," conceded Regers.

Dez scowled, forcing words from his pinched lips, one that he evidently found distasteful and seemed hesitant to relay. "Somebody leaked info to NOA, sprang the news of an invasion. Largest mobilization of defense ships in the history of the free colonies according to Colonel Grescon."

"You don't say. Now who'd do that?" Regers said with a somewhat sour twist to his mouth. "Something you ain't telling me, Dez?"

Dez swallowed, as if fearing the sharp edge of Regers' wrath. "Thought you'd be interested in knowing, the tip came from a good samaritan out in *The Dim Zone*. Our own, Yul Vrean. NOA was here questioning us, the Colonel, in person. Soon as they heard of this Vrean fellow announcing himself as working for Cyber Corp, they came knocking at our door. *Quenrix* is lost, the planet dead, the people enslaved. Vrean tipped off to the NOA that *Xares* is the next target on the fringe of *The Dim Zone*. Vrean's commandeered some bug ship and is acting as a spy. With others. We don't know how he got there or engineered this. He hasn't been made yet according to NOA."

Regers whistled through his teeth. "Ain't that pretty? Guess *Xares* is our #1 destination then. And when were you planning to tell me all this, Dez?"

Dez ignored the threat in Regers' eyes. "Since you've helped me secure this mechno which is worth a bit of money to us, I'm giving you this tidbit for free. I'd ask, in return, that you bring Vrean in alive. We didn't leave on amicable terms. He'll know what happened to Mathias and the others—him and his crew led by his cyber-ghoul captain-bodyguard, Goss. Like it or not, I can't run this company without the help of that bastard Mathias."

"You're too modest, Dez. Not a problem. Happy to help out. I'd go into the bowels of hell to get back my old dear 'friend' Yul."

"No doubt."

Deakes gave a strangled cry and grabbed at Regers' arm. "Now hold on. Are you loco, Regers? We're talking about flying off to a nowhere zone and taking on an enemy fleet, not just some day trip to some abandoned planet in *The Dim Zone*."

"Let go of me, Deakes, unless you want a metal knuckle dental job."

Deakes backed off. Jennings stood silent.

"We're going to *The Dim Zone*, whether you like it or not, bug fleet or not, then we're gonna spend our reward money, ie Dez's money, in as flamboyant a manner as possible. On booze, broads, flashy casinos, high-risk bets, everything under the sun. It'll be a lark, like Mekeroid on steroids."

Deakes grumbled. Jennings' fist worked, his other hand clenching tight.

"What's the matter, Jiminy?" asked Regers. "Got a bee in your bonnet?"

"No," said Jennings, "I don't know this Yul fellow from Adam, yet he seems a decent enough fellow tipping off the NOA. Not to mention the insanity of us flying off again into the zone of those brutes."

Regers gusted out a sigh. "No wonder you were stuck in that bug tank with no hope of escape. You're a pansy ass. Gotta break you of that habit."

"Come on, this way," said Dez. On a signal, one of the guards prodded Regers along.

Regers' mood did not improve as they mounted some steps, passed through various electronic fields and check points with red-eye scanners then piled into a small elevator. They dropped more floors and exited into a concrete command booth about thirty feet square, furnished with a load of high tech equipment and four engineers: two men, two women who sat around a luminous circular holo display offering a panoramic view of a war-torn street in startling clarity. The four scientists, headsets circling ears, tapped fingers on holo keypads. Regers was unaware this was the same command booth that Dez had attended earlier, inviting the colonel to witness a demo.

Artificial yellow lights mimicked a daytime solar glow from the domed ceiling. Regers' eyes roved over a ruined parkland to the right of the bombed out street. At its edge, about twelve feet off the ground, hovered two vertical-standing, coffin-shaped mechnos like that back on Remus, but considerably smaller. "What the fuck is this?"

"In this demonstration," Dez began, ignoring Regers' crude outburst, "we pit one enemy against the other. The mechno armatures you see before you are deliberately made smaller than those of Hresh's. That's a sealed war room, ten feet thick of hypertilized titanium. We can watch their interactions from this sealed command booth as they cannot break out and cause mischief here." He signaled to the holoview. Jennings' eyes opened wide, clearly daunted but impressed. The holoview zoomed in to enhance details.

Regers stared down upon the scene with undisguised amazement. He hadn't realized Dez was running such a high-end operation. That the scientist had rigged something up of this caliber this quickly was a testament to his expertise and resolve. Obviously the man and his team of eggheads had been working non-stop days and nights on the project.

The two mechnos lifted higher into the air, alerted by some stimulus. A scavenging bird?

"Each mechno has been infused with a Xesian moth," Dez continued, "an insect similar to the feral dragonfly that assaulted us on Remus. Both are live specimens contained in protective titanium shells, as you can see.

Some have been bred and formed into quasi moths and butterflies. We have a dozen so far in secure vaults."

Jennings pawed at his brow. "You kidding? You deliberately spawned these monsters? Do you like flirting with death?"

"I think not. They're an asset to be used by those who can harness their power."

Jennings shook his head in disapproval and shock.

"These creatures drive the armature of Hresh's cutting-edge, experimental technology. My team of researchers enclosed them within these apparatuses where they perceive each other as a protector of their common habitat. At no time in our experimentation has any moth displayed hostility to the others, a good sign.

"We've simulated war conditions similar to real life—notice the bombed street and ravaged parkland. We've even gone so far as to inject forms of indigenous fauna into the environment, like those turkey vultures, rats and wandering hyenas to make the moths feel more at home."

Regers noted a fresh-water creek to the left and a foul, brown-colored one that ran up the middle with bloated bodies of various animals Dez had mentioned. Shell-pitted air cars littered the banks, hoods and wheels missing, hydraulic arms of cranes smashed, mangled backhoe scoops, rusted engines; lengths of metal siding and slabs of concrete lay strewn among the weeds and the rubble, and out into the street.

"Ah, you marvel at the contrasting conditions of the streams. The polluted stream serves as a reminder to the moths how fragile their ecosystem is, something to fight for, if need be. The creatures need some sort of fresh water supply to hydrolyze the fat in their food, similar to the dragonfly on Remus which was able to synthesize ozone from the atmosphere. Don't ask me how. The thing's makeup is completely beyond our knowledge base. One of the moths' only weaknesses, as our scientists have determined, is its susceptibility to poisoning, like from that polluted stream."

"You sure like to hear yourself talk, Dez. Why you telling us all this?"

"The first test will be against a land foe...two rivals actually...competing for water and space."

Deakes turned to Dez and hissed in a hollow voice, "What you got going here? You plan to sic metal moth on bloodsucker cricket? Bug on bug." He laughed at his own joke.

Dez blinked with a far off look. "No joke, Deakes. There's more to your statement than you think. The Xesian insects seek comfort like a security blanket in their metal shields, as does a snail in its shell. They excel with their armor. Outperform all our other mechno models."

Regers gave a caustic snort. "Don't know about you, Dez, but I've no intention of piss-assing around talking about bugs all day. We're on a program here to pillage and burn, hunt down a fink."

"Not going to be anything left to pillage, Regers, if those squids and their allies get their way. Unless we do something about them."

"Says who?" sneered Regers. "Why's everybody trying to be such a god-damn hero?" He threw up his hands. "You want to spend the rest of your days stuck in a bug tank or squeezed to shit by skulking squids? Go right ahead." He turned to stalk off, but the guard kept him at bay with his E1.

A heavy metal door slid open on the side wall to reveal two cages of nearly-identical beasts pacing behind the outer bars. Massive, hairy, four-legged creatures, behemoths in their own right, with razor-sharp fangs like the saber-toothed tiger. Each harbored white matted fur like the polar bear, spread thick along hide and limbs but sporting a long, muscular trunk, like a prehistoric elephant's protruding from the fanged snout. Regers guessed this was useful for bashing obstinate predators, projectiles, trees or any other impediments.

The iron bars lifted. The first brute was released into the test ground. It loped in sidling fashion, massive head swinging from side to side toward the creek. The beast halted on three legs, lifting one to sniff at the air. A minute later, the other creature lumbered forth, released from its cage. It approached warily and assessed its rival. The mechnobots veered in, hovering above the ground to study the two intruders, at this time evincing only curiosity. The wall slab slid back, cutting the beasts off from their cages.

"What the hell are those things?" demanded Deakes, his eyes watering.

"The test subjects are *ursilars*," said Dez, "a cross between an ice age cave bear and mastodon, both whose DNA we dug up in old paleolithic sites in remote glacial areas on Earth. Extremely territorial, violent and deadly. You would not want to be in there with them, Deakes. It's unlikely that even your blaster could take out one before it charged you and ripped you to shreds. No predator alive today can take down an ursilar, nor would any in its day, except maybe one of its own kind. That's why we have two to make the arena more *interesting*." Dez gave a dry chuckle. "Needless to say it cost us mega yols to bio-generate these beasts, cross their DNA in effective ways and incubate those that you see before you."

Jennings opened his mouth to say something but Dez waved him off. "Not now, Jennings. Just watch." The CEO's voice achieved a pitch of higher intensity.

The first ursilar paused from its crouch at the creek, lapping up the fresh water. Turning, it gave a low growl. The two beasts circled each other.

Dez cackled in triumph. "Both are alpha males. Yet one has the aggressive edge. See! The blood-matted fur on the other's pelt is fresh and the area behind its ears and back of the neck, is even fresher."

The ursilars sprang at each other, rearing on their hind legs. They batted and swatted at each other with killing force, such that Jennings went rigid in response to the clarity of the video feed. Claws distended and curled to rend fur and flesh, as each sought out necks and vulnerable bellies.

The mechnos glided in within a few feet to observe the altercation as soon as the beasts' struggles brought them dangerously close to the fresh water stream. The weaker one's left hind foot sloshed in the shallows. A stimulus.

Dez sprang up on the balls of his feet. "The moths perceive a threat to their small, stable environment! Watch! If the one beast kills the other, its blood may contaminate the water supply. Maybe even drag the other's grimy, matted fur in deeper."

Mechno #1 swooped in with impressive speed to bash the lead beast out of the water. The beast rolled and lurched up on its hind legs then swatted out a clawed paw at the mechno. Mechno #2 bunted the other beast to keep it clear from the water. The ursilar, thus challenged, gnashed its fangs and roared as the mechno countered by extending a robot arm to clamp on the raging beast's forepaw and drag it up the shore. The beast went berserk, its six-inch claws tearing at the titanium armor.

To no effect. It gnashed and swatted until it began to tire. After a while it realized the futility of its efforts. The mechno released the ursilar. It tucked tail between its legs and lumbered off among the ruins to hide behind a pile of twisted metal in the bombed-out street.

The mechno left it alone. As long as the beast didn't venture near the water, it remained neutral. But the other beast was not compliant. It ran beneath the hovering mechnos, rearing on its hind legs, swatting upward and roaring at the top of its lungs. The second mechno reached out and dragged it by a hind claw far up in the air, then let it fall from a fifty-foot height where it thunked on its head, snapping vertebrae and front limbs.

Dez rubbed his jaw in speculative wonder. "Very interesting. Cooperation, and success in less than two minutes. Remarkable. I'll pass this holo footage onto my behavior analyst experts for processing." He spoke into a recorder disc pinned to his white lab coat. *"Mechno #1 kills its aggressor while leaving the other alone. Both mechnos exhibited mutual cooperation though visual and auditory cues. Though there never appears to be any signals transmitted between the two. Again, remarkable. Perhaps a psychic link between the species? Not impossible. We may never know."*

One of the engineers gasped. "Sir!"

Dez's eyes flicked back to the holo view. "Wait now…this is unexpected."

Mechno #2 had detected the cowering ursilar rustling among the metal and concrete rubble and moved to accost the survivor. Was it evincing second thoughts? Dez, perhaps worried about the cost in securing more ursilars for testing, grabbed the nearest assistant by the arm.

"Recovery operation! Code yellow and evasive security restraints!" Dez cried.

A white-faced engineer touched some buttons on the virtual holo pad. Within moments the two mechnos became docile and descended to the ground, placid as picked plums.

"What did you do?" exclaimed Regers.

"Initiated emergency measures."

Dez signaled to another operator. A grey-haired woman touched another holo tab which lifted the containment wall and the ursilar hastily scurried back to the safety of its cage. The mechnos, still not fully recovered from their daze, zigzagged up into the air.

"We figured out a way to semi-sedate them," said Dez. "We pipe calming soporific into their air mixture. But that may not be effective too much longer. They keep adapting and resisting our manipulations. Like just yesterday, the mechno on the right, driven by a moth with greyer tinge on its wings, dropped behind the ruins of a communication tower as a way to avoid our cameras during a key moment. To this day we have no idea what it was up to back there."

Regers grunted. "Go figure." Secretly, he was amused at the degree to which Dez got excited over every piece of trivia related to these bugs.

"As I mentioned, we've managed to breed more dragonflies. Actually, they are more quasi-moths than dragonflies. Each brood is a unique variation. Never the same batch. Possibly an adaptive survival trait. What do you think?"

"Not much. A bunch of bully bugs dressed up in metal suits beating on innocent prehistoric beasts," growled Regers.

Jennings had nothing to say.

Dez frowned, his mood one of detachment. "From time to time I allow lay people like you to witness the experiments. Sometimes these observers offer valuable insights, most often not. My motives for showing you this simulation are twofold: scientific curiosity and recording a gut reaction. Your visual cues and body language are being recorded by hidden cameras as an extra layer of data for my research team—" He cleared his throat. "The irony of this demonstration is complex and part of the reason I called you to witness this. As you know, these are *Lepidoptera* spawned from the plant pods you and your friend Yul harvested from Xeses in *The Dim Zone*."

"How could I forget?" snarled Regers. "I only wish Yul was down in that arena—and that I had been present to deliver the pods myself, to stuff them down your throat, rather than being stuffed myself in a bug tank on an alien moon." He peered with loathing at Dez. "No thanks to the indifference of you and your lunatic boss, Mathias."

Dez winced and looked away. "We made copies as best we could, Regers, of the hardware and inner workings of the armature we brought back from Hresh's installation. You've been paid handsomely for your efforts—so quit complaining. The armature houses a 'brain', or containment tank—'Bio-Imagron' as Hresh called this quintessence of the technology."

"What the hell is that?"

Dez gave a nervous chuckle. "The interface between alien and machine. In the case of the mechnobot and dragonfly, the 'Imagron' is like a vault-like container, positioned in the mechno's center. The one you saw on Remus was ruptured. The subject, the dragonfly, the 'Bio' in Bio-Imagron, could slip in and out at will. To devastating effect. I'm not sure what Hresh had planned, but he wanted to keep the beast contained in the vault, not fly free…to make it a slave that he could use to his advantage to control the outer mechnobot. The alien's feral intelligence and natural instinct for survival could guide the advanced hardware in case of attack. Its predatorial instinct could be used to drive the AI circuits and outwit unruly enemies such as a Mentera flagship. Quite ingenious, if you ask me—the ultimate military application. As much as I dislike the man, it's a testament to Hresh's near genius and creative imagination. According to his last notes left at Cyber Corp, his prototype was successful. After he fled the company with the crucial design plans, he continued his research of the Bio-Imagron on his own, down in *The Dim Zone.*

"My kind of man, an enterprising thief."

Dez wrinkled his nose. "Oddly, the 'Imagron' was still functioning, despite the rupture, though Hresh's model clearly stipulated that the alien be entombed in the sealed chamber indefinitely."

"You're repeating yourself, Dez. Sign of old age?"

Dez gnashed his teeth. "Onward to test #2."

"What this time? A rhino and dinosaur mix?"

"Test 2 is another containment scenario. To test cooperation, pecking order, degree of feral aptitude, fight or flight tendencies, and other adaptive mechanisms."

Both Regers and Jennings flinched in bleary-eyed resignation.

Dez paged somebody on his communicator and pointed a finger as a short, stocky man walked into the room. "This is Jessel Vrand, one of our senior remote mechno drone operators. Vrand is contracted from NOA."

Regers peered at him closely through critical eyes. Military brush-cut, marine-trained, if he ever saw one. With no words spoken or expression revealed, the man fitted his fingers around the holo controls floating in midair before him. The dome of a ceiling in the test chamber opened to inject a new mechno into the mix, larger, but of similar quality and design like the others.

"Vrand will operate this mechnobot, a shielded, impregnable hulk, similar to the other two. The mechno, I dub MXTR. It will test the mettle and ingenuity of Xesian insects so that we can pattern their behavior."

Down the mechno glided, a shape not dissimilar to the upright slab-shaped molar from Remus, only more intimidating. The others paused, their anti-grav units keeping them a dozen feet above the clear water stream. Vrand's mechno jerked forward into the first mechno's path.

MXTR's questing external arm prodded this more docile one while hovering over its turf. Alien mechno-moth #1 did nothing, but waited in curiosity for the intruder to make the next move. Vrand propelled his charge ever closer. Without warning, mechno #1 lashed out its robot appendage to bash MXTR aside. The move did nothing except knock Vrand's drone vehicle backward. Vrand unleashed robot fire on the aggressive mechno's armature. Bright rays deflected off the gleaming titanium. Vrand got MXTR out of the way. He worked the controls with aggressive intent and smashed the hulk forth to bring mechno #1 down into the water. Now a show of flagrant aggression, this act at last brought its twin, the more dominant mechno #2, surging in to defend its habitat.

"Up the ante," commanded Dez. "Quit toying around, Vrand. Push these titanium hulks to their limits!"

"As you like." Vrand's grim smile did not escape Regers as the NOA man sent mechno #1 tumbling through the stream.

Vrand's mechno boxed #1's turret with its outstretched robot arms and sent it spinning back on land. The second hovered angrily to retaliate while its dripping peer jerked to its upright self again. Mechno #2 swept in to dive bomb the aggressive intruder.

Vrand's bot forced mechno #2 on to open ground, firing hostile beams from its turret to land square on its central frame. Two hyenas got cornered by the shore. Running amok, they were pegged by fire and lay dead in the shallows. Both mechnos took the abuse, but riddled with stray blasts, mechno #2 was propelled backward. It swayed then toppled while mechno #1 smoked and sizzled.

The yellow flares penetrated mechno #1's armor. Energy beams sizzled and sparked off its metal. Robot arms flailed wildly, heated to dangerous levels.

The mechno lay supine in the dirt, smoking, unmoving. But then an amazing thing happened. The metal started to melt in a rippling pool in the mechno's center. A hole sprouted like a termite burrowing out from within.

"Shut the power down!" cried Dez.

"It's useless. Look, they're burrowing out, flying free," cried one of the engineers.

A grey-winged thing burst out of the dissolving armature and shot high up into air. The other was also burrowing out of its metallic prison, then it came rocketing out to smack headlong into MXTR's offending armor. The thing pierced through the titanium. Vrand's bot spurted and sparked, then fell face first in the dirt.

Vrand sagged back, licking his lips. "Fucking hell. That's not supposed to happen."

Dez stared in dismay. Regers and Deakes laughed out loud and high fived each other. "Fucking A, Dez! You're a real hero. Plus one for the moths."

The moths flitted around each other in a strange flurry. Their habitat lay now in disarray with smoking metal and some of the animal bodies caught in the crossfire, floating in the creek. Other wildlife—wild foxes, hyenas and rats—ran amok, spooked by mechno blasts and deafening clamor with the sizzling mechno half in, half out of the clear stream.

One of the moths flew too close to the other in its wild frenzy and smacked it head on. The larger moth, under attack by its peer, feinted. It dodged a gnashing strike. While the other was caught off guard, the larger lashed out, teeth and claws catching the victim's neck and ripping its head off. Strange, multicolored fluid ran out of the decapitated moth's neck as it spun helplessly in midair then fell, flopping in circles in the dust. The thorax twitched. It was still alive for some moments, pumping out life fluids, then lay still. The surviving creature landed and rolled the carcass in the dust with its two front legs, spitting a gummy liquid on it from between mandibles and weaving some kind of fantastic thread from thorax. Round and round it wrapped the thread as would a spider, then clawed a hole in the soil not far from the shore where it shoved the head in and the dead, unmoving thorax. After covering up the hole with its black, fidgety digits, it patted the earth and proceeded to clean its mandibles, as if in a primitive burial ceremony.

The scientists gaped in incomprehension for this was something totally unprecedented. They were first time witnesses of the fact. The moth emitted a high-pitched sound, like a flute, or some sort of eerie banshee call—the first ever recorded of the alien species. In a burst of fantastic speed it hurtled up to the domed ceiling and smashed an area of metal. The blow took out the hidden camera with its bullet-shaped head.

The holoview flickered then went dead. The scientists stumbled about in pandemonium, gazing at one another. The creature had effectively nuked two impossible adversaries in a matter of minutes. Now it was champion of the arena.

Dez's mouth sagged. "What the hell? How did the thing get out of its Imagron? You must have blasted it too heavily, Vrand."

"No way," the operator grumbled. "Those were only force 6 rays."

"Then they must have secreted acid!" Dez cried. Red suffused his cheeks.

Mutters and grunts coursed through the scientists. The first hints of panic spread. No way of knowing whether the moth-alien predator was still contained in the war room or had somehow burrowed its way out of the containment sphere.

"Those are ten foot thick, solid titanium walls," Dez mumbled to himself hoarsely.

"You going to take that chance?" asked Vrand.

"Surely, it could not get out?" He bit his lip. "Vrand, you take Biz and Mastri out to the beast access ramp and see that it's secured. I'm alerting bio-hazard. Use the access tunnel on level D4 if you need to. Be careful!"

Vrand gave a low grunt and strode briskly off.

Dez's mouth quivered. "They've never done that before—how can it be possible?—" he trailed off, his hand shaking.

Regers slapped him hard on the back. "Dez, you're a wreck. Surprised you?—I told you not to fuck with those bugs and look what you did, you got a whole rodeo show going here that's going tits up. I was lucky to get my money when I did—a million yols for getting that scrap metal to your yard. Now you've got a colossal mess on your hands."

"They can't do that," babbled Dez.

One of the remaining engineers muttered, "They just did."

"How can they be that intelligent? How'd it know the camera was there?"

The engineer shrugged. "Something alerted it to the camera."

"Think! There's no logical reason for it. Or reason for them to attack their brethren, actually, the opposite, there's safety in numbers, Darwin's survival of the species."

Regers stared at him as if he were daft. "It's a fucking alien. How do you expect to understand it? Your dimestore psychology models and R&D experiments mean jack shit to it."

Regers could see that Dez was clearly out of sorts. "Loosed the beast from Pandora's box? What's to stop them from installing themselves in a FTL ship and blinking off between the worlds? How then's your Bio-

Imagron thingy gonna save you? They'll bust through that like rats chew through cheese."

Dez stared unblinking as if in a sleepwalk.

"Your problem, not mine." Regers shrugged. "If you were trying to scare me with this moth freak show so I wouldn't come after you sometime down the road, it didn't work. That said, I don't want to be a hundred light years within you or any piece of your operation." He made for the exit. "Come on, Deakes. We've got our own battles to fight. I've had enough of this circus act."

Chapter 22

The Zikri war Orbs circled in orbit above *Xares*, a rose-tinged planet, home to some 200 million people. The Mentera fleet drifted a score of miles away like wolves before a flock of fat sheep. Its thousands of mantises, aphids and destroyers gathered in no less menacing configuration. Now they drifted in a slow spiral ready to swarm down upon the planet.

Invasion of the hapless world was slated in minutes. A red light signaling a Code Critical flashed on Admiral Nrog's communicator.

An armed detail of four massive Zikri entered the battle command bridge, tentacles glistening.

"Sir," the lead security squid chittered, "a rogue ship has been captured and brought aboard Orb destroyer SP01 *Uglik*."

"Who? One of ours?"

"One of the Mentera ships. We flagged it earlier. The ship we presumed malfunctioning that took out Mentera aphids and one of our rearguard Orbs. We tractored the ship into locking bay and managed to break through the hull, discovered it manned by three rebels, two human and one Mentera…the same ship set out to comb *Kraetoria* for intruders."

Nrog's motilators bristled in anger. "Those stupid Mentera and their non-existent security." He twitched. "Transport the spies aboard via amalgamator"

"As you wish."

"Anything else to report?"

The lead security squid's train of thought shifted with its parting polyp of a mouth. "Some peculiar Mentera recorder has been discovered aboard. The rebels claim ignorance of it."

"Bring the unit for examination."

"Right away, Admiral."

Nrog whistled a fluting chirrup and patched through to First Officer Jring of the Mentera fleet.

Jring's singsong voice sounded over the com. "A successful coup, Admiral. Both of us should be pleased with our achievement. One hundred thousand prime slaves have been shipped to *Carcarus*, a far world for factory tanking. For you, quite a score of factories and resources gained from one human planet."

"Yes, quite, *Princeps*. Yet another matter concerns me. Some news of a security breach—in your ranks," he added with a disturbing air of menace.

Jring clicked his mandibles.

"A rogue ship, two humans and a Mentera. I've detained the spies for questioning. Another special item has been retrieved."

"Why don't I come aboard and take a look?"

"I was expecting no less."

Jring signed off.

Nrog paused in moody reflection. Zikri and Mentera, recent allies but age-old foes since time immemorial. Wary of each other's propensity for violence and treachery. Could he trust Jring? Odd that Jring hadn't captured and dealt with these spies earlier.

With haste, Nrog glided down the dim-lit hall to the interrogation chamber with his detail of security squids in tow.

* * *

Miko, crouching in painful posture, saw a flash of amber light as several forms emerged from the U-shaped amalgamator along the far wall of the interrogation chamber. *Princeps* Jring himself hunched forward, with gold bands on his pincer arms and hind legs. Four locust guards scuttled in tow, gripping lumo blasters. Nrog gave them a hasty greeting.

Miko's spirits sank to new lows as the direness of his plight hit home. A humid, slightly rank odor permeated his nostrils in the maroon murk, courtesy of the mossy dark brown plant stuff caking the walls, somewhat bioluminescent. The Zikri went in for creepy. Star and Usk crouched at his side, damp, blooded, wild-eyed, but with no less fear and resignation. Five Mentera tanks loomed to the side…green-glowing aquariums filled with characteristic eerie green waters, three empty, one containing a husky, gape-eyed Daulk, and another with some horned, bat-like insect and three crab-

164

like creatures with jellyfish streamers. The significance of three 'empties' was not lost on Miko.

On a signal from Nrog, guards from both races stepped forth to affix circuits, small coin-sized translator units, to the captives' bodies: one on Usk's antenna, one each behind Star's and Miko's ears.

"The invasion must proceed as planned," Nrog told Jring. "These spies have somehow alerted NOA. I feel it in my motilators. We must not lose our advantage, Jring. If we wait too long, our window of surprise will be lost."

"Agreed," chirped Jring, "yet a small delay in conducting some security checks will not cost us, Nrog. I see no NOA on the horizon, or any visible threat."

Nrog spurt out an angry chitter. "For now! Hostiles may light-drive in at any moment. There may be more of these spies about." He turned to face the prisoners. "Who else is with you?" He shuttled closer. "Answer! What other ships are working in collusion?"

Miko maintained a grim, tight-lipped silence. While the blood pounded in his ears, Usk and Star stared at the luminous tanks, though Miko could see the shiver run through Star's slender shoulders and almost palpably hear the beat of her heart.

Jring turned with brisk energy to his chitinous aide. "Kerut! Analyze all recordings between Mentera vessels prior to Quenrix. Start with the ships from Kraetoria."

"Aye, *Princeps*." The aide, a squat, heavy-plated locust in tight dark-green protective garb, moved aside to spew chitters into a coin-sized communicator pinned to his antenna.

Jring's piercing red eyes bored into Usk. "It distresses me that one of my own kind is behind this fiasco, Nrog. Give the rebel to me. The culprit will be probed and sentenced to our tanks for intravenous feeding. Likely for workers on one of our space stations. Notice the rebel has the telltale red band on his head. A common mark of a deviant or convicted felon."

"Interesting," mused Nrog, grazing a tentacle tip across his prune-wrinkled mouth. He stared down at the traitorous crouching insect. "What have you to say for yourself?"

"I was wrongfully accused." Defiance flashed across Usk's eyes.

Jring scowled. "Your crimes of treason and murder trump any crimes here, real or feigned."

Usk made no comment. He stared with a hollow expression.

"Give me five minutes with this traitor." Jring clacked his pincers. "Our interrogators will make putty of him."

Nrog flicked out a motilator. "No. He's my captive, Jring, and on my ship. Your brutal means will have to wait—I'll have Basilursk, my torturer, have a go at him."

Nrog's lead torturer gave a raspy acknowledgement. A ripple of excitement undulated through the squid's upper body.

Jring seethed, but he held his pride in check and decided not to push the issue.

"Before you all die," Nrog said to the prisoners, "tell me, what is this blue crate you carry with you? It glimmers with an unwholesome glow." Nrog's unsettling gaze drifted on to Miko.

Miko hesitated. His eyes flicked to the blue box. The device sat guarded by two of Nrog's squids. Usk glanced about with nervous apprehension. Star whimpered in her space boots.

"Answer the question—or face my torturers!"

"I believe it is the vessel of the *Masters*," Miko said.

"Ah, the *Masters*," parroted Nrog with contempt. "I've heard of this creature. Some entity that haunts our ancient tunnels...what a lab assistant on Kraetoria was babbling about before he was murdered by some test subject."

"Apparently a Zikri," Jring interrupted. "The unusually large specimen who still prowls your lab tunnels, according to my intel."

"Maybe." Nrog glared in silent acknowledgement.

Miko licked his lips. *Such a creature could only be Audra.*

"Bring forth this 'Master', if you please," instructed Nrog.

Jring scuttled forward. "Take care, Nrog. The box could be some bio-viral weapon or trap."

"Relax. Our scanners have detected no explosives or organics. Lumo circuits of some sort, maybe some other material, yet wholly identifiable."

Jring stirred in unease.

Nrog waved Miko on toward the crate. "The invasion will be delayed until we learn what this spy mission was...who sent them and what this device is."

Jring chirruped. "That's self-evident. They are spies of NOA. The device came from Kraetoria, our mother world. It is none other than some old lab equipment that my troops discovered and packed in a ship for further study under my lieutenant's orders."

Nrog rippled his upper motilators in doubt. "None of this makes any sense, Jring. What were the intruders doing on Kraetoria? Why would NOA send three amateur saboteurs, disparate picks in my opinion, into our remote base? This box is a weapon of some sort." He rounded on Miko. "Speak up, human!"

Miko clenched his fists and shook his head. Even if he were to tell Nrog the truth, these creatures would kill him. Death was the only outcome and only moments away.

Nrog tipped his motilators forward and slapped Miko toward the box. "Move! Activate the device."

"I know not—"

Nrog cast a suggestive leer at his torturer.

Miko swallowed. A stream of words gushed from his lips, "Only that at one time we activated such a box by pressing a panel, with a luminous knob, perhaps—"

Nrog flicked a motilator toward Usk. "What of you, insect? Do you know how to summon the Master? You crouch there like some deep sea turtle. Do you not know how to activate this box?"

Usk wavered a drooping antenna, an indication of the negative.

"Basilursk, torture these hostiles. Start with the human girl."

"Wait!" cried Miko, desperate and flush-faced. "I'll see what I can do."

He limped over and squatted before the pale-glowing box of mystery. The enemy guards glided forth, not trusting Miko or his moves. Mentera weapons lifted. Miko studied the device. The knee-high box was featureless but for a series of wide, grooved indentations on its right side. He passed his fingers lightly over them and the bare, smooth side and top. No effect. The box was unusually heavy for its compact size. When he tried to lift it, it took most of his strength. Easier to slide, he mused. But tilting it on its edge allowed him to scan the underside.

Nothing there. The other guards pressed closer, chitters in their mouths, curious as cats. Jring's aides trained blasters on him. Miko tried various prods and knocks on the outer surface—to no avail. Only blue hard stuff, but it felt slightly warm to the touch. Just as he was about to accept defeat, an eerie peach glow lit on the box's side and projected a conelike beam...a familiar form stood illuminated: the simulacrum.

An ugly figure, floating three feet off the ground.

The locusts recoiled and trained lumo weapons. Nrog's squids flung tentacles at it. A humanoid creature of some sort: tall with yellow eyes and hairless hooded skull. The thing was neither male nor female—some androgynous creature, with short forelimbs and long bare feet graced with four hairy toes. Like some giant, humanoid, primitive ape.

The image swayed and leveled its otherworldly gaze at Nrog. "Greetings, creatures from a far future age. I see Miko has introduced you to me."

All gathered shuffled back in surprise.

"What are you?" Jring crowed. He shook his locust head, recovering his composure. "State your purpose." Though his truculent demand fell short as only superficial pretense.

"As you wish," came the AI voice, with something of an imperial timbre. Its horrid grin lit an improbable face. The being's words translated into three languages via the devices attached to the presiding creatures' antennae, tentacles and ear buds.

"I am the simulacrum of the ageless *Masters*," it intoned. "A proxy, hidden on Kraetoria for an age. Our race is gone. Yet our essence lives on in the form of electronics and synthetics like what you see, though it be beyond your grasp."

"We'll be the judge of that!" Nrog snapped.

"Perhaps, but the truth must be spoken. You will discover that I only speak in truths."

"We shall see," Jring said. "Start with an explanation of your presence on Kraetoria."

"That is a discourse too lengthy to deliver. Suffice it to say that our presence has been not without advancement. Furthermore, it is a joy and privilege to behold such marvelous creatures of the Masters' design."

"What do you mean? Do you suggest *we* are a product of your Masters' whim?"

"In a word, yes."

"Where is your proof?" Nrog sputtered.

Miko felt a cold shudder run up his spine. He could not help but recall the disturbing revelation conveyed by this luminous creature in the bunker on Kraetoria—that humans were created from the same source. Grown in vats, bred as experiments down in some hidden lab on Kraetoria. Could humans and godless Zikri and Mentera have been created from the same essence? The prospect chilled Miko's to the bone.

"You mean even us, humans?" Star wailed.

The proxy grinned back at her. "My database recalls your distress in our last meeting, human. You seem to have trouble grasping that everyone has a creator, even myself."

"Answer the question!" Jring persisted.

"My circuits advise me to ask you this instead, *Princeps*. Do you think your allied war is merited enough that its fruits will outweigh the cost?"

Jring scoffed. "Of course. Why else go through all this ordeal and ally ourselves with such violent creatures as the Zikri?"

Nrog glared, as if such words stung. His black, beady eyes glowered with a tinge of malice.

The proxy continued with curious amazement, "Do you not think these humans will rise up and retaliate against you? The same whom you persecute, kill and enslave for food?"

"They are weak and insignificant," declared Nrog. "Tadpoles to be scooped up in nets."

"Like these humans who have single-handedly slipped through your net and defy you?"

Nrog gave a rumble of scorn. "They are nothing but a pack of lowly fugitives, nobodies. A broken-down NOA spy, some human female from a backward planet with no military skills, a rebel locust missing a claw. It's laughable."

Jring spoke up, "And yet, here they are, Nrog, infiltrating our fleets, killing your soldiers with the help of the rogue Zikri skulking about our own shared planet on Kraetoria. They steal our ships and kill our pilots."

"That's not entirely true. We are both stooges here, Jring. How many of your own locust guards have been killed by these ragtag rebels?"

"The numbers have not been ascertained."

The simulacrum slapped its ape-like hands on its thighs in a gesture of satisfaction. "It delights me to see you at loggerheads."

"Shut up," chittered Nrog. He glided before Miko who glowered up at him. "I will ask you again, human, who are you and who sent you?"

Miko licked his lips, seeing Nrog's minions arching tentacles toward him, ready to throw him in a tank. "I am a NAVO officer. Lieutenant Miko Almstran. Usk and Star are my friends. I picked them up along the way."

"NAVO doesn't exist!" roared Nrog.

"They did, at one time," refuted Miko. "They are NOA now. I came through a time tunnel with that rebel Zikri you search for on Kraetoria. We got caught in a gravity whorl while taking off in time-drive while under attack. We crashlanded on a far world, *Rogos*, passing from amalgamator to amalgamator, finally to land on a Mentera station and long story short, were shot down over Kraetoria."

There was a stunned silence. Nrog shrilled, "You lie!" He advanced on Miko, lashed out a motilator, slapping him across the room.

Star surged up and hobbled to Miko's side where he lay on his belly, gasping in anguish. "Brute! Leave him alone!" One of the Zikri guards caught her up in its slime-pocked motilators. She squirmed, pounded fists uselessly in its iron grip, and battered it with her heels. Her legs dangled a foot off the ground.

Miko rolled over, wheezing out a curse.

"Let me go!" Star shrieked. "Why don't you die, all of your foul race!"

On a flick of motilator, Nrog urged Basilursk forward to snatch at Star, dragging her kicking and screaming toward the first of the empty tanks.

"No!" rasped Miko.

Too late. The Zikri dipped a tentacle round her mouth to stop her outcries. He carted her before the glowing glass. Glistening tentacles lifted her up and over the brim.

With its powerful front motilators it held her under the pale green brine while she thrashed and kicked, her ashen hair askew. A wild look of terror was branded on her face. She struggled. No use.

Miko crabbed to his feet, striking out and yelling—but slimy tentacles held him back. In teary-eyed horror, he watched as Star convulsed in back-arching agony as she drowned. Floating, suspended in green fluid, she stared out from behind the glass, her lips parted in a small O. Bubbles trickled from her mouth to the surface. He gave a wretched howl as Mentera blasters arced his way.

Chapter 23

Usk spat out white fluid and backed away as Mentera lumo blasters leveled on him.

Nrog's shadow fell on Miko. "I trust this is a warning for you to show proper deference. All will go the easier for your locust friend and the female."

"I'll kill you," rasped Miko. He started forward, but Nrog's motilators kept him back. He stared helplessly at Star, every cell in his body wanting to lunge forth and strangle Nrog with his bare hands.

"I hardly think so. You and your rebellious friend are in no position to do that."

Jring called, "Enough of this charade, Nrog." He signaled to his aide to apprehend Usk.

The simulacrum, bearing silent witness to all until now, glanced in idle interest toward the tank with Star and the other creatures bobbing placidly in the pale water. "Intriguing, intriguing. Treating your guests so disrespectfully. Bravo, Admiral! By plunging your naysayers in tanks, you hope to gain their fear and respect. You have not won against them by going the way of the brute. You'll only make them angrier, and angrier. Perhaps this is what you wish, but it won't save you."

"Says who? We've choreographed this invasion to crush the humans completely, confirm our supremacy."

The simulacrum shrugged. "Perhaps. Logic dictates it will work, but too many variables cloud the issue. Despite your energetic leadership, I daresay, foresight is lacking, since you have not considered all the variables. You've set yourself up for failure."

"Failure? What failure? Have you foreseen any aftermath of this war?"

"Perhaps. But you doubt my very existence so..."

"Admiral," interrupted Jring, "do we have time to waste conversing with this memory module?"

"Quiet, Jring. I want to hear this imposter."

"Very well," said the simulacrum, "look what the powers to be have orchestrated. We have rolled the dice and played god, as The Masters. Created monsters like yourselves, and now the cubs have come to play with sticks and stones and fire and steel to beat in the heads of their brothers."

"A flowery allusion," derided Jring, "but a vast oversimplification. *Masters*," he scoffed. "Why beget such a disparate pantheon of species? It's as impossible as it is improbable."

The simulacrum grinned its ape-like grimace, if such were possible. "Is it so outlandish as not to be obvious? Like all dutiful parents, to see the children play, then fight and wage war with one another, at last to triumph over all the others. The cycle repeats itself while the other tribe rises up and conquers its rival. The ultimate cycle of the ages. War, peace... Peace, war. Rulers rising, rulers falling, then to rise from the ashes yet once again. On and on forever and ever. Just as it happened to us. I find the irony amusing."

"I find no irony in any of it," chittered Nrog.

"Then you have no sense of humor, Admiral, and have much to learn." Nrog bridled, but the simulacrum rippled its shoulders in what might have been an indifferent shrug. "The journey is long, Admiral. Yes, very long. Yet time is infinite...and much of it is an illusion."

"Enough riddles," snapped Jring. He piked up a gold-pincered claw. "I opt we pull the plug on this bombastic automaton and dispose of the prisoners."

Nrog lifted a motilator. "Not just yet, Jring. There are pieces of this puzzle which still remain unanswered. Like, for example, where do the humans fit into all this?"

The simulacrum clipped out an ape-like grunt. "That's a question I am forbidden to answer."

"Answer the question, proxy, or risk annihilation," threatened Jring. "We will plumb your innards, and short-circuit your *cerebus*."

"As I mentioned before, you will wait a long time, *Princeps*. The information you seek is buried so deep in the lattice of my memory crystal that it would take a million supercomputers a million years to find such information."

Jring clacked his claws. "Impossible. You speak on the edges of hyperbole."

Miko did not like the sinister glow on Nrog's face—or Jring's. How to exploit these two leaders' mutual rivalry and hatred? So much different than Audra, this commander Zikri. Weaker, smaller in girth, but as ruthless, if not more deadly.

He kept glancing with hollow heart over to Star who floated in pathetic passivity in the hated locust tank. Her hazel eyes glazed, blank orbs staring forward, unblinking as a speared fish. Her arms floated elbows out, as if she were comatose.

He must get her out of that tank! But how? She was sealed in, paralyzed by the water. He was weak, defenseless, with no weapons or means at his disposal. Where were his wretched powers of invisibility when he needed them? How fickle the universe was!

As he brooded, one of Jring's guards caught up the cable hookup from Star's tank and plugged the end into a circular indentation at his navel. The other end remained affixed to the plug and circuit box at the tank's top. A sallow light glowed from the circuitry and the Mentera began to feed off Star's essence.

Miko stared in sheer horror. The locust's back straightened, his head lifted high, lips parted in a satisfied sigh as Star's eyes took a murky dip and her whole body collapsed inward in the fluid's suspension.

Miko could not bear the sight and he sagged, defeated, numbed by despair. His heart thickened in misery, his drive zapped, and he roared out in anguish, "Noooooo…"

Nrog flicked motilators in triumph on seeing his pain. He looked over at Jring with satisfaction.

The simulacrum continued with a sigh. "This allied invasion of yours. Nothing but games on a star-lit stage, albeit ones spanning light years. The Masters are watching. They've been watching for an eternity—though have long passed into ephemeral husks. It comes as no surprise to us, this war of yours and the anticipated outcome."

Nrog clipped out an outraged chitter, clearly despising the simulacrum's arrogant claims. "So, you have mapped out its outcome?"

"Of course. What do you think?"

Miko glared at Nrog, nursing a silent, seething wish that the luminous creature of the Masters would launch a firebolt and fry him.

"So, what is this outcome then?" Nrog sneered, his motilators flexing with suggestive menace.

The proxy smiled, a grim, disturbing rictus of a simian smile. "Such knowledge is beyond your limited intellect. Any disclosure would affect your part in the overall drama to come—it would set in motion a variation of the *observer effect*, altering the predicted outcome."

Nrog's aide rustled at his commander's side. He spoke to him in a whispered guttural. "Sir, permission to dismantle this device and forcibly extract its secrets."

"Granted, Basilursk. But not until I question this creature more."

"As you wish."

"It will do you no good, Admiral," warned the simulacrum. "My circuits cannot be decrypted, or reverse-engineered, or even backtraced. Part of our advanced design was to install a *pleuron* node."

"What is that?"

"A backtier whose very nature defies description. Consider your most advanced neural networks, those are but puerile snakes and ladders pathways to what the *pleuron* offers."

"We Zikri are masters of decryption," Nrog sputtered. "We revel in taking things apart."

"Not as masterful as you think. How successful were you in decrypting these humans' transmissions in real time?"

Nrog choked, as if wondering how the thing knew that.

"These humans, in fact, are just harbingers of your own doom. Even while you plunk them in tanks, others gather forces. Never underestimate the weakest link in your chain, or the smallest resistance to your supposed, invincible forces."

Nrog's face grew blue with rage. "I don't care for your sanctimonious lectures."

"No lecture, Admiral, simple facts."

"Basilursk, shut this box down this minute. And kill these humans and the bug, if they are to be our 'demise'."

The simulacrum smiled. "Even if you kill these specimens, it makes no difference. The die is cast. There are others who have picked up the torch."

Nrog laughed at the creature's assertion. "At the moment ten thousand

Zikri and Mentera ships are poised to storm the free colonies and subjugate every human man, woman and child. Tomorrow it will be a 100k."

"What do I care who wins this fools' war? The Masters are beyond death. You, as creatures of flesh and blood, cannot see that everything works according to clockwork formula. Before the Masters shed their mortal bodies, they learned how to transcend the laws of cause and effect."

"That is impossible," jeered Jring. "This genesis prophecy of yours is likewise preposterous. Who are you to tell us how it is to end and what has passed? What we're capable of grasping? You're a synthetic droid, nothing more, some voice programmed from the past."

The entity responded in a toneless monotone. "I am everything—I am the future, the past, and the present. You cannot grasp the totality of what I am, what I have become, and what I will continue to be."

"Gibberish," grumbled Jring. "The Mentera will endure and outstrip all the races of the galaxy. As of this moment, engineers of ours are constructing a planet-size Ark—*The Ark of the Future*—a vast blimp full of Mentera, our youngest and most gifted progeny. To be outfitted with unlimited food in the form of humans and untold resources and technology. They will reach out to the farthest ends of the galaxy and spread the Mentera seed!"

Nrog's polyp of a mouth gobbled. His motilators worked, somewhat paler now, as if his warrior sense only now perceived the sinister intentions of his allied partner's race.

Miko knew in an instant that Jring had been goaded into revealing his master plan.

"So, it has all come to treachery!" Nrog roared, lifting fore-motilators in menace. "This ape-like thing from the past is an instigator, these human rebels are saboteurs, even you, Jring, and your skulking brood are fickle and ready to gobble up everything in the galaxy." With exasperated venom, Nrog glided over and grasped the blue simulacrum's box with his six motilators and flung it far across the room.

The device rolled and smacked but remained undamaged. The projection continued to glow, but its beam shot out a lopsided ray, canted the simulacrum some thirty degrees to the floor. Its smiling face looked much unfazed by the aggression of Nrog, and *Princeps* Jring watched on in silent amusement as his counterpart seethed and glided over ready to strangle Miko and Usk with his uplifted motilators.

Miko braced himself, his fists balled, as he cast Nrog a venomous glare, awaiting death.

But fire thudded against the hull.

Nrog shrank back on his motilators. Crouching in a protective stance, he motioned to his attendants. His four aides sprang to attention. The locust that had been feeding, unhooked himself from his intravenous cable and jumped over to Jring who withdrew his gold-plated lumo weapon, hunching on his hind legs.

"Sir! NOA," chirruped Basilursk. "They've come in on light drive. They assemble their fleet before our ships."

"How many?"

"Reports indicate over eight hundred."

Nrog gave a sinister chitter. "Child's play, Basilursk. Engage them. Full strike. Jring, get your forces down to *Xares*! We'll take over the planet and our Orbs will incinerate these NOA upstarts."

Jring hastened to comply, nattering on about the loss of their initiative. "I told you so, Nrog. We've lost the element of surprise."

"Viewport up!" Nrog motioned. A vivid curved holo screen of some unknown technology shot up around them in a wide arc.

Miko's eyes gaped. This was a circle 360 technology, some amalgamation of holo gas, light and color. The dizzying view made him feel as if he and all gathered were projected into space right in the middle of the battle."

Nrog gave further orders to his minions. They lurched forward to obey.

The NOA ships arrowed in. Long thin tapers, smooth hulls, globelike belvederes dead center, shaped like the submarines of old. In a trailing wedge, they spread out to flank the Orb flagships.

Orbs hurtled to surround the foremost fighters. Miko cringed as Zikri uro bombs flashed out from spiked fuselages and smashed into NOA fighters, penetrating submarine hulls and capsizing shields, while the Mentera began their sinister descent planetward.

"Bridge, evasive action! Get *Viscurg* moving," barked Nrog into his communicator. "Alpha wing team, take out those lead fighters! Destroyers, don't let them flank you!"

Some of the NOA broke through the spiderweb and fired in a tight ring on the enemy. *Viscurg* shuddered to new assaults while sister flagships fell under heavy fire.

Orbs regrouped. They unleashed sprays of hitherto unknown anti-matter technology down on the fighters. White light with jagged edges splashed across the holovision 360. Some kind of disruptor beam, Miko guessed. Dozens of NOA ships went up in flames or were rendered powerless, zapped of their power.

An exultant leer came over Admiral Nrog's face as he chittered on, pointing at Miko. "Look at your pitiful resistance! Blown to dust. Losers of a dying realm." He lifted a stinging tentacle bristling with muscle and smashed Miko across the room. "All you humans are weak—and stupid."

Miko groaned, rubbing his ribs, as he struggled to rise. He shook the daze from his head and wiped his lips. "We will not fail," he croaked. Usk scuttled to his aid, ready to fight, though he had only one claw.

Nrog chittered out a laugh. "You've already failed."

On its canted angle, the simulacrum gazed on in watchful silence. "Not necessarily. Aggressors always have a propensity for underestimating their enemies who will give their life blood to take out their oppressors. You need only study the patterns of history, the chronicles of warfare, your own race's wars, their bloody history and those of your allies."

Jring scowled, one antenna drooping in growing alarm. The holo view flickered out, revealing mossy walls once again. Before the nearby amalgamator, the *Princeps* scuttled to crouch poised, ready to transport himself back to his own ship. "We did not request an analysis of our military tactics."

"You're much too polite," rasped Nrog. He glided over. "Fly back to your nest, see to your fleet, Jring, and hope that no more resistance comes our way."

Jring and two of his guards vanished in a flash of amber brilliance as the U-shaped amalgamator whisked them off.

The simulacrum appeared to absorb the changing situation with an air of curious amusement. "My database and nth-order light-AI virtual network is equipped with data from a hundred million worlds, Nrog. I'd have thought you'd have taken advantage of it at this moment."

"I could care less for your networks. The time for idealizing has passed. We crush these overweening NOA!"

The simulacrum's primitive brow seem to crinkle in interest.

Miko only wished he had a weapon in his hand. A starship at his disposal. He would rend these foul squids from tentacle to tentacle. This unpredictable power of his, blinking out, leaving him defenseless was useless, unless he could somehow manifest it at will. Such a potent gift wasted.

He staggered to his feet. Basilursk and his bullies came gliding in, tentacles twitching to encircle him and Usk.

Chapter 24

Regers paced the bridge aboard *Grendel*, his E1 slung over his shoulder. "We're minutes from that dimhole *Xares*."

Jennings, resenting the perilous mission, hissed through his teeth. "You realize you're getting mixed up in something over your head."

"Have no intention of getting caught up in a bug war, Jiminy. But if it lands us a chance of netting that fucker Yul, I'm in."

Jennings snorted while Vincent grinned. "You've never told us the full story of this Yul bastard."

"And I never will, Vincent. All you need to know is he and I go back a long way."

"Whatever beef you have with this man," said Jennings, "I don't want any part of it."

"Thanks for clearing that up, Jiminy. It's a hell of a lot deeper than you think, and you're neck deep in squid shit as it is. You do what I tell you. Nothing more, nothing less. As in, if I say 'jump', you ask 'how high'? Without a care of how much squid shit you may be swallowing on the way up, got it?"

"Like hell I will."

Regers nodded to Vincent. Vincent jammed the muzzle of his E1 in Jennings' mouth. Dragging knuckles across his peach-fuzz head, he brought his head in close. "Listen up, Jennings. It's better for your health."

Jennings fumed, licking at his bloody lip. Regers turned to Deakes. "We've got full power, Deakes, a fast new ship, and plenty of firepower and booze aboard. I won't kid you, we're going to have a lot of trouble out there. Feel it in my bones. Bugs to the left of us, bugs to the right of us.

The main objective is to get in and out as fast as possible."

Deakes blew out air from his cheeks. "Whatever you say, boss. You know my feeling on the subject."

"Attaboy, Deakes! Always loyal. Let's shape up, bitches! We're not going to waste time quibbling or shedding tears. We've got a hell of a lot of bug gunk to wade through and vengeance to wreak! Jennings! You got something to say? Guess not. With a mouth full of bleeding teeth you'd better save your wind. Of all these bastards here, you're the slowest learner I've ever seen." He shook his head in smiling wonder. "You'll learn, Jiminy, if I'm not your Uncle Regers."

Grendel came out of light drive a safe distance away from the bug fleet poised ready for battle. "I've a feeling the most interesting gambits'll be down on Xares—from there we'll find our quarry when those locusts start landing cargo vessels on the surface. Ramra, keep ship intercept open for human transmissions. Our Yul boy's probably going to be squawking on the blower to NOA before long."

"Right, boss." Ramra nudged Jennings aside from the nav panel. "Move over, Jiminy. You're hogging the console."

Regers laughed as Jennings slurred his words through a sore mouth.

Deakes pointed to the rose-tinged planet below on the holo screen. "From the sound of our friend Dez's hare-brained scheme, I bet they plan on planting those mechnos down there somewhere in the cities. The dragonflies hate their habitat being disturbed. When they see trouble, they'll take action."

Regers shrugged and muttered under his breath. "Like a few moths in fancy armor are going to take on a whole bug fleet. I'll believe it when I see it, Deakes."

"You said Dez mentioned NOA's pegged our boy flying a mantis ship?"

"Yeah, which means we'll follow the bug swarm down to planetside and listen in."

"We still got the squids to worry about," Deakes cautioned. He made a sweeping gesture at the holo view crammed with clusters of hostiles. "Look at those fucking Orbs. Thousands of them. While the bugs kill each other, the squids'll plug a bomb on everyone's ass. Nuke us all, squeeze the bejeesus out of us."

Jennings just shook his head in disgust. "You guys are bloody clueless."

"Got something to say, fuckface?" growled Vincent, sidling closer, rattling his rifle. "Why not offer it up fair and square, instead of pitching insults?"

"Enough, you SOBs," said Regers. "Concentrate on getting this vessel down to planetside without alerting the enemy. Look, the bugs are on the fly." All eyes turned to the holo view. Thousands of aphid fighters spiraled down toward the planet with mantis scouts and raiders, a swarm of swarms.

Ramra frowned. "Why aren't the squids following?"

"Backup? Dunno." Regers grunted. "No chance NOA's going to make any difference against that horde with a few mechnos."

"Don't underestimate them, Regers," said Jennings through a mouth of swollen gums.

"Ain't my war," said Regers. "I could give two shits."

But a part of Regers felt hollow at such words. Damnedest thing.

Am I starting to go soft or something?

* * *

The Mentera fleet spiraled toward Pandara continent's most affluent major city, Kibalsh. Yul pawed with frustration at the controls still locked on autopilot. He looked over at Cloye and the innumerable red blips spread over the tactical holo map. He had no clue of the fate of Miko amidst that horde. He'd lost contact with the former NAVO lieutenant back on Quenrix. Fenli's groans became palpable through the com. The man gnashed at his ill choice in coming back to this hellhole. As luck would have it, his controls were locked on target below as well. The fluke of his nav ever being free again looked unlikely.

Cloye grazed Yul a meaningful stare. A savage glint pooled in her eyes, her slender fingers moving over the touchpads, itching to peg off bugs. Hresh was as white as a ghost. His jaw half swung wide, as if he were ready to puke. Perhaps the man foresaw his own doom in the steep descent of the Mentera ship, the canted angle of the stars, a dive to the human planet below...a doom coming up fast.

"Let's make it good, folks," said Yul. "These may be our last moments."

The bug fleet, rapidly descending, was just minutes away from the atmosphere. Yul saw the flashes of ship fire and advance warnings of ship battles far out in space.

"NOA, finally!" cried Yul. "They attack the Orbs. Took their sweet time."

Hresh hustled to the nav, his white face suddenly suffused with hope. "About 1500 of them!" He worked the locust scanners. "They're taking on the Zikri forces. Small numbers by any comparison, but better than nothing." His thin shoulders quivered. "Not faring too well."

Yul stared at the wide holoscreen to see submarine NOA hulls flaring to dangerous levels as Zikri blasted their shields and flanked them. Some Zikri Orbs blipped out, blown to ashes by return fire, but not nearly enough.

"Can't worry about it, Hresh. We've got our own battles ahead. The allies're going ahead with the invasion. We're seconds from contact."

Attack squadrons swept down to the Kibalsh's main city center in similar blitzkrieg MO as Gibras on Quenrix.

The locust fighters streamed in, a long line of offense mantis and aphid shaped warcraft. The city loomed ahead, a pale smudge on the horizon. Strange rust-colored clouds hung low in the midmorning sky like long coral snakes . Sky towers, airways, industrial complexes, took form in the light haze. The hapless millions padded about on their day-to-day business, oblivious to the menace fast approaching. If only they knew what hellfire was about to hit...The Mentera stealth craft hurtled closer, cloaked under radar. A planet-wide warning had been issued with strong advice for civilians to evacuate the city to underground bunkers, but few of the skeptical masses had actually heeded such broadcasts. The Xareans were simply a naturally sceptical people. The ruling class, taking little action, considered these warnings 'boy-cried-wolf' threats.

At last, mobilization of air and ground forces came, as the enemy ships registered on their tracking devices. Fire from Xarean advance guard slashed out. Yul's mantis ship rocked.

1700 NOA defense lightfighters faced the Zikri and Mentera vanguard. They split, half staying up to deal with the Orbs, the other half chasing after the descending locust swarm: a solid wedge of ships, weaving in and out of enemy space like two sets of rival hornets. Some shot up in flames, others skidded off to destroy incoming craft while aphids targeted buildings below, causing small fires on the surface. But the Mentera destroyers and Orb flagships remained high up, deliberately forcing the defending NOA to split ranks. Pandemonium erupted on both fronts.

Full nav control came back in the Mentera lightfighter. Yul gave a gasp of relief. He banked to avoid a stream of NOA fire. A NOA transmission came crackling through the com: "This is Eagle Base 1. Do you read?"

"Copy," said Yul.

"Vrean, you're in one of the bug ships, right?"

A familiar voice. Bjen Stone? "Yes, why?"

"Target the decoy mechno we dropped in Cirrus Square. You can't miss it—it's an upright slab of armor off Galihine street. A time bomb waiting to go off."

"Say again?"

"Shoot the thing! It's priority, Vrean. Pure titanium, shielded, you can't harm it. We need to make it look as if an ambush is in progress from an enemy vessel. Whatever you do, get the hell out of there after the first hit. Don't engage it—if you know what's good for you."

"Copy that." Yul dipped away from the convoy, his lips set grim.

"What the hell are you doing?" rasped Hresh. "The bugs' scout craft'll come after us."

Yul ignored him. "I see the target, Eagle Base. Moving in." He sighted on a blue-black upright hulk and hissed through the com. "Fenli, you too, quit your bellyaching and make yourself useful—Lure the locust ships to the mines. We're made anyways, soon as we step out of line. Don't fire on them or you'll have a freakstorm up your ass."

"Roger," croaked Fenli.

Yul banked in a tight sweep down a wide street, breaking ranks for the first time from the Mentera convoy. In the middle of the road on a square patch of grass divider, loomed an ominous hulk. Cloye set fingers tapping on the weapons grid. Bright silver patterns arched from the Mentera mantis craft and deflected off the mechno's gunmetal hide. The thing was knocked backward. The blue light on its forward turret blinked on. In sudden activation, the unit hovered a dozen feet above the grass and took pursuit of the offending craft.

Cloye, rasping in defiance, sent more silver fire shimmering off its hulk.

"Bonzai!" Yul fell back in line with the other craft. He accelerated ahead toward the vanguard. He knew he had to get a safe buffer between him and the pursuing mechno. The other ships trailing behind were lit up by the beams lashing out from the mechno's turret.

"Seems we've stirred up a hornet's nest."

"Don't get too trigger happy, Cloye. NOA warned us."

"Tell that to Fenli," croaked Hresh. "Looks as if he's bagged some targets of his own."

Yul peered at the flickering holoview. Two more of the hulks that Fenli had pegged off were now tearing after him in pursuit.

"Holy hell," Fenli's voice rattled over the com. "Got some angry wasps on my tail."

"I warned you, Fenli!" Yul spoke into the com, "We nailed the targets. Fenli got two more. What the fuck are those things?"

"Devils in disguise," NOA said. "Pure titanium, courtesy of Cyber Corp. Powered by plant pod hatchlings you brought back from the outer zones."

Yul's face dimmed a shade of grey umber. His grin turned to a lopsided grimace as a shudder of comprehension ratcheted up his spine. The thought of what those things could do chilled his blood. This was biotech graced with the ferocity of an alien intelligence, beyond anything he had ever encountered—and driving the titanium hulks. The irony of it brought phlegm to his throat, no less the sheer improbability of the current moment.

Mantis fire arced out of the back of the convoy at the mechno. Nothing seemed to faze it. It came weaving up, dodging the deathly streaks and firing high-intensity beams back with savage force. It thrust in at impossible speeds, smashed the rear of the Mentera brigade, severing ships in two, shearing off fuselages, wings and rear thrusters. Ships went careening off to strike the surface and explode in the streets below. The hulk passed through the smoke to pursue the remaining ships.

"What the hell—? NOA, can you confirm what I'm seeing? Is this hulk for real—that I'm not dead in some twisted dream?"

NOA's reply cut off in mid-sentence. Instead, a voice, familiar and not, intruded on his reverie.

"Yul, baby, is that you? Talking to your boyfriends? Your goody good NOA?"

Yul's lips parted in a frown. He blinked, as if hearing a ghost from the past.

"Don't you remember me? No, you don't, do you? But I'd recognize your smarmy, whiny voice anywhere. Old Regers is here to collect his dues." A clown's laugh came over the receiver. "Come out and play, Yul boy. Uncle Regers's coming for you. Fuck your sweet ass nice and pretty."

Yul half choked, hardly daring to believe what he was hearing. "Regers?" His bull throat worked, swallowing dry air. "You died down there—on *Phebis*."

"Oh, ho. Maybe I did, maybe I didn't. Me's the man! A hundred lives for old Regers. Prepare for a sweet reckoning, Yul. Get the grease out. Whoopee!"

"Who is this nut case?" Cloye rasped.

Yul's eyes swung to the tactical holo view. A blue blip came hurtling out at breakneck speed, a rogue ship diving out of the multitudes, veering their way.

Yul gazed in awe, not without some trepidation. *Regers*. Could it be? No way. The cannons were locked on their much smaller ship. A pink blot of fire blipped out at them.

The ship rocked to a concentrated blast. Warning yellow lights danced across the console.

"Friend of yours?" grumbled Cloye.

"Damn that fucking Regers! He's actually going to take pieces out of our hide. Can't he see who the real enemy is here?"

Cloye set the target lock. "Give me the word, I'll nuke him."

"He's no friend of mine, Cloye. Blast him."

"With pleasure. Mentera are sending suspicious eyes our way."

"Forget the Mentera. Concentrate on Regers. Fucking bastard. He's going to spoil our whole ruse."

"Thought you said we were already made?" muttered Hresh.

"I was wrong. How the hell did he...?" Yul croaked. He wet his dry lips. "The signal's encrypted."

"Ever hear of a decrypter, bozo?" Regers jeered.

Yul scowled down at the receiver, not realizing he had a live channel still with Regers.

"*Grendel* rules. This is state-of-the-art shipcraft, Yul baby."

"What the fuck's he talking about?" muttered Cloye.

"He's a madman." Yul shook his head. "Crazy as a loon."

Skimming recklessly over the streets, past ships, round bends and ruined apartment blocks, Yul tried to lose his new menace. Brilliant bursts peppered around them. Shields fell. Now other Mentera craft, perceiving Regers' vessel as hostile, took pursuit. But Regers state-of-the-art Roamer was more than a match for the inadequate mantis fighter he was flying. Yul cringed. He suffered through the irony that he was glad to have Mentera hostiles on his tail.

The street was coming to an end. Surprise. A sheer wall of stone.

Yul slammed the lightfighter up and over for a better view. A lofty wall fifty yards high, glinting of reinforced concrete. Set in a rough oval, it covered about a quarter of the city's perimeter and looked over the grubby tenements. What was it for? Some kind of semi-transparent dome rose shimmering over the wall to further enclose a ghetto of decrepit buildings beyond.

Mentera heavy bombers and RPG drones rocketed in. Some ships bounced off the force-field of the near-transparent dome and went spinning out of control. A shield of some sort.

Yul blinked as an explosion of white light hit hard somewhere down below.

Transformers and power grids went up smoking and burning in ruined heaps outside the wall's perimeter. The shield was down. It crackled and sizzled sparks where the edges used to meet the top of the concrete wall. The locust ships flew in, through the smoke, fires and electrical arcs while Regers' Roamer went ballistic. Mentera cargo holds opened and dropped payloads to pepper the streets.

Masses of people scurried for safety, panicked out of their mind, hoping to evade the effects of the pressure bombs. Yul banked in for a closer look while citizens swarmed in denser configurations. Maybe they could lose Regers in the twisted streets in this protected quarter. The shield had been constructed of some semi-opaque flexible material, an electro dome, some technology similar to ship defense shields. The locusts wanted badly to penetrate this inner quarter. Why? Higher density of people? More fodder for the taking?

No time to ponder. Regers had sighted them again. His ship came roaring through the smoky haze, a streamlined blur cutting through grey webs of confusion.

Chapter 25

Regers clamped a hand on the bridge's console beside Deakes. Multiple bogies came soaring after the Alpha Roamer in the tactical view. "Deakes, blast their asses."

"I've told you, Regers," grated Jennings. "You're in over your head here. How long before those bugs get wise, gang up and blow us all away?"

"Dez got us a suped-up machine—extra shields, tactical AI, quad cannon, all the bells and whistles and trimmings. Not even one hit yet."

"Until one of those bug fighters snags us in a trap and slams us good."

"Ain't seen it yet. I'm savoring every minute of ham-stringing this Yul Vrean. Bitch must be quaking in his boots. Look at him run!"

"Yeah, maybe because he's got red hot bogies on his ass too," said Deakes. "Including a stealth Mentera bomber. They must have made him, figured he's a spy."

"Good. Hope they nuke him. Though that too won't matter much. We can outrun these filth puppies. Outshield 'em and outwit 'em."

"It's insane." Jennings mopped his brow with a frustrated groan.

Shabby soot-covered tenements whistled by, row upon row, and the odd warehouse with sagging chimneys. Disheveled figures ran amok in the streets below at the roar of the ships hurtling overhead.

"Looks as if we're in the slum district," said Regers. "See those ragamuffins in lepers' garb running about as if they haven't a coin between them?"

"Yeah. Seems as if the rich folk had something against the commoners and boarded them up in a kind of quarantine," Deakes remarked, "via some electro-shielded dome. Bugs made short work of it." He laughed.

"Haha…the dumb bastards," chuckled Regers. "They never knew the bugs'd be their saviors, freeing them from their pens. Come out, come out wherever you are, Yul baby. You can't hide from me."

Enemy fighters and NOA jetted across the sky. Rectangular hulks too, the mechnobots.

"It's those badass drones of Dez's," muttered Deakes. "How many did he build? Only so many of those bug-wasps or moths, whatever he had, to drive 'em."

"Maybe he bred more," Vincent suggested.

Regers looked at the young thug with pity. "They don't just grow those aliens on trees overnight, idiot." He swatted at his head.

Vincent ducked his head, scowling.

Deakes pointed. "I got a line on Vrean. Target locked."

"Bombs away."

The torpedo flared out and tagged Vrean's mantis's stern. The vessel lurched, blue-green flares dashing off her shields.

Regers wet his lips in satisfaction. Payback! Always a reward so sweet when it was within grasp. "Good work, Deakes. Hit 'em hard again!"

The Roamer sprayed fire flares. The mantis fighter jumped again at *Grendel's* assault and it yawed, spinning out of control to crash halfway down the street.

"Victory!" Regers shook a fist.

As dust stirred, enemy fire sprayed and startled human spectators crabbed away for cover, expecting the ship to explode, or catch on fire. The lightfighter's port side lay angled up against a slum apartment block, jabbed through broken windows, its nose cracked and bent out of shape. Thick black smoke curled from its crumpled back end and starboard middle.

Regers clenched a first. "Circle back and finish 'em off, Jiminy."

Jennings complied, guiding the Roamer back to the crash site.

Before Deakes could sight in for a killing blow, another ship burst out of the low-lying clouds, reaming them with fire. "What the hell—"

"Who the fuck's this? He don't fly like any bug," cried Regers. "Must be Yul's buddy come to hinder us. Blast his skinny ass!"

"Right, boss." Vincent targeted the incoming ship while Deakes recalibrated for long range shots.

Regers called, "Deakes, forget it. Ramra, take point, scan that ship's innards for weaknesses. Looks like a special op bug tactical vessel to me.

Both of you take out this fuck then we'll come back to finish off Yul and his pals."

Grendel sped after the rogue mantis. It left their victim far behind. Rear cannon fire spat back at them, catching their bow shields, sending warning lights flashing on the nav panel.

"Jesus, this bitch's a real hot dog. Some cocky crawdog. Give it to 'em, Vincent."

Tongue clenched between teeth, Vincent locked on the escaping craft's rear impulse engines. The special op ship wobbled in midair. It must have been malfunctioning, for it *slowed*. Or maybe the pilot was overconfident and misjudged. *Grendel's* firepower was more than it could handle...the mantis's shields were pummeled by Vincent's and Deakes's onslaught. The fuselage lit in blue and went down.

Deakes and Regers catcalled in triumph.

"Want me to finish it?" Deakes rasped.

"Naw, don't waste any time on that shitbox," rumbled Regers. "Jennings, get back to the crash site."

With a curt nod, Jennings sent the ship around to the back streets many blocks away.

* * *

Yul roused from his stupor. The sound of bleeps and buzzing noises echoed in his ears. All bad sounds. His body ached. He lifted himself with difficulty and pain from a broken pilot chair. No broken bones, but his brow had suffered a good hit.

Oh, yeah, they'd crashed. His head did a little jog as memory drifted back. He unhooked the harness around his shoulders. Cloye stirred beside him, her shaky fingers clutching her safety strap. Her face was ashen. She gave a groggy moan and attempted to roll over on her side.

Yul staggered over to a slumped form lying across the bridge by the far wall. *Hresh.* He felt for his pulse, lifted an arm. Nothing. The scientist lay eyes up, in lifeless sprawl.

Yul visualized events as they had happened: the flare to the stern, the loss of power and emergency systems as the ship careened out of control and rammed against the building. Hresh had not been able to belt himself in in time. The impact had sent him flying across the bridge like a straw man, snapping his neck.

"A quick death's better than stuck in a tank," Cloye muttered. She staggered to Yul's side.

"Let's go, Cloye. We've got some surviving to do."

"I agree."

"Those bastards'll be here with guns to finish us off. I know Regers. He'll be on our tail once they shake their pursuers."

He grabbed an extra E1 from the broken rack and tossed one to Cloye. She limped after him.

The emergency cargo port was jammed. Yul hoofed it in with a savage kick. He shuffled through, dragging Cloye with him. Smoke poured in, stinging their eyes.

They debarked the broken craft, getting as far away from the crackling hull in case it exploded. The sounds of sniper fire greeted them in the streets.

Eyes stinging, Yul squinted up in the pale sunshine. A war-torn mess of broken masonry, twisted signposts, streetlights, fallen bodies, whispers of hostile movements lurked in the daytime shadows. Hunched figures like rats broke for cover. Stun rays lashed out, the smell of fear and sounds of capture by locust ground troopers eager to snatch a body or two. A bleak day for Xares...

Cloye's face was soot-grimed, her left eye blackened and bruised. A cut ran along her upper right shoulder. She looked like a raccoon.

Yul's joints creaked to new stiffness. He flexed his mechanical arm, glad of its strength and its 1.5 factor of strength. He'd need it in the moments ahead.

He gripped his blaster, glad of the extra slung at his hip. "Let's move out, Cloye, before locusts—" Jesus, there was Regers' monster stealth craft hanging in the air! But wait, another mantis craft. A special op ship, barreling down on him with sleek neck, extra cannons and oversized bridge. *Fenli.* "Run!"

    * * *

Grendel swooped low and hovered over the wreck of Yul's crumpled mantis flyer.

"Don't see Vrean jumping out of his tin can." Regers frowned.

Jennings grunted. "Not picking up any life readings."

"Why should you? They must have died."

"Not necessarily, Vincent. We have to go out there and check. I need closure on this."

Ramra pointed at the holoview. "Fleeing figures at 6 o'clock. By that dilapidated tenement."

"Well, I'll be a fucking baboon. Ramra, zoom in."

He flipped the holo's controls to show better resolution: two figures, one man, one woman, staggering like wind-tossed scarecrows along a black line of debris for shelter.

"It's him," muttered Regers. "I'd know that husky ratfink and his boring face anywhere. We go in—on foot."

"Hate to tell you, Regers," said Jennings, "but that last hit knocked out our gyros. We're going down."

Regers hissed every lewd word ever to leave human lips. "Land this crate then, you fuck—We're going in on foot."

"Then what?"

"Shut up! Just land it."

A jerky landing jarred them back in their seats. The impulse engines sputtered then hissed a dying lament as they came to a shaky halt before an overturned air taxi. The smoking underbelly landed struts down about a hundred yards from the ruins of Vrean's crumpled mantis craft.

"Bastards must have slipped into the walled slum north," muttered Regers. "The alleys're too narrow to fit our ship anyways. Deakes—you, me and Vincent are going in as a team. Jiminy, what's the status of the amphibious portable vehicle Dez outfitted us with?"

"Sensors show it's operational."

"Good. Ramra you take the APV and cover us." Ramra's mouth worked while Deakes and Vincent griped about being on land patrol. "Don't trust those bugs not to waylay us. Jennings, you guard the ship in case we can fix it. No, wait—" He scowled. "Don't trust you with *Grendel* on your own. Better you come with us. We'll set the electro shock mechanism on the exterior to discourage any scavengers."

They hopped out onto the dusty ground. The rust-brown, camouflaged APV whirred at Ramra's touch. It floated over the four standing beside the defunct *Grendel*. Ramra, sitting in the pilot's seat, saluted Regers through the glass. He turned to give them a wink and a thumbs up.

"Give a kid a toy to play with and he's happier than a pig in shit," muttered Regers.

Deakes squinted. "Think he can handle it?"

"He better." Regers shrugged. "Whether he can or not, Deakes, is besides the point. I need you and Vincent on the ground with me. Still don't trust Jennings here enough to drive an assault vehicle."

"Why don't you get one of us to—"

"I told you already." Regers said briskly. "It's decided. Deakes, Vincent, Jennings. Let's go."

Chapter 26

Yul and Cloye dogged it in a slum city within a city, now a prime target of the Mentera slavers with the dome breached. Sounds of mayhem and blaster fire echoed from the soot-grimed stone. Yul cringed, his ears rebelling at the sounds of wartime terror: shrieks, screams, cries of dying, pain and mad laughter turned to heart-wrenching sobs. Stun bombs dropped from Mentera scout raiders on various parts of the city. Hordes of the population lolled dazed. Trams, monorails, air buses came to a standstill as private air-cars fell out of the sky. Communications went dead as the Mentera pulse waves fell upon the city along with the brunt of the Force 2 jammers. The city was a ravaged war zone, a booby trap waiting to happen: buildings reduced to ruins, fallen live wires, thousands dead in the streets.

The survivors were easy pickings for the locusts after the blitz, the signature Mentera-Zikri MO, same as the last planet. Men, women and children who'd escaped the stun blasts fled through the streets in wild, mad panic. They sought any shelter, from dark holes amidst the fresh rubble, to open sewers blasted open by enemy guns. Other more intrepid defenders grabbed up guns and whatever weaponry they could—mostly chunks of metal from the heaped-up rubble. They organized themselves into makeshift vigilante groups, fighting Mentera stormtroopers as buildings toppled and power stations crackled and smoked. The fraternal street gangs had the best chance of surviving, but Yul reckoned those groups were too few and far between to make any appreciable difference in this free-for-all apocalypse. Endless streams of locusts poured out of the landed lightfighters or wide-bodied convoys, clutching lumo blasters or stun guns in pincers, scouring the streets and buildings, dragging fresh captives into slave ships.

A city turned mad within moments by hideous creatures from far worlds. Looting and rapine. Crimes committed by no less unscrupulous domestic scavengers. The ugly underside of the modern city had reared its warted head.

What happens in an orderly world when every day routine goes to shit? When hard-working citizens are thrust into topsy-turvy madness, anarchy, dark impulse. When quiet, mild-mannered Ned on your neighborhood block becomes a killer and rapist overnight? When the good at heart, and the sensitive soul, realize that every breath, every moment of life is a waking luxury?

Is it all just illusion? Yul remained locked in a semi-daze.

*Show your face, ghoul of nightmares past. Don't be shy…There's a bucket of blood for everybody…*He shook his head, urging his brain to snap out of its weary funk.

"Yul, you okay?" Cloye grabbed his arm, steadied him.

"I'm okay. Everything good."

"For a second you looked half zoned out, like you were losing it."

"Yeah, just feeling woozy. Probably when we hit that wall."

She held his head in both hands. "We're alive for the moment. I don't know why we're still standing on our two feet."

"Because we're survivors, Cloye," said Yul hoarsely. "Part of our nature."

Cloye sucked in a heavy breath.

Yul's vision swam. He snapped himself back to reality as another bleak space threatened to wash over him. He had experienced such washouts before, fighting out in war zones, battling squids in *The Dim Zone*, defending the crippled *Albatross* from ambush, caught between gangs out in Aldebaran, pinned down by snipers in besieged Catawaln, other grim scenarios too numerous for his cloudy mind to recall.

Hresh dead. Fenli down. Miko likely in the same place with all his crew. Only himself and Cloye left to fight this bitter war. Stranded on a doomed planet with only their blasters and wits. Not enough to win against these fucking bugs and squids.

But soldier on they must. They were not quitters. Of all people, he was glad to have Cloye at his side.

As they passed a ruined tenant building, a balcony gave way. A crumbling concrete slab slid down and almost brained them. They ran crouching for shelter down a deserted alley. Vacant for some reason…danger? A trap? The Mentera had cleaned everything and everybody out here.

Yul licked his lips. He moved on through the garbage and rotten filth and rubble; Cloye padded ever-alert at his heels. They came out into a dirty square with scattered groups of ragged survivors staggering about, labored of breath. Hostile fire flashed out from up a radiating alley. A brown, rag-garbed man fell at their feet.

Cloye recoiled. She dropped in a crouch, her rifle gripped. "Let's get out of here." Defiance lay pasted on her dusty lips. Yul nodded. They pushed on past straggling groups and fallen bodies. *The dead were of no use to the Mentera. Easiest to leave the bodies rotting in the streets.*

Deeper down into the narrow, winding alley they plunged, with aim to get as far from the lurking slavers as possible.

Yul's face wrinkled at the sight of three more bodies, torn, charred and twisted in the rubble. These were the sketchy remains of two men and a woman, one singed by blaster fire, the others hit by burning fallout. Passers-by, garbed in ragged wool and cotton, surged past, heedless of those crushed by falling debris.

Life reduced to ignoble mockery. What did it all mean?

"If we get out of this in one piece, Yul," said Cloye, "you and I are going to have us a lie down and make love till we can't move."

Yul turned, his mouth worked, her words hardly bearing meaning to him in this grim moment.

"Call it a celebration over death," she added.

Yul licked his lips, admiring the suggestive curves of Cloye's slim figure. Soot-grimed and battle-torn, she was all woman, sexy as hell, foul-mouthed and ornery, but surely, a looker.

He hooked a hand on her shoulder, the touch sending heated visions into his skull. He shook them off. No time for distraction. "Got to get past that open space, Cloye. Looks like a main drainage conduit, or some kind of vehicular culvert. May be a safe way out of here."

They skulked out of their dim alley as the daytime light of Xares streamed down, harsh to their eyes and surreal in the grim, besieged streets of the city.

Now halfway across the square, with burning vehicles and flutters of movements, stun fire lashed out from the grimy shadows. The surrounding blackened tenements and shabby shops with iron-barred glass, could not help them.

A grim huddle of survivors lay pinned down behind a fallen air bus, twisted and crumpled on its side. Must have been chased into the slum quarters and shot down. Six or eight figures crouched behind the smoking metal from what Yul could see. A squad of a dozen locusts scuttled ever closer, long lumo-blasters clutched in sharp pincered claws.

He and Cloye ran around a mound of rubble and bodies, crouching low. They dug themselves in behind a pile of broken bricks, offering covering fire to the doomed before the slavers could flank them.

Blue fire fanned from their gunmetal muzzles. Bug heads separated from chitinous bodies in smoking yellow-blooded heaps. Only one hostile was left, staggering about, bewildered. The creature fanned its lumo-blaster left and right while one of the besieged, squat, brawny skinheads burst out and brained it with a meat cleaver. He pulled out the weapon from the skull and chopped the thing square in the back.

The locust fell, in a quivering heap. The offender stomped on its neck, cracking it, whooping with glee.

Yul grimaced "Come on. Let's go. There're more coming in at three o'clock. God help the survivors. Run!"

Shot gun blasts came from behind him where the others were pinned down. While making their escape, green fire lanced from behind, catching Cloye on her left side, grazing her. She slumped to a knee.

Yul ran over to her. "You, okay? Where'd you get hit?"

"My whole left side feels numb. Fuck, fuck." She slipped another notch lower to her other knee.

"Damn it. Just what we need." Yul grabbed her up. "Come on, Cloye, we have to get out of here. More bugs are coming. Quick! Grab on to my shoulders. Cling to my neck."

She wrapped her good right arm around Yul's neck, and they half loped across the rubble square, weaving amidst the rubble and flashes of green fire. Yul lifted his rifle in the other hand and peppered back answering fire while hobbling with Cloye toward the culvert. "Down!" he hissed.

They crashed headlong to the bomb-streaked asphalt as more locusts came running. On his belly, Yul lay fire into their masses. Dust and metal kicked up around them.

"Jesus, they're creeping around us from everywhere! How'd they sneak up on us so fast?"

"I don't know." Slowly she flexed her hand. "Feeling's starting to come back in my left arm."

Four hostiles beetled forth, black-green, shoulder-high menaces, scuttling on hind legs, determined to take them as prisoners. Yul laid down fire before they could get too close.

He dragged Cloye with one hand behind an overturned air car, then leap-frogged away, drawing them away from her. "Over here, you fuckers!" He waved his hands, roaring.

They wore no suits, these locusts, for better speed. As a horde they ran, like a swarm of wild locusts would fly. Mentera craft soared overhead. One mantis-shaped craft dipped low and dropped an oblong grey package. Not a gift. A pressure bomb. It never made the ground. It exploded fifty feet overhead, catching Yul full on in the first wave. He clutched at his head with a grimace of pain. He sagged to his knees, as his world went slipping sideways, dim as a crypt. When he opened his eyes, a blurry scene met his eyes, vision opaque, not quite right. He squinted, seeing double, like looking through a fishbowl lens, his ears echoing with thuds and booms and low frequencies like a seashell roar, but slowed down like a recorder machine losing power.

Cloye, shielded by the air car, had been spared the brunt of the blast. As five crickets skittered in with lumo-blasters, she sprang out of her daze, surprising them. She fought like a demon, slashing out with her combat knife, then jabbed another in the throat. Yellow fluid jetted over her space kevlar suit. Lifting her rifle, she grabbed at the sagging corpse, using it as a shield to shoot around it. Her muzzle sprayed mortal fire, felling locusts. More came. On she staggered, roaring a kamikaze curse, using the puppet locust as a battered shield, nailing locusts right, left and center. She left the street littered with Mentera bodies.

Stunned human onlookers gaped in awe from the sidelines by the grimed, ruined shops as Cloye dealt death and a squat spaceman with a killer E1 scrabbled to a military crouch and lay mayhem at anything that moved.

Cloye scrambled over to Yul's side. He shook his head, mouth opened in a gasping yawn to clear the cobwebs from his ears. "Fuck, that hurt."

"You alright?"

"Not really…but good work," he rasped.

"Get up." Now it was her turn to help him. "Run!" She covered him, kneeling, spraying fire, while he pegged hostiles coming in from behind.

They hobbled on, ducked into a twelve-foot wide, gaping culvert sighted from before. Shadows crossed both ends, puddles of brackish water massing in stagnant pools. The two advanced, but warily. Yul felt some blood coming back into his brain; though each step was slow, the next was slightly longer and more self-assured. Already a bad feeling brewed. But where to go? Green flashes of Mentera fire spurted behind them. Amplified echoes of Mentera blasts sounded from back in the square.

Rat-like creatures skittered underfoot, squeaking through tapered, whiskered snouts. Yul winced. They were about fifty feet in, making good progress at the half way point when he jerked back, bringing Cloye to a standstill. A brisk movement startled him in the blue-shadowed gloom. Accompanied by a furtive sound that was not their boots sloshing through dirty puddles.

"Yul! Behind you." Cloye loosed a line of fire, clipped one stalker between the eyes. But two more were on her, wrenching at her gun arm. Her last wild shot ricocheted near a reaching figure and buzzed the head of another.

One of the skinheads behind Yul roared, "Hold up! Put the gun down."

A set of eight skulkers scuttled forth, four on either end of the culvert, trapping them in the middle. They gripped improvised clubs and cleavers. The same crew of skulkers who they'd recently liberated, offering covering fire. "Son of a bitch!" croaked Yul.

He spat fire that sprayed up water at their feet as they dove out of the way.

Skinhead roared, "Drop the gun or pay the penalty!"

Street gang? Two skinheads, three long-haired thugs, black-haired, two blond. One woman amongst them, bleach blond with sides of her head shaved and long tail at the back. All had black and red bandannas over their heads.

"Hand over the weapon, spaceman!" blurted Skinhead from the place where the culvert shadows ran deepest. "Or girlie gets a face full of metal." They'd wrenched the gun from Cloye and held her in a stranglehold. "Spike and Marv are in need of such items."

The gang members sauntered up confidently as if they owned the whole sludge pile of this inner city.

Yul cursed himself for being taken so easily. He let his blaster fall.

"That's it, smart man." Skinhead kneed Cloye forward. He waved his sawed-off blaster. Why he'd used a cleaver earlier to kill the locust was beyond Yul. Aside from the skinny ruffian who gripped Cloye's weapon, the headman was the only one who held a gun: some short bully with an eyepatch and small rooster cob of brown hair up the middle of his egg-white skull.

"Kick the weapon over here where I can see it. Don't get cute."

Yul complied. The echo of his E1 clattered in the puddle-soaked dinginess, painful to his ears.

"The other one too."

Yul grimaced. He pulled the compact from his belt with reluctance and tossed it in the same place.

Cloye hissed at him. "You dumb shit! You should have wasted these scum and let me die."

Yul shook his head.

"You! Spaceman. Pzt." Skinhead jerked a thumb at Yul. "Park yourself over here." He motioned to a place between slant-eyed Marv and rake-thin Spike.

Yul hesitated, took a step closer. "Way I see it, we all have to cooperate here, chief, if we're going to survive. Last time I checked, a swarm of locusts were coming down to toss all our asses in tanks."

Smacky spat out a wad of phlegm. "Maybe. But one step at a time." He shouldered Marv ahead, glancing nervously back at a flicker of green fire that flared from somewhere out in the square.

Yul scanned his enemies. Nine of them in sour moods, with itchy fingers on weapons, wearing blood-spattered denims and synthetic leathers, ready to kill and run, get some payback for their losses. The dog-eared crew clutched a combo of kitchen knives, meat cleavers and wooden clubs, hand-crafted, and bits of twisted metal.

"This how you repay someone trying to save your skins?" jeered Yul.

Smacky smoothed out his rooster cob. "That you back there? Well I'll be damned, spaceman. Thankee. You're a life-saver for sure. Reckon my sawed-off jammed and I couldn't use it to peg any of those crickets off any more than killing pigeons through a pea-shooter. Working fine now."

"Name's Yul. You can thank us by giving us back our weapons."

Smacky laughed. "Not just yet, 'chief'. Don't trust you more than a wooden nickel tumbling in a slot machine. Until you prove to Smacky you're loyal, that you're not going to drive a metal pin through his eye, we keep 'em safe."

Yul grumbled. "Smacky's your name? Look, there's an alien invasion and we're—"

"Preaching to the choir, spaceman. Think I don't know what's going on in my backyard? Think I'll divvy up these weapons to my crew. I like my shotgun, quirky as it is." He crouched and tossed Yul's weapon at his feet to two of his redneck crew. "Marv, Wilb. Catch! You can fight over it."

Marv won. He gave an ear-to-ear, gap-toothed grin. He eyed the weapon like candy. "Gracias, Smacky! This one's got double action, and heavy gauge."

Smacky nodded, pleased that he could light up the lives of one of his ragboy crew.

Cloye muttered a sarcastic rejoinder, "Don't think either of you yobos know one end from another."

The taller and larger stepped forward with a menacing grin. "Who you talking about, girlie? Your spaceboy friend here?" He swaggered in closer.

"Relax, she's right, Marv," Smacky conceded. "Who taught you how to work an energy rifle?" He pulled it from Marv's grasp. "You do it like this, see?" He recalibrated, gripping the stock and adjusting the firing arm, then waited until the green light sighted and stopped blinking. He sprayed a burst down the culvert, deafening everyone. Tossed the weapon back to Marv. "You try."

Marv beamed, licking his lips. He snuck in a quick wild shot at a startled rat-like thing darting for cover in the culvert's end. Likely had some nest there.

Smacky gave a weary nod. "Marv's poor aim'll be the death of us all."

"Smacky, you should give me the gun, not Marv," another long-hair suggested.

Smacky waved him off. "Don't pay to linger here. Bugs'll be after us before long and zap us, take us up in the sky, like they did Nora and the kids."

With grim looks and grumbles of hatred, the gang trudged through the shallow puddles to the far end, herding Yul and Cloye along like cattle.

"So what's your plan, Smacky?" Yul asked.

The gang leader squinted into the saffron light streaming in from outside. "Not rightly sure, Yab. A bit of this, a bit of that. Probably some duck and dash before the day's out. We'll keep on moving through the night, pegging off bug scum with these new weapons. Reckon they'll be gone before long."

"Think you're not factoring in the reality. It's never over. The squids'll be down soon, and they'll make the locusts look like angels in a bishop's wet dream."

Smacky sneered. "What do you know? Squids, octopussies, crabs, we'll keep fighting them in the streets, air, and through flame."

"As you should. But think you're going to need a better plan than the one you got, drawing attention to yourselves, hobbling on through the night."

"And what may that be?"

"Getting ships and firepower to level the playing field. Capturing as many ships as you can: aphids, even the locust mantis fighters."

"You seem to know a lot about this, Yab. Thing is, none of us knows how to drive a starship."

"Me and her do." He jabbed a thumb at Cloye. "If we work together, you could get us—"

"Shut up. I know your tricky little games, spaceman. Get us all keyed up in hopes so you can plug a shell in our backs and fly away, leaving us all stranded. No, Yab, think we'll do it my way."

"Suit yourself." Yul shrugged and looked away with a frustrated grimace.

Without warning, Marv shot another few test rounds back down the culvert, making everyone's ears ring again.

"Hey, this ain't no firing range," Smacky thundered. "You warn people before you fire that gun, hear? Give me that." He smacked Marv in the ear and snatched back the rifle.

Marv slunk back and put on a simpering face.

"Real smart there, moron, get your kicks out of killing a few helpless animals," muttered Cloye.

Marv shot her a feral stare. "Black beauty, that's what we should call her, Smacky. What with the blackened eyes and sooty cheeks. Like a regular weasely *marbikin* come up from the sewer pipes."

"Good one, Marv."

They all laughed. Cloye told them to go circlejerk themselves.

Spike snickered. "Black beauty got a mouth on her."

"Shut up, Spike." Smacky motioned them out of the culvert.

The dank shadows gave way to a wide traffic circle and what must have been a city park, littered with garbage and now, slumped bodies. More broken up shops and dingy low rises hunched at the far end. Behind them a row of sooty buildings rose over the culvert and what Yul guessed another city street in behind the buildings. At one time the city had been affluent, judging from the formal structure of roads, parks, apartments and squares.

Members of Smacky's roughneck gang blinked under the raw light as if seeing real sunshine for the first time. The dome's semi-transparent material had filtered their source of radiance for who knows how long. Out in the natural light, Yul got a better look at them. A degenerate crew. Skid row types. All wore chewed-up denims and frayed leathers. Some with teeth missing and parts of ears clipped off or torn. Their faces were sullen and cracked with seams and bare arms and necks were grimed and cinder-sooted, fingernails caked in dirt.

"They keep us holed up here like hogs," muttered Smacky. "Fuck 'em. Now that their dome is gone batshit, I say we make a move on the rich side of town. Take what's ours."

There were here, heres and grunts of approval. The young woman, dirty, white-knuckled, long-necked, and the loudest of the lot, cat-called out like a street whore. "Sure thing, Smacky! First time the dome's ever gone down. We got some payback coming so long as we slip by these bugs."

Yul did a face-palm and sucked in a breath. "That's an egg brained idea. You're not thinking clearly."

"Who are you to tell us anything?" Wilb said, edging in with a cleaver.

Yul cautioned the angry man with an upraised hand. "You want to die? There's Mentera there, probably more than here, and soon there'll be squids, thousands of them, looting the place and taking more of you as slaves and looking for resources to capitalize on."

Smacky squinted at Yul as he scratched at his scarred chin. "Don't reckon you know as much of the ground reality, sheltered in your fancy ship up there."

"I know lots."

A rustle of boots crunched on the pebbles up ahead, alerting them.

That and the whirr of a flying engine.

"Quiet down, you loudmouths," said Smacky. They hunkered down behind some rubble and twisted sewer pipes. Behind them, a monument leaned on a drunken angle. The handiwork of Mentera pressure bombs.

Nose in the dust, Yul balled his metal fist, hoping for an opportunity. Cloye crouched, breathing heavily beside him. He caught snatches of the conversation.

"Gonna find that chump Yul and slit his eyeballs, Vince. Keep looking, Deakes, and quit whining about *Grendel.* Ship'll be fine. We can always get Jiminy here with his slide rule to fix it."

"I don't know, boss. Getting a funny, bad feeling here."

Regers! How the hell'd he catch wind of them so fast?

Some amphibious vehicle, a rust-painted globe, hovered eight feet above the rubble, twin blasters trained their way. It jet-thrusted closer. All edged noses deeper in the dirt.

"Want me to fry that thing, Smacky?" hissed Marv, lifting his rifle, clutching at Smacky's shoulder.

"Nah, don't try." Smacky shrugged off the arm. He pulled the muzzle down, his voice a dull whisper. "Those are armored plates. Rifle fire'd just deflect off it. Tip him off and they'll make bread dough of us. They smell like military types. Mean. Can tell by the way they strut and hold those guns. The other fuck though, whitey with the pale, ghost-like face, looks like a newbie. Doesn't even know how to hold a gun. Looks scared shitless too, as if he's gonna shoot his own damn foot."

Marv snickered.

"Shh! Want to give us away?"

Marv glared. "You're the one yapping—"

"Shut the hell up."

The airborne vehicle slid through the air like a greased lizard. Yul hoped that the pilot didn't spy them from his loftier angle. Seconds passed. Nope. The operator was another newbie.

After the four foot soldiers trudged by and the air vehicle passed into the next street, Smacky thumped Yul on the shoulder. "Who are those guys? Some friends of yours?"

"Guys you'd rather not meet," murmured Yul.

"What do you mean? You seem a little tense, Yab. That posse is offworld, like you. Can tell from the dicky accent. Out for your blood, spaceman? Yeah, they're out for your hide. Can smell the fear from here. Man doesn't get all worked up over a few fuckboys passing by when there're bugs galore on the loose ready to slap ass in tanks."

Yul's fingers clenched. A new sheen of sweat broke out over his brow. "You don't want to mess with Regers."

"Regers, is it? Ratshit, he'll soon be. This is my turf. Nobody comes in unless I say so."

"Yeah, like the locusts?" sneered Cloye. "Not looking much like anyone's turf to me." She waved an insolent hand. "Mostly bug-fucking ground from where I'm looking."

Smacky rolled over closer, one eye scrutinizing her with a critical glint. "You speaking to someone, sister?" He reached out to clout her but Yul caught the hairy arm in a metal fist. "Relax, chief. We've got other problems to deal with than slapping women around."

Smacky pulled himself away, "I'll bitchslap who I want."

The blond gang girl of the group snarled, raising a misshapen club of home-crafted wood.

"Back, all of you," Smacky commanded. Scrambling to his feet, he whirled his gun like a parade leader. "Think I'm up for a bit of knock on wood. In the mood."

Yul held up his hands. "Bugs are on the hunt and you've got a lot of wild and crazy people about. Better things to do, Smacky, so let's think it through."

"Trying to tell me another thing I don't already know, spaceman?" He fingered his sawed-off rifle.

"No need to get blast happy on us." Yul gritted his teeth. Of all the lowlifes he had to get waylaid by, it had to be these mouthbreathers.

"Mick, you got any explosives left?" bawled Smacky.

"Fresh out of bombs, sorry, Smacky." He scratched at his brown-tousled hair. "Wasted them on the last bug ship that came down snatched Artha and her brats."

"Shit, we'll have to get back to camp then." Smacky blew air out of his chipmunk cheeks. "No way we're going to blow that EV without heavier weaponry."

"Your call."

Chapter 27

The ragged group ducked back into the daytime shadows, retracing their steps through the scattered pockets of survivors and the endless rubble. Smacky and Wilb prodded Yul and Cloye along like pet animals, hustling them toward a low-rise apartment flat, the lower level bombed and the glass shattered. They stepped across broken glass to a stairwell half clogged with masonry and broken bricks then down to a cut-out gap: a doorway of sorts covered by a thin strip of canvas.

Smacky and Wilb herded Yul and Cloye into a large, one-room apartment.

"Inside," Smacky ordered.

In the gloom, Mick and Marv lit some kerosene lamps.

Yul opened eyes wide to adjust to the murk. The place was a shambles. Lingering reek of molder, sweat, and rankness to go. Fist-holes in the walls, crumbling plaster, a cracked holo screen tacked on a nearby wall. A warped floor, broken bottles, bits of old fried meat and busted plates, ale-stained garments slung across a low, ripped-up couch. This rattrap must have seen some wild parties and drunken fights. A pile of charred embers sat in the center of the room on a thin, raised sheet of metal. Yul frowned. What could that be? His brain unlocked the mystery: a communal campfire. Some jerkoff had built a fireplace with a jerry-rigged stove pipe, soot-black, and installed an electric fan to draw smoke up the air vent. Could actually see these yobos smoke-cooking weenies and marshmallows all day when they were as drunk and high as glowworms.

The girl went over to the mangy couch and plopped herself down and helped herself to some gummy brown stuff stuck in a broken dish.

Yul moved further inside. A small workbench with electric components and circuits lay against one wall, having the look of an amateur electrician's workspace. Odd. Spike cleared a space on the cluttered bench to set a lamp down.

Yul turned at a sound to his left. Struggling under a beat up table were three Mentera strung up in chicken wire. The table's legs acted as posts to barricade them in. The creatures chittered and sputtered, spitting white fluid from their clacking mandibles. They pulled at their chicken-wire bonds, though it cut into their black and green chitinous hides.

Yul choked. "You aim on rustling up some cricket stew, Smacky?"

Smacky just chuckled. "Mickey here wants 'em as pets. On account of how they shot up his place and took his pa and sister away in a big space blimp. These bug-rats were the last of their squad before we gunned them down and took them prisoners. Now I told him you can't make pets out of such bloodsuckers, but Mickey's an optimist and an obstinate one, ain't you, Mick?"

"Sure thing, Smacky. Bet your ass."

"Good, then—"

"Nice," derided Cloye, shaking her head.

Smacky padded over, eyeing her with deeper curiosity. "You've got yourself one sharp-edged tongue. Rough crowd here, and rough times, tough situation, miss. How far you want to play it?"

"How deep can you go?" she challenged.

"Woo hoo." There came a flurry of cat calls as the ruffians slapped their clubs against the scored plaster walls. Smacky hissed for silence.

Yul stared in horror upon a situation rapidly escalating out of control. What could he do to stop it? He moved to her side to catch any heat he could and caught her sly look at him. A dangerous game, but Cloye seemed to know what she was doing. She had not been a Cyber Corp spy for nothing.

"I think you should waste this chick, Smacky," grumbled Marv. He shoved Yul aside. "Don't like the sound of her, or her slutty looks. As much as I'd like to make use of them. She almost tagged me back in that culvert."

"I second that," said the gang girl, still smacking her lips. "Don't need no more than one sassy gal here."

"You're just jealous, Lace," said Smacky, "over another choice piece to share among the ranks."

Her mouth dropped and her face grew livid. "Am not, Smacky!"

"You know I just say everything straight as it is, Lace."

She shook her head, still fuming.

"Don't give me that saucy look. You're like a four-year old."

Cloye's lips curled in a snicker.

"What's so funny, bitch?" called the girl.

"Just remarking how gentlemanly your bully boy friends treat you. You going to stand for that talk? How you expect them to respect you?"

"Yeah, Lace, you going to stand for that?" mocked Marv.

The woman shrieked and sprang at Cloye, made a claw grab for her eyes. The move startled Cloye. She turned aside as sharp nails flicked across her cheek, nails that drew blood.

"What the fuck—are you loco?" She grabbed the girl's hair and flailing arm and let the gang girl's momentum crash her into the two yobos behind her.

Lace was up in a flash on the balls of her feet. She sprang forward like a sprung coil. The others gathered around stomping their feet, clapping their hands, hooting and hollering, like a bunch of ranch-hands at a stampede.

"Hey, boss, think we got ourselves a cat scrap here!" yowled Marv.

"Hot damn!" cried Wilb.

Smacky stood apart, lips set in a firm line.

Yul dropped his head and sighed. The young female hood reached and pawed again for Cloye's eyes. Cloye feinted to the side. She kept those nails back then jabbed an elbow into the girl's midriff, knocking the wind out of her.

Lace gasped. Before she went down, she hooked a foot under Cloye's left leg and the two crashed to the floor. Yul heard a distinct smack.

They were rolling around like a couple of momma cats on a spring day, with the young one kicking and biting, cursing like there was no tomorrow, when Wilb hitched his squat, rank frame in like a happy gnome. "You show 'er, Lace! She's a real scrapping tigress, our Lace is." Smacky growled, bare arms laced across his wide chest while Marv whistled encouragement through his gap teeth.

The two rolled close to Smacky and he kicked Cloye in the ribs. Cloye wheezed out a hoarse curse and lost momentum. Yul started forward but Spike held a gun on him. Tired of the game, Smacky hauled Cloye up. She drew back a fist, sucking air through her split lip, ready to lay into Smacky for putting boots to her. She clubbed him good just above the left ear.

A heavy red welt began to brew, but he blocked Cloye's second fist, looking to do something nastier. Yul moved in despite the gun trained at him and blocked Smacky's blow.

"Enough already." Smacky faced Yul in sullen mood. "Okay, your bitch bests mine. Bravo. Nothing to see here, folks. Move along." He slapped the others away, shoulder-checked Wilb and Marv back. He turned to Lacey, snatching at her wrist. "You happy now, Lace, you dumb slut? You go off shooting your mouth, get your ass whipped. Clock you up a bunch of bruises, lose you some pride, skin and a front tooth."

Lace spat out an uprooted tooth, wiping her bleeding lip.

"Smacky, my arm hurts. Don't pinch it so hard."

"I'll pinch it if I want to. Here, lemme see." He squinted at her bruised forearm, poked and prodded around at the swelling and she yowled some more, sucked in a pained breath at his rough touch.

"It's nothing, girl. Just a chicken scratch. Maybe a small sprain or two. Nothing to bawl over."

Her eyes brimmed with anger. "What d'you know, Smacky? You some doctor?"

"Don't talk back to me. It'll heal."

Marv tapped Smacky on the back. "We ought to—"

"Shut up. I know what we ought to do, Marv. When I need your tongue I'll pull down my leathers. We're heading out, Lace. You can stay behind if you're hurting too much."

"Naw, Smacky. I'll be coming. Boring as shit in this filth crib."

"Suit yourself. Yab or Yulb, whatever the fuck his name is, is coming. Get your woman cleaned up, and wipe that smug grin off her face or she'll be eating it. And get your ass moving out the door. Mickey, bring all the explosive gear you can carry." He kicked at bottles, tin cans, old ale-stained clothes. "Sick of this fucking dump. Told you bastards to clean it up, and what do you do, sit here and yak out more filth from your gobs whenever you get high and wasted."

They made for the hall and moved up the rubble and plaster-strewn trail clogging the stairwell.

"Don't like that redneck crew on our turf," Smacky mumbled. "Seen it in all the holo movies. About Armageddon. Planet goes to shit. Guerrilla warfare in the streets. Turf wars to the end of time with some highbanger moving in, trying to take over the local creed. Blows the head off the competition, sets up shop and becomes the new head hog. Seen it a million times. Only one Smacky round here, that's me."

"You tell 'em, Smack," said Wilb.

Smacky turned at the half-sagging railing. "Don't call me 'Smack' or I'll smack your fucking ass. Want me to call you Wib instead of Wilb?"

"No, wouldn't like that, Smacky. No need to get sore." Wilb shook out his shoulders. He looked away with a sullen grin.

"Why don't I get a gun?" Lace bawled, keeping her distance from Smacky, eyeing Cloye with contempt.

"Because you don't need one, Lace. And I don't trust you with a gun. You'll blow off somebody's head."

"Aw, Smacky, you always give Mickey the good stuff," she whined.

"*Give Mickey the good stuff*," he echoed. His eyes scrunched up like raisins. "Don't 'aw Smacky' me. What is this, kindergarten?"

The others guffawed. Wilb grabbed her in a head lock and gave her a stiff, hard noogie. "Hey, cut that out, you dipshit!" Lace cried.

"Knock it off, you asswipes. Move out!" Smacky slapped some heads. The pale light showed ahead through the broken glass that gave way onto the street. "Enough horseplay. Day's still young, we've got some bugs to hunt."

The young blonde hesitated, rubbed her head and swatted at Wilb, nursing her sore arm. "Think he should get punished for that. Why I always get beat on?"

Marv hunched in toward Smacky and muttered, "Don't you think it's a bit risky out there after the last bug blast? We've already got some crickets here to play with—maybe, Spin the bottle, Matchsticks, Blow the gasket. Whole pile of smash to smoke. You know how kinky Lace gets after a bit of Zombie." He grinned and nudged Smacky in the ribs.

"Are you fucking brain dead? There's a war out there and you want to play Spin the Bottle and smoke smack?" He herded Marv, Mickey and Wilb out with a rough push and painful prod of his gun.

The others lanced Marv a scowl.

Chapter 28

A view to the street showed no improvement from the last time. An aphid and NOA fighter had crashed down and more humps of unmoving bodies lay in heaps. Yul looked on with little hope. Casualties during the Mentera raids.

Smacky groused. "Gotta put a stop to this. They've infiltrated our turf. Not to mention they've snatched friends and innocent citizens."

"Very noble of you," said Yul.

"Yeah, I think so…and don't get too glib with your two-toothed remarks, spaceman. You're already in enough trouble as it is."

"Smacky, I say we—" bawled Lace.

"Shut up, bitch. Move!" He grabbed a hankful of her hair and herded her through the broken glass and into the street.

The bright light stung Yul's eyes. He took a deep breath, paused to get his bearings. The square was as before: overturned vehicles, scattered mobs of people, distant screams, the thump-thump of locust blasters.

His eye caught a sparkle of metal across the square. Out of the third floor window of a soot-grimed apartment building, some amateur sniper had gone ballistic and was taking pot shots at anything that moved in the street below. Dumb fool.

Smacky danced to fire that had him kicking up his heels like drops of oil on a frying pan. "Jesus H Christ…Get the hell out of here!"

All of them made a mad scramble for the downed airbus. Yul hunkered down, his back sideways to the bus. He saw dead faces with staring eyeballs peeking out at him from the blood-grimed glass.

"On my count." Smacky heaved himself erect. They scrambled for better shelter after him while Spike and Mick gave back cover fire.

The shooting stopped. A body slumped out of the window, doubled over the sill.

"Good shot," commended Smacky, "whoever took out that screwball."

"Nailed that smarmy bastard myself," crowed Spike.

The situation was completely screwed, Yul concluded. These Mayberries were going to fuck up badly and get everyone killed. If he couldn't get away from them, he'd have no chance of surviving. He and Cloye could make a break into the ruins, for safety, provided some other menace didn't catch up with them first. Only a matter of time before those bloodsucker locusts swarmed in and blew the shit out of the bottom of the barrel. He glanced over at Cloye, saw she was taking the situation very coolly, especially after her cat scrap, wiping at her split cheek and flexing her wrist. Smug too. Never one to be intimidated.

A high-circling Orb came angling out of the sky. The thing was spiked like a murder ball on the end of a demon's mace. Copper-colored, menacing, though the crude armored outer plates were closer to the color of old bronze.

"Holy shit, Smacky!" cried Wilb. "What the fuck is that?"

"A squid ship, what you think? We got ourselves an alien party. Guess Yab was right."

"Holy Jesus shit fuck."

Yul sighed. Jesus shit fuck was right. What to do now? What else could go wrong?

Back the other way they loped off, opposite from where they'd entered this doomed square. Ever vigilant, Spike kept Yul and Cloye covered. Not much wiggle room for a breakaway. Even if they could give old Spike the slip, Smacky'd blast their asses in a flash. Whether their new meandering course included commandeering a ship was anyone's guess. The man seemed impervious to suggestion and had an agenda of his own.

Unfortunately, one that brought them closer to hell. Around a bend came the low whine of a small flying vehicle, an amphibious vehicle, with globular fuselage, and twin AK4 blasters. The thing hovered overhead, covering the four men below as they walked like street kings.

A dark figure in the lead on ground pointed at them. *Regers*. He mouthed words into a com. The APV twisted and turned as bright fire splashed out of the twin guns mounted on either side of the turret.

Yul dove for cover. On the way he shoulder-checked Cloye out the way. She fell in a heap at the foot of the alley.

Others weren't so lucky.

Shells sprayed by, reaming the air. The excess bullets skimmed off down the alley.

The APV angled in. Yul gave a cry of warning.

"Now, Mickey, you fuck!" bawled Smacky, ducking behind a rubble pile.

With a grim leer, Mick lobbed the first artillery shell at the incoming APV.

For a moment the air froze. Then *kaboom*.

A major pressure blast hit the APV dead on and set it spinning out of control to the ground. It lay in a crumpled heap. The pressure wave and fragments from its hull knocked Regers and his crew backward.

The smoke cleared and Yul peered in apprehension. Whoever was in the APV was toast.

Smacky squinted into the sun, signaling Marv and one of his henchmen to poke around the ruined glass and smoking, twisted metal.

"Hody ho. Anything interesting? What'ch you got, Marv?"

"We got one dead Jakru, horns and all, lying in the cockpit."

"Anything else?"

"Just a fancy assault rifle, an E1 mangled up with cracked stock."

"That ain't doing us no good, Wilb. Why even mention it?"

"This fusebox and weapons kit has live ammo we can use."

"Good man, Marv. Wilb, you get up there and help the man yank it out." He gestured. "Spike, you and me'll head over and take out the rest of those gun lords. Don't want them creeping up on us from the back and blasting us. Spike, you with me?...Spike?"

But Spike lay in a spreading pool of his own blood, eyes staring up, blood draining from a chest wound, pierced by shrapnel.

"Ain't that a shitter," said Smacky, scratching his head. Two more bodies lay unmoving, the long-haired brothers. Lace prodded them with a finger, a sniff and grimace, like a curious grade-school kid.

Smacky fiddled with his stock's firing mechanism. "Fucking thing's jammed again. Should've taken Marv's weapon." He looked around, kicked at the dust. The blast had leveled all sign of anything. "Where are those fuckers?"

Yul stared grimly. Anxiety grew in his gut.

"No matter," said Smacky. "Get those explosives out of the APV. Reckon we'll need them."

Yul grimaced at the irony of the adoption of a plan he'd suggested all along.

"Back to the crib."

"But Smack—"

"Back, you fucks! We take this bomb, rig it up back in the crib."

Try as they might, they couldn't find hide nor hair of Regers. They had disappeared in a trail of blood.

* * *

Deakes eyes darted about. "Regers, this is fucking dangerous."

Regers motioned him on with his gun, ignoring the pain in his mangled half ear, torn by shrapnel, as they crawled on their bellies away from the blast. "Only the good things in life are, Deakes. Damn that crafty Dez, installing egg shell armor on that APV. Last laugh's on us. Get moving, Deakes. Stay low, you other two," he rasped back at Vincent and Jennings. "Don't want them tagging you too."

Deakes shook his grime-faced head as they rounded a corner. "Ramra dead. Creib dead. Just me, Jennings, you and Vincent now…and Jennings is looking the worse for wear. Want to add three more corpses to the count?"

"Ain't going to be more corpses if you quit jabbering and we get this job done."

Vincent grinned through his sweat and grime, "Yeah, Uncle Regers gonna take care of us."

Deakes gave a hoarse sneer. "Uncle Regers is going to be sucking bug dick before long."

"Shut up, Deakes. Enough of your vulgar talk. Down!" Regers pulled Deakes's shoulder. Three figures were hunching their way through the rubble: blocks of masonry in a square of fallen buildings. Smoke curled from piles of bodies. Hydro wires had fallen. Electrical fixtures lay exposed and sparking.

"There's those fuckers now, creeping like weasels along the line of that derailed tram line. Think they're going to get away from old Regers? Fat chance. There's probably more of 'em, I count six now. Looks as if they're carrying something. Probably parts scavenged from the APV. Fucking packrats. Yul must have bagged himself some new friends."

Regers nudged Deakes. "You slip over there, head them off. Vincent and me'll go straight in."

With a grunt, Deakes disappeared on the left flank of the battered square.

Regers broke off in a dog trot. He spat a round of fire ahead of the skulkers, trying to hedge them toward Deakes, but they ducked into a back alley. "Shit."

Vincent came up behind Regers, face grimed and blood-streaked, his voice hoarse. "Should've pegged those rats, boss, rather than try to take them alive."

"Hindsight, Vincent. We'll get them."

Following like weasels on the hunt, they set after Yul and the others at a loping run. Deakes joined the three as distant booms echoed across the dismal cityscape. Mentera craft haunted the skies, long mantis shapes firing down stun rays like grasshopper spit. Sticking to the sidelines, Regers and his hounds dodged from rubble pile to pile or ruined vehicle or half crumbled building to building, tracking the fugitives to some shelled apartment complex with front windows blasted. "Bonzai," Regers croaked between his teeth. "Deakes, Vincent, you first."

Chapter 29

In the dim kerosene lamplight of Smacky's den, Mick and Smacky peered over the scavenged ammo box and its prickle pod of wires on Mick's workbench.

"Hurry the hell up, we don't have a lot of time."

Mickey rustled away at soldering some leads. "Yeah, yeah. Only so fast I can go, Smacky."

Smacky darted anxious, half-slitted eyes at the door and the gloomy confines of the decrepit apartment as if every shadow was a foe in waiting. Marv's weapon had been jammed, ever since they'd lost Spike's in the free-for-all. Yul could understand Smacky's anxiety. Only one working gun between them. Still, one gun was enough to keep him and Cloye from leaping at Smacky's throat.

As if guessing his thoughts, Smacky waved his cleaver at Yul. "Keep those prisoners covered, Wilb. Don't want them jumping us."

"Why don't we just fucking kill them?" growled Wilb.

"Because I said so, This Yab bastard's given us some good intel. While he's useful, we keep him. The woman—" he stared with an evil grin "—well, she can have her uses at a later time."

"You should kill her too," Lace wailed. "Fucked up my arm."

"Quit your whining, Lace."

Yul debated trying to reason with them, but dropped the idea. If Regers was still on the loose and caught up with them, he and his thugs'd make mincemeat of Smacky and this motley crew.

"What's that?" Smacky whirled, ears perked, raising his hand.

Fire flare sprayed through the doorway. A grey muzzle poked out and a burly form's bald head with it. Smacky gave a cursing cry, his cleaver raised. He charged the dull shape from the side.

Deakes, blood-grimed in his kevlar, caught the descending meat blade. He yanked his E1 about just as his muzzle picked off Mick who was scrambling in the background for a knife to hurl.

Yul sprang sideways to pull Smacky off Deakes's back before he got himself wasted by crossfire.

Too late.

The next figure through the door blasted Wilb to ratshit as he raised his rifle. Another muzzle lifted and nailed Marv. Both slumped in puddles of their own blood. Cloye scrambled for the meat cleaver but Deakes kicked it away. Jennings stood mute, a ghost in human form. The girl, Lace, wailed, hands clutching her ears. "Stop! Stop!"

"Cry all you want, little girl." Regers patted her on the head. "Momma ain't gonna kiss and make it better." He stared about in the dim, crypt-like gloom. "Deakes, you okay?"

"Yeah, just got half my finger chopped off by this chicken shit rooster boy." He hoofed Smacky in the gut. The gang leader lay supine, deader than a doornail, riddled with shells from crossfire. Deakes worked at wrapping leather around his stump of a finger, stomaching the pain and muttering curses.

Regers chuckled. "You ought to be more alert, Deakes. Surprised you fell for the old chip and charge back there. These boys like to play rough."

"Well, let's just say I'm not as spry as I used to be, Regers. I'm off my game, after having a pressure blast in my ear." He gnawed at his bloody knuckles.

"Happens." Regers leveled his gun at Yul whose lips worked and his fists clenched. "Well, Yul, the happy deserter. Long time no see. How's it feel, friend?"

Yul spit out curses.

Regers peered crosswise at Jennings who still stood mute, rifle down, pointed at the floor. "Jiminy, you're quieter than a church mouse. Anything to say?"

Jennings just stared, unblinking, the whites of his eyes dull in the kerosene lamplight.

Regers gave a wry grunt, jabbing Vincent in the ribs. "See, Vincent, I told you Jiminy'd learn his lesson. Doesn't even want to call NOA now, or cry for backup, or help that poor dying turd over there, crawling in his own blood."

Vincent gave a raucous laugh.

Cloye, fingers twitching, itched to make a move but Yul flashed her a warning glance. He took a stealthy step sideways, looking for a weapon to grab, but Regers motioned him back. "Forget it, Yul boy. Don't try it. You're dogshit as it is."

"You kilt Smacky," the girl wailed, scuttling over to kneel by her gang leader's side.

Regers frowned down at the shredded corpse. "Looks as if Smacky or Smokey or whatever the fuck his name is, ain't going to be doing too much more rough-housing in the next while."

"No, he ain't, is he boss?" laughed Deakes, stamping on the lifeless arm. He hooked a meaty fist around the sawed off weapon, tossed it to Vincent. "There. Extra toothpick for you."

Vincent showed a grin full of brown teeth. He cocked the weapon, gave it a go. "Useless, jammed." He threw it aside where it smashed into some broken plates.

Regers slung his rifle over his shoulder and sighed. "So, this is the local clubhouse." His feet shuffled about and beady eyes roved around with critical inspection. "Shithouse more like it. Wouldn't let a pet rabbit run loose in here. All that work and 'em all dead except the girl and a few bozos back there." Vincent reached for the girl. Regers warned him back. "Nah, leave her. I don't like her meat anyway. She can play amateur ham radio operator, chew on some hashish and twiddle herself." He gave a hollow sigh. "How the day has run sour. Ramra fucked. Who's next?" He glared around with a quizzical expression.

"Hey, locusts at two-o'clock," Deakes shouted. He motioned to the table.

Regers grimaced. He peppered the chicken-wired captives full of fire. Heads and pincers went flying in sheets of puce-yellow blood. "No, not no more, Deakes. This is bug-crushing day." He scowled, face curled in a sneer. "These creepos are sick here, harboring crickets. What the fuck are they playing, bug rape?"

Yul saw the desperate gleam in the other two gang members' eyes, huddled in the shadows, thin, ragged, unkempt hoods. He shook his head in warning, as if they'd try something stupid, like make a run for it.

"Mickey wanted them as pets," the girl whimpered. "You kilt Mickey."

Regers looked down at her with a sad sigh.

"What we going to do about her, boss?" asked Vincent.

"Bring her topside into the light. All of them. The stench in here is killing me. Honestly, Yul, don't know how you stood it, why you didn't break out of this crib with fists flying."

There was shuffling of feet and muttered grunts.

"Any time soon, you fucks," sneered Regers. "Move your feet, Jennings, you slack bastard! Sick of you turning zombie on us."

The four mercs brought the prisoners out at swift speed. Lace and two other no names shuffled along, the latter mumbling curses. Cloye and Yul remained silent. Vincent led the way, rifle fanning the shadows to deal with ambushers. Deakes and Regers took up the rear. All the while Lace giggled hysterically. She danced about, sing-songing out-of-key nursery rhymes.

Regers rolled his eyes and muttered a few dark words. "Girl's getting a rude awakening to the reality of life—one big violent ant farm."

Squinting through the broken glass, they stood in the lobby, staring out at the bright, open square. No stragglers in sight. Seemed as if any wandering locals had learned the hard way to stay away from this death zone.

The air battle had taken a new turn. Sleek submarine shapes of the NOA fighters now slid across the skies like brown leeches harried by a swarm of aphid and mantis fighters. Orbs drew in, armed to the teeth with lethal uro bombs. They raced after the newer threat, the smaller, lighter NOA craft. Space fireworks lit up the near distant skies; dogfights erupted everywhere, feints, dives and luck to play a role in deciding this battle. Yul gritted his teeth. He hoped, but knew his was a small hope that so few could win against so many. But if those damn mechnos could do their job...

Regers was about to motion them out toward the nearest overturned airbus when the girl sprang up in an unexpected fury. She laid teeth into Deakes's wrist, prompting a painful howl as she wrenched at his rifle. Deakes pistol whipped her down but she was up like a cat, snarling, as if she felt no pain. She scrambled, hands and knees off into the dust like a crab with the other two gang members fleeing at her heels.

Vincent's muzzle flashed. It slammed the slowest in the leg. The three stumbled off, groaning, cursing, the last hobbling on one leg. "Mother fucks, die in hell!" he called back.

Vincent sprayed fire, kicking up dust at their feet. They dogged it behind a crumbled corner of an alley. Vincent went to take after them but Regers held his arm. "Leave 'em. That girl's so hiked up on smack she'll live through anything, like a rabid animal. Our prizes are here." He pointed in the fading light to Yul whose chest heaved. "Well, well, my good ole buddy Yul. Taking up with a pack of chicken shits to fight your battles. Shame on you."

Cloye went to snatch up a piece of iron pipe, but Regers waved her back with his gun. "Uh, uh. Spring chickens get their wings clipped."

Yul grunted with disgust. He cursed himself for not taking the initiative earlier. He started forward, but Regers was faster.

"Back the fuck up, Yul. Four to two, we got you covered. You too, young lady. Unless you're itching for a pisshole full of E1. Think you can immobilize three marksmen before one blasts your ass?"

Cloye stepped back. Regers came up to her, squinting in the pale sunlight, licking his chops as the sun struggled between thin clouds.

"Well, well, a mighty fine spring capon. Perfect for a late afternoon dessert treat, eh Vincent?" He yanked the piece of pipe from her hand and tossed it into the rubble. His eyes roved over her wide hips, buxom chest and pouting jaw, his own jawbone outthrust in challenge. He turned to Yul. "Didn't think you had it in you, Yul, having a lady like that. Always pegged you for a pansy ass." His lascivious eyes raked Cloye again with deeper scrutiny. "I might get ugly old Deakes here to do her in front of you, just for kicks, see how much anguish it causes you and what kind of man you really are."

Cloye snarled. "Try it, fucker, see what happens to your nuts. I'll squeeze 'em off like cherries from a tree."

Regers burst out laughing. He doubled over, slapping his thigh. "Oh, you know how to pick 'em, Yul! My kind of lady, foul-tongued and sweet-assed. Sexy as hell, even grimed and blooded up. Woo wee! This day has certainly picked up considerably." He piked his rifle to the sky. "Captain Regers on the prowl! Bags one spirited wench and a surly boy toy all in one go. All the better. Might save this vixen for a special day. Blood, guts, burnt-out cities, squids and bugs getting their asses kicked. Mayhem left and right and some fine tail to go." He shot off a few rounds in the sky.

"Settle down, Regers," warned Deakes. "You out of your mind? Don't want to attract any more squids and bugs than's necessary."

"Enough noise and guts to go around a hundred lifetimes, Deakes, so don't matter what I do."

Deakes looked around with nervous eyes.

"Aw, don't be such a pussy," Regers snorted. "Let 'em come, Deakes. Place is infested with bugs as it is. Kill 'em, crush 'em under our heels."

Yul stared. Seems as if Uncle Regers had gone a little off the deep end.

Deakes scowled and twisted about. He made a wide sweep with his rifle back the way they'd come. "Think we better get back to the ship, Regers, even if it is screwed. Safer there. What you going to do with Yul? Slice his nuts off? Take him back as prisoner? Don't know about you, but I'd feel safer with armor around us. Think about looking for a new ride out of here. NOA could pick us up as looters and opportunists."

"That's an awful lot of babble from you, Deakes. Ramra's dead face staring up at you back there got you spooked?"

"Just cautious."

"Yeah, sure. I'm just savoring this precious moment. Treasure it, Vincent." He put an arm around the younger thug's shoulders. "There won't be any better time or place here and now to enjoy this moment of triumph."

Vincent's lips curled in a sanguine grin.

Blaster fire licked out from the rubble. Regers instinctively swept his rifle barrel back and forth. Yul tensed, his metal fist flexing.

"What the fuck?…Vincent, go check it out."

Vincent scrambled off into the shadows of the wall breasting the rubble-choked sidewalk. More fire echoed off the twisted mortar and leaning buildings. Vincent came back, hissing air between his teeth. "It's that smarmy fucker. The one we gunned down earlier. He's out there running loose, must have alerted the bugs and squids."

"Your friend," Regers snapped at Yul. "He was tailing us, one we shot out of the sky. Must've gotten sentimental and came back looking for you after crawling out of his downed copter. Should have dropped a bomb on his ass while we had the chance. But we were too busy chasing you."

"Squids coming at four o'clock," grunted Deakes. Six sets of eyes lifted to the sky. "We can't get back to the ship without a major firefight."

"Ain't that a pickle. Another shootout."

"Told you not to fire those shots." Deakes groaned. "Regers, doesn't anything faze you? I mean, anything?"

"Nope. Reckon I died a hundred deaths back in that fucking bug tank. Don't feel an ounce of fear. How you feeling, Deakes? You're looking a little pale. Old man fear giving you the shakes?" He laughed. "Killing the old geyser named 'fear' makes a man invincible, you know."

"Or stupid. Let's get the fuck out of here."

Regers motioned the two prisoners on. "Move, you two, if you want to live a little longer."

Yul gave a surly grunt. He heaved himself up through the rubble. Jennings took up the rear, as if resigned to death.

As they loped away from the incoming fire, Regers hitched himself closer to Yul. "Had Vincent go easy on shooting your ship down. Boy's a regular marksman. Deakes here, boxy-faced badger's a little heavier on the trigger."

"Let the woman go, Regers," Yul rasped. "She's innocent. You and I have our beef. Let's have it out."

"Mighty brave of you, Yul. As I see it, so brave of you to leave me dying back in the trenches in that shithole Orb too."

"Let's put it this way, Regers, if you were in my shoes, would you do any different? Just can't picture you stopping to pick up and carry a dying Yul Vrean a mile or so to the ship. Frue was hurting. I left you with the last bit of suit adhesive. I could only save one of you. At least Frue had a suit."

Regers gave a grim laugh. "You got a way with words, Yul. Maybe it's just my imagination, but I'm thinking I deserved as much dignity as chirpy little Frue."

"Yeah, so did Greer."

Regers snarled. "Greer was an accident. I was flying high on Devirol. Offing him…was a mistake."

"All fine and nice to say it after the fact."

Chests heaving, they hoofed it down an alley, half covered with twisted beams, girders, broken piping, then down a water-slicked patch of torn-up asphalt to what looked like a muddy canal. A stone pedestrian bridge, clumped with bodies, gave access to the far side, cluttered with fallout, where more grim tenements stood huddled together.

"You going to try to lose them down there?" Yul snapped at Regers. "Doesn't look promising."

"Not seeing too many other options."

"How'd you make it out of the tank room?"

Regers showed a mouthful of teeth. "I'm the cockroach that doesn't die. Don't have time to swap war stories with you. Let's move our sorry—"

Yul struck like a sledgehammer. He smashed into Regers' right side, sending him reeling back. He twisted his torso to latch vengeful hands on his weapon.

Regers' rifle went off, ricocheting off the sooty wall. The weapon went skidding out of both men's grasp. Regers squawked as Vincent and Deakes leveled rifles at both men, neither able to get a clean shot.

"No!...leave him," Regers roared. "This ratbastard's mine."

Deakes trained his muzzle on Cloye. Vincent covered Yul. Yul and Regers circled each other like a couple of prowling tigers. Yul leaped in, grabbing Regers by the neck. Regers ducked, twisted out of the hold. They both locked machine arms together, vying for advantage.

Sweat dripped from Yul's salty skin. Muscles bulged and veins popped on each other's temples. Regers seemed to give way...A spurt of Yul's fantastic strength powered by state-of-the-art mechno force, running half way up to shoulder, courtesy of Cyber Corp, had Regers panting.

In a dream-like trance, Yul's mind flicked back to the ironic significance of this freak encounter between him and Regers, two quasi-mechno men with metal prosthetics.

Yul landed his full weight on Regers and drew back his arm to smash Regers' face in. But stun blasts came arching over his head, zinging dangerously close to his ear. He rolled off with a curse. He snatched up Regers' weapon, firing at anything that moved.

Orbs were in the air, coming down closer now. Three were within firing range. They must have gotten word to clean up the mess the locusts had started.

Now it was back to old times, allied against a common enemy. He and Regers, against the squids, like on *Albatross*.

A blue streak came whizzing down from the sky and took Vincent full in the throat. He toppled back, choking. His life force drained out in seconds.

Regers gave a dismal cry. "Vincent, you sorry bastard! You didn't have it in you to survive." He staggered to his feet.

A small horde of tentacle-waving Zikri came gliding in, powered by lower motilators and what might have passed for primitive feet and tail. No weapons. Such was the monsters' way. Just pure strength and sheer muscle. Yul only knew that strangling force too well. Once those motilators got around one's torso, better chance getting out of a python's grip.

Two of the loathsome creatures drew in on either side of him. Yul blasted the first grey, writhing shape, but the other got a piece of his arm. His rifle went spinning out of his hands. Cloye sprang in to grab it. Regers, without weapon, was caught in the slimy grip of a hulking Zikri. His two henchmen opened fire on the advancing squids but were steamrolled in a grey mass of teeming flesh. They were swiftly overwhelmed. Cloye blasted squid meat, sending mangled chunks into the air. A slimy guard lunged for her, but Yul squirmed out of the grip he was in and smashed his metal fist into the ropy face, sending it spinning sideways. It gave Cloye the split second she needed to blast the alien thing to hell.

The move cost him. The suffocating grip of another latched onto his chest, slowly choking the life out of him. His grip relaxed. The squid tightened its sickening, deadly embrace…then started dragging Yul toward the waiting Orb.

Blaster force ripped through the air, decimating squids as new forces joined the fray. Yul, his head swimming and vision blurring, caught a glimpse of a half-familiar figure hobbling out of the haze. *Fenli?*

Cloye blasted squids left and right. She whirled in a cartwheel over a whipping tentacle to roll up on her knees and blow three squids to shredded pulp. A tentacle lashed out, whipped by her amber hair. The slimy loop knocked her sideways. She blocked martial-arts style with forearm, ducked a follow up coil with a quick arm movement then lashed out with a fierce roundhouse kick. A kamikaze yell vibrated in her throat. Fresh fire from her muzzle clipped the squid constricting Yul. The thing jerked in a marionette's dance and sagged. Yul staggered forward, unraveling himself from the rank, twitching coils.

Regers fought like a wild man, kicking, clawing, yelling. Too many of them. The squids hustled him and his other companions, the man he called Deakes and the pale ghost of a man Jennings, toward their ship. Regers slapped out with boot heels lifted a foot off the ground.

Yul stumbled forward, scooping up Deakes's rifle, trying to get a clean shot. No chance. Too many hovering squids by the Orb to save him or his henchmen. The cargo port was sliding open, taking slaves.

Cloye pulled him back. "You owe that creep nothing, Yul. He came back to kill us, reduced us to this…"

Yul hobbled into the shadowy ruins of the street with Cloye, her amber hair slick with sweat and grime. A new ally to their cause trailed behind—Fenli. He was breathing heavily, wrapped in a numb daze. The cargo door to the Orb slid shut, and the squids and their fresh catches banked into the sky, but circled twice, with cannons aimed their way.

* * *

Away from the gangsters' hideaway Yul, Cloye and Fenli stumbled through the corpse-ridden streets. The aura of death hung heavily at every twist and turn like a thick cloud blanketing the city.

Fenli stared into space with a faraway gaze. Burn marks etched across both cheeks. The man's grey space garb was shredded and streaked with black cinder marks. His hands shook. *The man should be dead, by all rights.*

Yul slapped him on the back. "Good work, Fenli. Snap out of it, flyboy. We've got a long run ahead of us."

"Yeah." The man blinked and shook himself alert. He looked ten years older, but alive. Some inner fire kept him on his feet.

The three scrambled through the debris of a city made unreal by devastation and rapine. Yul and Cloye were all too glad to be free of Smacky and Regers. Yul looked up in the sallow sky as the NOA craft rocketed over the bombed rooftops. Fewer Orbs now. Could it be? Had NOA gained some ground? Too much to hope for in this precarious war. This was a grim, sallow day for humanity...

Yul shuddered to think of Regers' fate in the slimy grip of the Zikri. Cloye had said it all—he had it coming. The man was a menace. And now he was going to die all over again…

But in no way could Yul revel in such a fate for anyone, no matter his crime. Living a thousand lives, an eternity of dull, monotonous death, entombed in a Mentera tank. Perhaps that's why he had picked up that gun and tried to kill those squids before they carted the men away, men who were out to torture and kill him.

Chapter 30

Audra piloted the hijacked Mentera vessel into the endless ranks of the Zikri Orbs. A sea of burning ships, streaks of death fire traded from various vessels: aphids, Orbs, friends, foes alike, including NOA. Collisions, killer torpedoes, uro bombs...a chaotic melee...and now some strange rectangular metal hulks, handiwork of the NOA, drones that seemed to both take hits and pummel the strongest of the Orbs, ripping holes through their armored hulls. Audra shook her head in wonder. A strange universe indeed when such compact fiends could take down assault Orbs. A sign of the turbulent times of the future. From what signals she'd intercepted and decoded with the universal translator, she learned that Miko and his companions had been taken prisoner aboard the flagship *Viscurg*, Admiral Nrog's own flagship. Likely the most guarded and secure vessel in the fleet. An unbreachable hulk. But not impossible to penetrate...especially if her crafty powers were put to use.

From afar, she studied the activity around the flagship. Lucky for her, the vessel kept a central position, serving as the command hub for the rest of the fleet, processing and relaying orders to squadrons in the attack field. Those orders seemed to be doing little to win this war. An oddity in itself. Other Mentera vessels were docking on her broadside ports. So, why not her? After a bit of thinking and discarding some very rash actions, she came up with a plan of action.

She engineered a staticky response using the shipboard computer by splicing Mentera words together from previous recorded transmissions. Zigzagging amidst the Zikri and NOA ships, she piloted closer to the flagship, taking evasive action as much as possible to preserve her shields as they got bombarded by NOA crossfire.

The flagship loomed ahead, a giant among Zikri destroyers. Easily it was a half mile long, oblong versus orb-like compared to the innumerable spiked monstrosities in the field. Riddled with radiating rods, prickly com towers and attack cannons, she was a formidable sight, no less were the complex bays and loading docks on her scalloped sides shaped like underwater honeycomb caves in old cauliflower coral.

The chaos continued all around her while the NOA ships attacked the Zikri vanguard.

Audra played the voice recording back over the open channel, hoping her simple ruse would work. If not, there was always plan B, the unpleasant alternative.

"Structural damage critical. Air pressure dropping. Request dock access for repairs."

A pause came over the communication console. *"Request acknowledged. Dock in Bay 8 Eil ...(the rest was untranslatable)."*

A triumphant chitter vibrated through Audra's glottal cavity.

She brought the ship into the open bay, as the metal hatch closed behind her. Landing in a vacant space among the many other attack vessels, she prepared herself for the next phase of her operation. Much Zikri activity ensued. Military protocols had squids bustling up and down the walkways and catwalks, carrying out orders, loading and servicing ships of many designs: orbs and aphid-shaped lightfighters alike.

Hastily, she feigned a sprawled position in the pilot's chair, her left dangling motilator a convincing image of a recent skirmish, perhaps a victim of internal cabin burns sparked by an onslaught of enemy fire.

The starboard portal opened. Two Zikri glided in to investigate, evidently puzzled by the squat, massive form sprawled before the master console. When they hovered closer, Audra sprang like the killer she was, wrapping motilators around the foremost's head and snapping its neck. Before the second could chitter into its com, she lashed out with long lethal fore-tentacles. With coal-black eyes, she stared down at her handiwork. The two were loose masses of jellied flesh on the floor. Audra pursed her polyp of a mouth with satisfaction. Snatching up the com fallen from the last quivering squid, she managed to splice in words:

"Pilot dazed. One of us will stay aboard."

A pause. *"Affirmative. Report status as soon as possible."*

Audra chittered a prefabricated response. She stuffed the bodies in the forward compartment, then glided out of the portal, wearing the guard's communicator headband.

* * *

Miko crouched inches from Usk, both in fighting stances before the advancing squids. In the eerie glow of the nearby tanks, Basilursk and two squids surrounded him and Usk, tentacles outstretched, cutting off any escape. Nrog watched with half a black, prune-pit eye to the side, while chittering furious orders into his com to the bridge.

Basilursk sent out a questing tentacle. Human and Mentera flashed each other resigned glances as they awaited death. The end would come soon and terribly.

Basilursk pounced. He grappled Miko in an undulating strangle of motilators. Miko fought hard, smashing fists against the rubbery flesh lifting him. But it was of little use. His strength did not come even close to his fiercer opponent. Usk dodged a looping tentacle. His eyes darted in desperation to the U-shaped amalgamator. Jring was through, whisked back to his ship, but not as yet his last aide. A sudden burst of speed propelled Usk under the next whipping tentacle toward the pulsating and glowing transporter. He lashed out his good pincer at the locust's limb that bore a lumo-weapon.

There was an amber flash, a hiss of sparks as the insectoid's arm separated from its body, while the rest disappeared through the amalgamator, a wormhole jump across physical space. Usk snatched up the fallen weapon. He dropped in a whirling crouch to level fire at Basilursk's guards.

Squid flesh parted in bloody cords as the first two went down in sizzling heaps. The third bowled Usk over and caught him up in a whirlpool of tentacles.

Utter mayhem struck in a space of a few seconds. Another menace entered the scene. Its grey-black bulk burst through the convex doorway, a blurred shape, a hulk of writhing tentacles, smashing into the Zikri who was carrying off Usk. Usk went spinning out of the creature's grasp then hastened to crawl painfully away from the creature's flailing grip.

Miko struggled in Basilursk's crushing motilators, his feet kicking at the first touch of the Mentera water as the creature thrust, keen on plunging him into the nearest tank. But its husky torso sagged, as strangling coils fastened around its head and ripped it off and sent it rolling past the blue box with its obnoxious luminous proxy, still smiling with an ape-like face tipped on a slanting angle. The Zikri body slumped; Miko sprawled to the floor, his knees hitting hard. He gasped for air and looked up. The nightmarish face of Audra peered down at him. She stared with an infathomable expression. Perhaps one that said, *"So here we are, human. Did you think you'd seen the last of me?"*

In a fit of frenzied rage, Admiral Nrog launched his bulk at the intruder. Audra turned to meet his overzealous hulk. Tentacles locked with tentacles. Zikri and admiral tumbled end over end in a mass of rippling flesh.

Nrog's impressive musculature had developed over years of wrestling, but now they bulged under new pressure not yet experienced. His best was not enough, for Audra was of the older breed, trained to kill without prejudice and mercy. The female of her species was more vicious and in this contest, the better fighter.

She twisted out of Nrog's grip, uncoiling thick wads of strangling, python-like flesh that worked desperately to squeeze the life out of her.

In his half daze, Miko watched. The titanic struggle between two Zikri generations raged on, as he swayed to his feet. Staggering like a drunk, he scooped up Usk's blaster and with quivering hand, aimed it at Star's tank. The glass shattered in a burst of rippling spiderwebs. Shards of glass and green brine sprayed over the floor, sweeping Star with it. She rolled on the cold steel, choking, gasping for air.

Miko raced toward her. Circling her ribcage with both hands, he squeezed the water from her lungs.

Audra and Nrog dueled on. A fierce and ugly fight. As flesh ripped and tore, chitters poured from Nrog's prune-like mouth.

His strength was rapidly ebbing, no match for Audra's brawn, nor her cunning, as muscle and cartilage and tough rubbery sinew began to shred under her crushing ministrations. Nrog buckled under her weight, feeling his collapsing body succumb to her superior strength. He was at the point of breaking, when all of a sudden blaster fire rang out. A single flare, and the monster Zikri Audra jerked and spasmed.

A Mentera guard had skulked out of the shadows, gripping a lumo blaster. Miko's head turned in a daze. The locust thing must have come through the amalgamator. He looked around with wild surprise, guessing Jring must have sent the creature after his mutilated guard had come through the other end. More locusts spewed one by one between the horseshoe-shaped parallel plates. Miko tensed and raced toward the gathering enemies, lumo-blaster lifted in hand with a kamikaze cry in his throat. Blaster fire shredded advancing locust flesh. Pincers and heads flew in pasty clumps as his green fire did its bloody work. He dove aside, ducked as return fire came his way. With a raucous yell, Miko fell flat on his ass, leveled fire into the amalgamators, laying waste to their hated metal, until all were sizzling, blackened hulks. He sank on his haunches, panting, weak from the horror of it all.

A Mentera had killed Audra, or so the Mentera soldier thought. With half a red eye on the carnage behind him, he came skittering forth on hind legs to save the Zikri Admiral, his eerie eyes blazing, unaware that he dealt not with an ordinary Zikri intruder, but a lethal, guerrilla-war-trained soldier.

Nrog looked up in anguish. "Kill me, you idiot!" he rasped in a hoarse chitter. The admiral convulsed, tentacles splayed aside the hulk of Audra. "You—should have let—this thing kill me when it had me in its hold."

The chirruping guard lifted his weapon but Audra sprang up with murderous intent, snatching him in a strangling grip. With her last squid-like strength, she ripped his fragile chitinous body in two, helmet, suit and all.

Nrog gasped, unable to believe his eyes. He crawled in the blood and slime, pleading with his female adversary to end it. But Audra would do no such thing. She glided one jerky step and another toward him, gazing with burning singlemindedness. No pity or remorse glinted in those eyes. She swayed, her charred hide quivering in response to incomprehensible inner pain, then she tumbled in a rubbery heap.

She left Nrog there, bleeding out, feeling every inch of his agony, as she, too, dragged her own smoking, bleeding hide away, as an animal crawls off to a hole to die. Three of her motilators trailed uselessly behind her.

The ship rocked to another savage blast. More enemy fire thudded against the hull, now one without a commander to lead it.

Miko staggered over to where Star lay, half senseless, but recovering. He waved a hand in front of her face. He saw the briefest flicker of recognition as an eyelid fluttered open. A mouthful of green water spewed from her lips. She spat it out, wiped her mouth, heaving from the effort. She peered around in a semi-vacuous gaze. "Miko, where are you? Hold me."

He pressed to her side, his hand gently massaging her back.

"Oh, Miko, it was h-horrible. I could see you and I couldn't, like I was looking through a fish bowl. You were so far away." She reached out a feeble hand, clutched at his soiled uniform. "I tried to touch the glass but my arms wouldn't move."

"It's okay, Star, I'm here." Miko held her close, her wet, shivering form responding to his own warmth.

She gave an unwholesome shudder. "Each moment was like an age." Tears sprang in her eyes. "I couldn't move, then when that guard-creature plugged into me, I thought...I was fading away to oblivion, like some mist evaporating in sunlight. Then the scariest thing happened—I didn't care anymore. As if I could sleep in a vacuum forever."

Miko shuddered. A silent death. No pain, no free will, no nothing. He knew it well enough. Just an endless silence with no end.

He hoped never to experience the death of the tank again...

A whisper of movement fluttered to his left, then a rasping wheeze. He looked with new concern to where Audra crawled away slowly. In the pit of his gut, he felt a host of indescribable emotions. Remorse? Anger? Sadness?

He released Star gently and hobbled toward where Usk lay in a panting crouch. He gathered up his faithful friend and the two approached the quivering but mobile Audra.

Her black and grey hide was badly scorched, charred beyond repair, her tentacles sprawled in a frightening starfish pattern. The tips left traces of residual slime on the hard-plated floor.

Time slowed and then seemed to stand still. Miko gazed in stunned misery. From that grim day out in *Gollonus* so long ago when he had encountered Audra, waylaid by her scavenging Zikri Orb, he had come to know the Zikri and it felt like lifetimes ago. Too eerie now seeing her in this helpless, battered condition. Gazing at her slack limbs and near lifeless eyes, he knew he would never understand her motives or what went on behind those alien eyes. Her drive to unite with him, coupled with a desire to kill him, as a female black widow spider would, was an incomprehensible mystery. Alien and human genes had been spliced in some horrible misconfiguration, thus binding them in a way he could not fathom. It scared him more than dying here in this alien ship with no purpose or loftier mission to speak of. He could never escape Audra. Nor could she him. In life or death.

And yet, death was not in keeping with Audra's courage. Even beyond the grave, he knew deep in his inner being that she would haunt his dreams till the end of time. And if he were to sit here and watch her die in this miserable, ghastly place, those dreams would be only the more bitter.

The ship rocked to another savage blast.

Miko swore under his breath. "Here Usk!…Help me drag her to that largest tank."

Usk hesitated, recoiling at the violent, headstrong Zikri who had, on prior occasions, tried to kill him.

"Do it!" cried Miko. "If it were not for her, we'd be dead."

Usk chirruped out a protest. Reluctantly he hooked his pincer onto her upper body.

Miko's face twisted in anguish. His was a twisted logic. He grabbed at a slimy motilator and pulled Audra inch by inch toward the tank, almost cringing with the thrill of the familiar feel of sliminess that had used and abused him in times long past. No longer did he feel guilt for the symbiotic pleasure they had both experienced in their erotic embrace. In the fading gleams of her defiant stare, he caught a glimpse of surprise on a ropy face gone slack and ashen and an understanding passed between them. For the first time, Audra saw concern mirrored in Miko's expression, withal, a compassion for her, and her face relaxed in a contented sigh.

Miko did not know why he did it; he was not capable of such introspection right now, only that a strong sense of duty called.

In helpless horror, Star stared, as if unable to comprehend the scene unfolding before her. Her glazed-over eyes were clearing. Now she blinked several times as she recovered from her plunge into a liquid nightmare.

Using their combined strength, Usk and Miko painstakingly upended the dying Zikri into the largest intact tank. She sank, a dead weight, straight to the bottom, gulping lungfuls of nourishing water then drowned.

The blue glow of the simulacrum flickered to life. The AI proxy, projected on a sharp angle, lifted a pale hand and spoke once again in a didactic voice.

"What a tragic waste! A vintage specimen! Pity it couldn't have been saved for our AI scanners and virtual scientists to study."

"You're all monsters!" Miko cried.

"On the contrary, I don't exist, only as a facsimile of what was once a dead race who crafted you. We live on in the nascent consciousness of our children. Like your memories."

"I could care less," snorted Miko. "I have nothing to do with you or the likes of your genesis myth, whoever or whatever you are."

"On the contrary, you have everything to do with us, human. Without us, you would be nonexistent."

Miko looked away, hardly knowing what to feel. He had nothing to say. Only a wish to pull the plug on that miserable box forever. But he knew no such thing was possible. That the Masters were technically beyond any 'shutting down'.

The AI looked at Miko with some pity. "I am sensitive to your pain, human. I can commiserate with your hopes and fears. Maybe our aims are not mutually exclusive. I wish I could offer more comforting words at this moment, but I fear, being an engine of truth, any words would only be superfluous and prolong the inevitable, that a cruel fate awaits you."

A feeling of overwhelming despair flooded Miko. As he slipped to new lows, *Bzt*, his body blitzed out and disappeared. The surge of violent emotion had blinked him out of existence.

No, no, not now! His inward shriek landed on deaf ears. He was back in that zone, of invisibility.

No! He had to be with his friends, not in some useless realm of limbo! They had to do something, get off this ship! He gave a shudder of frustration. A blast of anger smote his being and had him willing himself back to his bodily form.

Bzt. In an instant he came staggering back to corporeal form, floating on his heels, his senses reeling.

Star trilled a note of horror. "What are you? You're not human!"

He wiped at his brow, almost laughing uncontrollably. It hit him in a flash how he could control the force of invisibility. He need only bring the intense emotions that triggered it to the forefront. Bleak despair to blink out...confidence and anger to blink in. Should he test the theory? No. Better to get out of here and not press his luck. Not long would it be before the lack of Admiral Nrog's response would bring squads of squids gliding in to investigate.

He grabbed up Star. "Come on, there's no time to lose!"

On shaky but determined feet, he helped the half-quivering woman to the doorway, thrusting an extra weapon in her hand, while Usk scooped up a fallen weapon for his own from a charred claw. With a quick backward glance, he left Audra in her healing fluids and Nrog and the dead Mentera in their creepy tomb, as a growing lump hardened in the pit of his stomach.

They clambered ahead down the bioluminescent hall glowing in leafy-green splendor. The locust's blaster kept steady vigilance as Usk led the way. About a ten minute haul to the space dock, as Miko recalled when they'd been forcefully brought here.

There would be squids along the way.

Chapter 31

Miko shuddered as he navigated the Zikri halls with their icky moss and creepers hanging from the walls. How they had come to love the damp, lush, creepy stuff when they originated on that dustbowl Kraetoria was beyond him. Maybe the simulacrum had lied about the common genesis origin, part of the overall joke of the universe. Had Nrog adopted a new home world on some lush swamp-infested planet?

There was no point in remaining corporeal. Usk would gain more help with him an invisible man than a visible one right now. He was just about to will himself to invisibility, when blasts pounded at the hull. *Viscurg* lurched to each blow. Star whimpered, still in her semi-daze, groggy from her drowning plunge. She clung to Miko's arm. "I can't get that ugly, cold, disembodied voice back there out of my mind...it terrified me. It spoke so clinically of us."

"Forget it, Star. It's just a machine. It'll be destroyed before long as will this ship."

As will we, if we don't get out of here, he thought...*The Masters. Pure fiction. Only survival of the fittest.* But he could not be so sure of that. His blood ran cold at the grim revelation dropped by the luminous ghoul-ape of an AI.

Star clutched her blaster in a shaky hand. "Worse though was when I awoke to you and Usk dragging that Audra *thing*."

Miko stumbled over a charred Zikri corpse. Booms rocked the hull. Usk's blaster took out more squids while he and Star leaped over the inert shapes. Star shirked at the carnage, gripping her blaster in two trembling hands as she fired wantonly. Miko's eyes roved to the ceiling as they sprinkled down rank clumps of moss with every shudder of the hull.

He pinched his eyes shut. He willed himself into that mind space of utter despair and desolation.

Bzt. He blinked out of existence. Only his blaster clung in midair, like a magical, floating thing. Focusing his will, he trained it down the hall at any approaching squids. Usk chittered in grim acknowledgement of having an invisible ally. He shuffled on in a half-hobbling gait.

In fits and starts, the three threaded their way down the grim hall of *Viscurg*, blasting squids where necessary. Just a few minutes more, Miko thought. He and Usk acted as a tag team. Star fired from the rear, cleaning up the extras. They approached what looked like a power center, a control grid of five blackened tower boxes arcing sparks from top to top. Squid technicians worked behind a protective wire cage in a frenzy to repair what Miko guessed to be a burnt-out transformer. They slipped past the repair crew undetected. The hall opened up into a wide oval gap that showed a murky yellow glow. Frenetic activity loomed beyond, a massive landing dock of sorts. This hall had been one of the many access points to the command dock.

Pandemonium reigned below. Hundreds of Zikri swarmed the loading docks: a mini spaceport of its own, a marvel in alien engineering. A massive eye-like portal loomed above, allowing ships to launch themselves out into the gulfs of space. More of the strange bioluminescent moss dangled from the ceiling. The crews inspected and serviced craft of all designs to impulse out to fight on the war front.

The flagship had been hit hard. A giant holo screen showed a view out into space: countless ships flying in and out on disparate trajectories. Also two strange rectangular metal hulks under fire, weaving in and out like miniature demons and smashing through the Zikri Orbs as if they were putty. Now one of the NOA drones came barreling toward the flagship, unleashing a giant moth before the outer armature disintegrated under shell fire. The insect swept on to ram *Viscurg's* hull, threatening to breach it.

Miko's mind raced. It looked very probable that Jring's dreams of some 'Ark of the Future' were rapidly disintegrating. A fleeting hope that maybe this alien invasion could be thwarted, percolated through his mind. Almost as suddenly, a dark shiver flashed up his spine at the image of the tens of thousands of humans already bound on that giant slave ship for a far world.

Only two mantis craft remained in the space dock. Tucked in beside a row of craft and a monster attack Orb. It was their only hope. Good luck getting to it!

An unspoken communication passed between Usk and Miko's invisible form holding the blaster.

Miko set out with bobbing blaster to distract the squids gathered there. He kept the anger and nail-edge panic bottled up just under the threshold of breaking. Just enough not to buzz back to human form at some random instant.

The floating blaster spat out green fire as it advanced upon the service crew of the Mentera fighter. Squid parts streamed every way. Usk and Star came quickly after him, padding in the wake of Miko's trail of destruction. Usk scuttled to the cargo hatch. An insectoid's feral grin lay etched on his face, as if pleased at the opportunity to pilot another ship.

In the cargo bay Miko's blaster dropped as he fully engaged his senses. He contacted that place deep within, the calm and the confidence, and felt his atoms resurging. In a flash of sprinkles of light, he buzzed back to his normal self. He swayed on his feet, clutching his head in a woozy daze, but remained otherwise intact. Star laid a hand on his shoulder to steady him.

A quick race to the vacated bridge. Without words and with deft efficiency, Usk got the ship up and running and moving out of the open portal. Ships were coming in from the depressurization bay at swift and regular rates. The great ocular slit opened wider and the mantis fighter rocketed out into the blackness of space.

A vast battleground of ships greeted Miko's eyes on the hijacked ship's viewport. A 3D gridlock of thousands of ships in every direction.

"Holy shit," he gasped.

"Let's get out of here," Star wailed. She wrung her wrists.

'Usk, planetside's looking good," said Miko.

"No, not *Xares*!" Star protested. "NOA will shoot this locust ship down."

She had a point. If NOA continued to hold their position, they would fire indiscriminately. "Is the light drive intact?" he asked Usk.

Usk chittered out a high note of affirmation.

Miko gave a sigh of relief. "We can't hyperdrive out so close to Xares. Try to reach Fenli and Yul."

Usk fiddled with the controls. Hailing frequencies went out to both ships. But no response. Only a hiss of white noise. Miko sighed. He gave Usk a sad look.

"They're gone."

"I'm sorry, Miko." Star looked at him with despair then at the holo view that registered hundreds of firefights going on. "What now?"

Miko grumbled, "We fight our way out."

Usk gave a defiant chitter. His good claw clacked over the nav panel, preparing the controls for engagement.

But just as the ship was about to set impulse for a wild flight, an unsettling scene greeted their eyes. More of the odd rectangular hulks weaved in and out of the enemy Orbs amidst the countless raging ships. With fabulous dexterity, the drones attacked. Whenever one of the armored drones looked as it was about to be blown to atoms by Zikri torpedoes, a strange insect—some half moth, half butterfly mutant—jettisoned out and came zipping after the offending craft, at astounding speed. Miko watched with undisguised astonishment as one smashed clear through an Orb's hull, armored plates and all. Squid carcasses floated out of the freshly-bored hole, frozen on contact with the frigid emptiness.

He'd never seen anything like it. The Zikri were getting pummeled by such creatures.

Renewed with fresh hope, Miko gritted his teeth.

What were those moths? An alien species? Some biogenetic weapon of mass destruction unleashed by NOA? The titanium hulks and their alien moths seemed to leave the submarine-shaped NOA ships alone. How such creatures could withstand vacuum or propel themselves through space at such impossible speeds remained a mystery.

Miko's biggest fear was how to avoid getting slaughtered himself. He hailed NOA and set up a mayday.

"Usk! Code Red! Launch an escape vector between those two Zikri Orbs. Ten minutes on full impulse and we'll be within range to light drive to *Altair*. Plot the best course!"

The Mentera ship lurched into the fray. All the time Miko had a shivery feeling Yul and Fenli were still alive. Clenching a fist, he resolved to find them. Or at least discover the grim truth of their fate.

* * *

Back in the bowels of *Viscurg*, all was in a state of flux.

Audra stared out of her tank, recovering from her grievous wounds, hardly registering the many Zikri scouts that scoured the interrogation room. All chittered aghast at Nrog's mangled body, the ruptured angles of his stretched and torn ligaments, the many dead, slain Mentera, the smashed and scorched amalgamators and the ruin of the nearby tank. They paid no heed to the lone Zikri floating immersed in the farthest of the four Mentera tanks.

Many high-ranking guards crouched to listen to Nrog's last wheezes. But the admiral's rasps made little intelligible sense. Chittering vengeful threats, the Zikri whisked by the charred and mangled black-grey shape in the green-glowing tank and glided on their way down the mossy hall, tentacles bristling, keen to find Nrog's slayers. The ship's crew had been put on high alert. But by that time all but one of the fugitives had escaped.

As the flagship *Viscurg* was further bombarded by NOA shells, a loose fragment of a heavy plate fell from the ceiling, smashing onto Audra's tank.

The glass shattered in a thousand shards as water poured out and Audra slid, half carried by the resultant deluge. Her fleshy lungs heaved, upchucking putrid brine. She crawled out of the jagged shards and chittered a ghastly groan—one of triumph though, even as sharp glass cut into her six motilators. Her lungs convulsed. The stark transition from dreary limbo to airy life was an intense experience. A dark awareness surged to her head. She was in the admiral's torture room. Of course…his mutilated body lay not a dozen paces from where she now sprawled and recovered her breath and senses. Other things resided in the tanks before her, horned and winged insects she could not name. The ship shuddered. Something akin to a grin wrinkled the ropy folds of her face. Across the room she glided, then down the mossy hall, with no need of subterfuge now. She was a Zikri, one of their race, but stronger, smarter. Evidence of the recent wholesale slaughter in the dusky, maroon-lit halls with their bio-luminescent moss coverings did little to faze her. Hers were nerves of steel.

The cavernous space dock teemed with squids bustling about, servicing craft and relaying orders. Vessels of many shapes and forms blasted off to fling themselves into the arena of war. On the open holoview the battle raged: red and green beams of destruction crisscrossing the black tracts of space and meeting shields, some penetrating through armor to targets within. Ships of multiple origins, NOA, Mentera, Zikri, weaved in and dodged out, delivering destruction upon one another: the submarine NOA craft, the triangular Xarean, ultra-light defense squads, Zikri Orbs and the Mentera aphids.

Audra glided toward the last sleek mantis left at the docking grounds.

She thrust open the hatch and entered the bridge, claiming it as her own. Better this than one of the Orbs. She could use this ship to pass through the Mentera ranks, thus avoid pursuit by her own kind.

A memory flashed in her mind: how Miko had made efforts to save her. Though grudgingly, he had followed through. She had seen it in the human's eyes, the struggle, the indecision. But he had acted with resolve. What to do with him? An age of subjugation and molding, bending him to her will had passed, and gone. The familiar impulse to hunt him down still surged through her veins, but now a new awareness dawned. The splicing of their cells by the shipboard computer on the NAVO craft had bound them in ways even her superior Zikri intellect could not comprehend. It had led them on an epic chase through the galaxy. For what purpose? Time to end it. The open galaxy lay ahead of her, hers for the taking...she would leave behind this unnatural war and the ghastly ruins of her misguided race. She wanted nothing to do with Nrog and his upstarts, despising what they'd become, and what she'd become in part, and their flagrant acts of terrorism against Miko's race.

Chapter 32

Regers' eyelids fluttered open. Glass enclosed him on either side. His heavy limbs floated in a liquid matrix. Ahead, beyond the thick glass, two Zikri worked at a command console, along with one of those dinky little locust munchkins.

A dim memory surfaced in the back of Regers' fuzzy mind. Of struggle, capture and pain. Deakes and Jennings, struggling in the iron-thewed motilators of squids like those that had hooked his own thighs, popping bone from sockets before he had slipped into welcome unconsciousness. The pain of snapping and searing agony had now gone.

A vague memory of cold green water lapped at his lank hair. Then drinking deep. A few lungfuls. Fighting, thrashing, to no avail. Then an eternal bath. A deep dive into silence infathomable.

Days, or perhaps years later, a snatch of awareness tickled his brain. He looked over to see Deakes suspended in a green tank on his left, Jennings on the right.

Well, he'd be a damned monkey! The three dumb-dumbs, side by each.

He could see squids still vaguely moving about somewhere ahead in the dim space of what looked like a ship's bridge. So, he'd been transferred to a locust craft. He recognized the cryptic design, the alien markings, the stigma-like toggles, artificial grav box and cluttered, low-sloping console. But why squids on a locust ship?

His mind worked with agonizing slowness.

Reckon he'd busted up an arm and a leg fighting those damn slime-bitch squids. All healed from what he could see, though he could barely lift an arm or a leg in this heavy soup. No matter how hard he willed it, no luck. No pain, just a blank, brain-dead type of numbness.

The ship impulsed above *Xares*. In the large holoscreen set above the control panel, he recognized the smalt blue disc of the human-colonized planet spinning below. Regers also caught a glimpse of a butterfly-moth taking a chunk out of a Zikri Orb. The pieces of the puzzle started to make sense. There'd been some fuck-up during the transfer of prisoners and all available ships had been called to fight the war in space. These nice squids had obliged, got caught up in the middle of it.

Lordy Lord. What was this world coming to? Jennings over there, gaping with a fish-white gaze, his face as long as a lank lizard's with a grimace to match, as if his mother'd puked all over his breakfast. Deakes looking like the ghost who denied Christmas, eyes two pissholes in the snow.

And what do you look like, Regers, you dumb ass fuck? Some princess at a honeymoon ball?

No, he wasn't going to be trading gags with himself for the next million years. He had to get out of this glass, monkey cage.

Not so easy with one's limbs quasi paralyzed.

The two squids jerked to some disturbance in the viewport and he imagined Zikri chatter gushing through the com speakers. The war must be going sour for the squids, they'd nowhere to run. All it took was one buggered up light drive and then it was all over. He'd known it himself.

Something slammed into the hull. The tanks vibrated at the impact. The squids and the lone Mentera jawed over it, not in good spirits, safe to say.

Why have bug tanks on the bridge, though? Oh, right…this was a bug ship, wasn't it? The crew could plug in, recharge on the fresh meat within.

Regers, you're slow on the draw here. Gears ain't working properly.

The short Mentera bobbed over on its hind legs, to check on the prisoners. It paused to gaze in the tanks. Its locust head dipped, yellow tongue darting out in interest while pincers twitched. One lifted to stroke the glass, until it snatched suddenly at the black cable that connected to the top of the tank. It snapped the other end into its navel.

Regers' eyes widened in horror. Not this tank, you grubby fuck! Pick Deakes, not mine.

But not to be. The locust hitched in, started to feed.

Regers slumped, feeling gutshot, as the Mentera lolled by the tank's side. It drank deep of his life energy, all the while Regers felt his bone marrow being sucked out of him as if it swirled up a tube and down a drain. He felt a terrible lethargy, as the bug drained his bodily and mineral resources.

Another violent shock jarred the glass: a deeper hit on the hull that snapped the cable at the tank's top and pitched the bug back on its heels. It cracked hard, chitinous carapace against the wall. The squids went careening backward against the tanks.

The glass shook. The tanks rocked, spilling water from the loose top of Regers' prison where the cable was. Regers saw a small hairline fracture develop down near the bottom of his tank. Green brine seeped out of the crack. Not much, but enough to drain the tank, if given time. Regers' face twisted in a leer.

Squids and locust scrambled back to the controls, oblivious of the seepage. The shoulder-high locust gestured at the others as if giving orders like a miniature overlord. One little munchkin giving two hulking squids orders. What was wrong with that picture? The squids seemed put out by the posturing and overweening command the locust had and were getting pissed, judging from the agitated wavering of their front tentacles. Shell fire flashed across the starboard shields. The lightfighter yawed. The tanks leaned on precarious angles, more water spilling out of the loosened plug tops. The Mentera ship slewed to port. The little munchkin ignored the warning. It seemed to be shrilling more orders at the Zikri. One of the brutes lashed out a stinging tentacle that sent the little dwarf flying. If Regers could have laughed he would have.

The Mentera leaped up on its hind legs in bristling anger and fumbled for its blaster. It shot out a beam, tagging the squid. Little bits of squid meat went three ways as it smashed back in a charred ruin, half its grotesque face now a sunken cavehole. Regers looked on, enjoying the sport. Its squid companion glided in and smashed the locust back against the wall, engulfed it in a sandwich of killing motilators. Not a pretty sight. Not before a green ray shot out like a greased eel and cracked Jennings' tank. Jiminy spilled out, all hands and knees sprawled akimbo, spewing green brine as he choked for air.

If Regers could bend over and smack the glass with his metal fist, he could accelerate the seepage. But he couldn't. The water paralyzed him. He could barely lift a finger or flutter an eyelid as it stood.

The squids were in trouble. Their well-wrought plans had gone to batshit, as somehow they hadn't counted on the dragonflies, moths, whatever the fuck they were, kicking ass and wrecking ships—coupled with Dez's insidious mechnobot armor, a lethal combination. Gave them the surprise of their lives.

The ship was failing. NOA was on their ass, no light drive or they'd have hyperdrived out of here long ago. At least, death was coming fast and all the prisoners would be bonfires rather than spend the rest of their days vegetating in a bug's liquid bath.

Careful what you wish for, Regers. You're not a master escapist for nothing. No reason to give up and die now.

The water was draining out at a faster rate. Lips peeled back, head exposed, Regers gave an oily smile, as now neck and chest lay bare.

He jerked a limb as more foul water gushed out of his mouth. Coughing out a briny mouthful, he clenched his teeth and winced. His head swam, arms and legs still immobilized by the paralyzing agency of the water and residual effects of the bug's feeding. Now his waist was clear and he crumpled in a ragdoll heap, head dunked back in the water.

Before his head had dropped though, he caught a glimpse of Jennings creeping nearby, trying to get a finger on the dead locust's gun. Good ole rat bastard Jennings! The ship lurched to a new attack.

The last squid worked its way back toward the console, jerking in desperate measures at the controls to save the craft from annihilation. Jennings halted, a shadow in the shadows, dripping brine. He was hunched and tensed, looking as if he knew he played a risky game should the squid turn and see him.

Life was returning to Regers' limbs in painful tingles. Fresh invigorating strength. Renewed resolve.

The water had drained to eighteen inches. He crouched down to batter at the crack with all his might with a metallic fist. One strike. Two... The glass spiderwebbed, gurgling out the last bits of water. He staggered out, his left leg catching on a jagged shard of glass and drawing blood. The squid turned.

His target was the blaster before it could wrap glue-slimed motilators around him.

The squid chittered a torrent of obscene syllables and bobbed over to deliver Regers a killing squeeze.

Jennings lunged.

Regers scrambled on stiff legs. The squid caught his left leg and tripped him. He gave a cursing cry. Jennings snatched up the blaster and targeted the squid before it could glide toward him and crush him as it had the locust. The thing rolled back in a smoking ball, fore-motilators whipping out, chittering and twitching in a most obscene fashion.

Regers grinned as he choked out a mouthful of water. His head rang to a seashell roar. He shook the cobwebs out of his skull and struggled to drag himself to his feet by hooking fingers on the console. The ship's defense gauge light showed shields dropping approximately to 30%.

He heard a choking cough behind him.

Jennings, scrabbling like a rat, pushing himself between console and locust gore.

"Not this time, Regers," Jennings rasped. He aimed the gun in Regers' direction.

Regers squinted, while a shadowy form moved out of the corner of his eye—a snaking tentacle, charred but not quite dead, unfurling out of the dim blue shadows by the artificial grav box.

"Jennings, you dumb fuck, look behind you!"

"Not falling for that trick, Regers. Get over there!" Jennings jabbed the gun, a luminous, blue, baton-like shape at Regers' chest.

A slithering wisp of movement darted. Then a flick, like the snap of a whip. The squid that'd been gutshot, lifted Jennings in a bear hug and wrapped its two still functional motilators round his middle. Jennings gave a fierce squawk and writhed and thrashed in dismay, his face a blurred, horrified white rictus, feet kicking with all their might, heels slapping on a slime-pocked torso as lower tentacles tightened in their crushing grip. His lumo-weapon went flying aside, firing off a round, nearly taking off Regers' head.

Regers ducked just in time. He snatched up the fallen weapon. In a wild instant, he blasted the squid, taking out chunks of tentacles, even as Jennings' eyes bulged and his guts spewed from his mouth under the strangling pressure of the squid's last death grip.

The thing flopped in a sprawled jelly mass, Jennings along with it.

Regers' lips curled in a distasteful grimace. That gave way to a savage yell of insane triumph. He was king of this castle.

"Die you motherfucking, shit-eating squid!" In a blind frenzy, he blasted it full of green fire as it danced and jerked, screamed and burned. He dipped both hands in the smoking blood and guts of the open chest carapace and ripped out entrails, and squeezed with all the strength of his metal hand. Black guck ran through his fingers and down his arms. He did a little ballerina twirl, stumbled in his dizziness, fell, ran the warm thick goop over his cheeks while all the time laughing such that tears dribbled down his begrimed cheeks. His eyes glowed pools of dark, blazing madness. "Uncle Regers always gets the last laugh! HAHAHA! Hear me, you fucking squids? Happy birthday, fuckers. You can't kill me. Try but you can't, you shitweasels! I'm the big bad horse thistle that keeps growing in your back garden! Try to pull me out! Just try it, you fucks!"

Laughing in senseless glee, Regers stumbled over to the nav panel. He tugged at knobs, hammered buttons, glared, squinted, cursed, as sensor lights blinked with dusky luminosity and squiggles of color, as the battle raged on. LU destroyers went up in flames, and lightfighters, bright balls of crimson, followed suit. Not quite all together, he had no inkling how to work the controls. He puked out more green water, wiped his lips, gave a series of sour belches. But he'd figure it out, Uncle Regers'd figure it out, if he had to raise that ugly squid over there from the dead and force it to pilot this evil vessel. Might even be other locusts on this tub, or even an evac vehicle cached somewhere.

Deakes stared out of the glass like a pickled herring. The thug was still mashed up pretty bad. Better to keep him pickling for a while yet, Regers mused. Green witch water would do him some good. Had some healing power which only the alchemists knew about.

Regers' left leg was throbbing badly from the fresh glass cut, but he'd suffered nothing compared to Deakes's injuries, including a leg bent on an awkward angle and his side pretty gouged up, as if his guts'd spill out any moment. Flesh was stitching up nicely though. The miracle water would see to that. He watched Deakes struggle to raise a finger, not nearly succeeding.

Regers wagged a finger of his own. "Yeah, I know, Deakes. Life's a bitch and then you die. Don't be a crybaby. Your turn's coming."

His eyes sighted once again on the mangled form of Jennings sprawled off to the side beside the dead locust with half its bug head hanging off. The reek of those fetid bodies would soon stink up this crib and toxify it. "Fucking pigshit, cricket-shit mantis. Just a matter of flying this crate out of here. And you, Jennings, a sorry sight. Jiminy, I told you'd get your ass plugged back in a tank and killed."

There Regers, had your rant. Now settle down and think this scenario through before you end up getting yourself completely fucked. No more Uncle Regers in this world is a sad world indeed. Besides, there's a little matter of unsettled business to take care of.

CHRIS TURNER

Epilogue

Yul looked over the smoking ruins of the slums. Downed alien ships lay in the streets, crumpled Orbs and mantis lightfighters bombarded by enemy fire, their hulls buckled and their dark metal lying across tenements.

A flurry of footfall pounded from nearby. Human militia, dressed in body armor with E1s clutched in gloved hands. They rounded up survivors and tended to the wounded. Yul hustled Cloye and Fenli to a dozen relief troops working between two piles of debris. He volunteered their services. A heavyset soldier directed them to a small group heading out to look for others.

Yul lay a hand on Cloye's shoulder and peered into her grime-stained face. Her pale blue eyes shone back with a determined gleam while Fenli stared in a daze. The experiences of the day had rendered him a changed man.

More activity reigned in the skies. NOA submarine-shaped bombers slid by like eels on the hunt for stray enemy to kill. But there was none left. It looked as if the humans had won this war. Yul's lips pursed grimly. He wondered what lay ahead in the years to come…

ABOUT THE AUTHOR

Chris is a prolific author of fantasy, adventure, and science fiction. His writing spans many genres: heroic fantasy, sword and sorcery and speculative fiction.

You can connect with Chris at:

http://www.innersky.ca/books/home